Unspoken Truths

- The Sphere UK Series -

Maggy McAndrew

Unspoken Truths
(The Sphere UK Series)
Maggy McAndrew
1st Edition, May 2024
Copyright © 2024 AMM

To my wife.

Maggy McAndrew

Chapter 1

January 10th - The Iron Lady

Olivia

Almost all the truly decisive moments in our lives are ours and ours alone. For others, it's simply another day, just like so many others. We will remember forever, they will forget without ever even being aware that there was something to remember.

I walk through the sliding glass doors and enter a new atmosphere. Anxiety turns into euphoria, and fear generates energy. I quicken my pace and grip the folder in my hand more tightly, while at the same time I'm invaded by a feeling of nausea, as if I'm going to vomit at any moment. I stop and look around. The hospital is so big, so confusing. Elevators, stairs, signs of all colours, and dozens of people occupy a seemingly endless entrance hall. Although I was here last week, I find myself having to ask for help at the reception.

"Hey Olivia! Good morning, welcome! How are you? Ready?" asks Assunción Martinez, the quality department director, a black woman who exudes energy and good cheer. "Don't worry," she continues, shaking her head.

I have no doubt that my face mirrors the uneasiness I feel.

"This just seems strange. You'll get used to it in no time. Before the end of the week, you'll already feel at home," she concludes, when we finally catch one of the elevators.

Today is Monday, but it's not just another Monday, it's the first day, the first day of a different future, I reflect, without being able to even come close to grasping the scope of what awaits me.

We enter my new office together. A large window, facing an inner courtyard, fills the space with natural light. On the wall, several serigraphs by new artists provide a splash of colour that contrasts with the straight, all-white furniture.

"We can't go on like this!" Shouts are heard coming from the corridor. "One of these days someone is going to die!"

Startled, Assunción stops mid-sentence and runs out. Not understanding what's going on, I follow her.

"Where is the head of anaesthesia, can anyone tell me? I'm not going to operate like this again!"

Finally, I can see who is shouting. A woman in a blue surgical gown, her mask hanging down around her neck, and the greenest eyes I've ever seen, rounds the corner. Behind her, two nurses try in vain to calm her down, but she completely ignores their presence.

Assunción walks quickly in her direction. I stand still at the office door, following the scene from a distance.

"Julia! Calm down!" Her voice sounds calm but assertive. When she reaches her, she puts her hand on her arm in a gesture of comfort, but above all, of restraint.

"I don't want to calm down, I want them to take responsibility! If these guys don't hire staff, we can't operate!"

"What happened, anyway?" Assunción asks, releasing Julia's arm.

"The same thing as last week, and the week before. I was in the OR with an anaesthesiologist and two interns, they called her for an emergency C-section, and as a result... I was left doing a valve replacement with the two kids. Damn it! I'm tired of this crap!"

"You're right..."

"I know I am, but when someone dies, that won't do much good."

Little by little, they move towards me and I can hear the conversation, which is now taking place in a more moderate tone, "The patient was complicated, he lost a lot more blood than he should have, and the kids had no idea what to do. You see... there I was, the man with his chest open, and them whiter than the patient himself. I'm telling you, it only didn't go worse because Raul who was operating with me reacted in time and took the reins. I thought the patient was going to crash. It can't be! It can't happen! It's not going to happen, at least not in my OR!"

"Come on, let's go. Let's go to my office," Assunción pulls her by the sleeve and she seems to accept the suggestion. As they pass by me, Assunción stops for a moment and says, "Olivia, sorry, I have to go. Don't forget, we have a meeting at four."

I'm left alone in the middle of the corridor. People move back and forth as if absolutely nothing had happened. I re-enter the office and close the door behind me. What just happened? Who could that be? I wonder.

I sit down for the first time in my new chair. I turn on the computer and open my email. What a strange feeling, a new address, and nothing in the inbox except for the automatic welcome message. I let myself stare out the window, watching the people crossing the courtyard without much attention. A meeting at four, and no one thought to let me know. I enter the hospital website and browse around. There are familiar names, and others I've never heard of. In general, the clinical staff is young and highly qualified. Amidst many other faces, I recognize the green eyes I just saw: Julia Garcia, the director of cardiothoracic surgery. At the top of the page is the posthumous photograph of the previous clinical director, Artur Navarro. He was a well-respected man, an internal medicine specialist, vice-president of the European Society, who died of a heart attack three months ago, completely unexpectedly. He was sixty-four years old, leaving behind a wife, two children and four grandchildren. It was a shock. The hospital kept his deputy as interim clinical director, but the administration decided that the new replacement should come from outside, and here I am. I anticipate difficult times ahead, Artur's memory is still very present.

I write and erase, write and erase, unable to come up with anything good. I try in vain to prepare something that might make sense to say at this afternoon's meeting. I know how important first impressions are and that only makes me more and more nervous. I take off my glasses and set them down on the desk, at the same time I'm surprised by my cell phone. It takes me a moment to locate it: 'Ursula'.

"How are you? Settled in?" she asks before I can even say anything.

I take a deep breath and almost feel her perfume. "What a surprise, how did you know I needed you now?"

"I always know what you need, remember? You should know that I'm present, even when I'm absent."

"It's true..." I answer, knowing that it corresponds entirely to what I feel.

"Are you sitting down? Close your eyes. Think of me... do you feel my hand?"

"Stop!" I interrupt in a falsely angry tone, "Not now! But we can continue later," I finish with a laugh.

"Right, if 'not now', let's talk about serious things, how are you? How are things going?"

"Well, I think. I mean, they just informed me that there's a presentation meeting this afternoon. They could have told me before, don't you think?" I sigh and put my glasses back on, tucking my hair behind my ear at the same time, "Let's run away? Spend the afternoon together."

"Uhm... it's not an offer I can refuse, Madam Clinical Director, but I believe duty calls!"

"Oh!... You're losing your touch! At other times you'd be the first to ask, 'Where shall we meet?'" we both laugh.

"It's the weight of responsibility. Thursday afternoon?"

The anticipation makes me feel better. I hang up the phone and look out the window, losing myself in memories.

I'm hungry. Of course I am, it's almost two o'clock. In a mechanical gesture I put my hair back and adjust my glasses for the tenth time. I reread the text

I started writing, it's terrible. I didn't come prepared for this, a crass error!

I go to the bathroom. I wash my hands and let the cold water run. I look at my reflection in the mirror, what will they see when they look at me?

I enter the amphitheatre at four o'clock sharp. It's packed with lab coats and I immediately regret not having worn mine. Again the nausea, the feeling of vomiting. I think of Ursula and the possibility of running away, I think of Javier and his cold words.

The chair of the board of directors gives a brief introduction and turns the floor over to me. A restrained applause is heard in the room, foreshadowing the difficulties to come.

It's my turn. I walk to the centre of the stage, thank them for the introduction, and almost instantly give up on following the paper I have in my hand. For a few minutes, I share my previous experience in managing the oncology centre and announce some of the plans I have for the hospital's future. As I speak, I feel calmer and more enthusiastic. My voice becomes softer and more melodious, almost like a seductive whisper. I finish feeling satisfied with myself, smiling and raising my eyes to face the audience. The moment is short-lived. The faces are stern, and several arms are raised, requesting to speak.

The first to speak is António Fuentes, the interim clinical director. His rough voice denotes the pain of not being the chosen one. In a warning tone, with a subtle hint of threat, he enlightens me about the hospital's specificities, reminding me that it will not be easy, perhaps not even possible, to apply what he calls "my" new models of clinical management. I feel a shiver run down my spine.

Before I can respond, another voice makes itself heard, this time coming from the upper part of the room. The voice has a very particular husky tone, a mixture of ice and heat, silencing all conversations. Without hesitation, she looks directly at me: "Doctor. Olivia Lopez, my name is Julia Garcia, on behalf of the cardiothoracic surgery department, I welcome you."

"Thank you."

"Those who know me are aware that I'm not one to mince words, and I go straight to the point. First of all, I want to say that I completely agree with my colleague. This hospital has its own reality, which I believe you are not familiar with. Well, the first thing I wanted to ask is if you intend to follow the functional unit integration model here, as you did in your previous institution."

The question seems simple, but it is truly cutting, and a hundred times more dangerous than all of António's aggressive speech. One thing is certain, she has done her homework.

Faced with my perplexity, she continues, without giving me a chance to respond, "By the way, since you are an anaesthesiologist, I would like to know if you intend to have clinical activity in the operating room? We have been having problems..."

This time I am ready, and before she can list a chorus of complaints, I interrupt her: "Doctor. Julia Garcia, thank you for your words and your questions. The way medicine is viewed is the central issue; creating functional units or not is a consequence and never a starting point. As for clinical activity, we shall see," I answer evasively, saying neither yes nor no. Usually, I am a frank person, but at this moment, I cannot buy wars, one battle at a time.

I focus my gaze back on Julia, who in the meantime seems to have become distracted, looking at her cell phone with a smile and a shrug. I cannot help but notice that when she smiles, her countenance changes.

§§

"You know, Fili, at that moment, I felt fragile and vulnerable..."

Fili interrupts what I am saying, "Usually, you don't give so much importance to what others think of you, Olivia. What is making you insecure? I thought changing jobs was a good thing."

"I was standing there, in front of everyone, I was the new clinical director, and I had no idea what to do. I felt so exposed, as if I were naked, I don't know, I don't know why."

I started therapy at a time when nothing made sense, when everything seemed to have no solution. In a short time, Fili, Filipe Rivera, became much more than a psychiatrist; he became a safe haven, transforming me as a person, giving me a confidence that, in many moments, earned me the nickname Iron Lady.

Fili raises his head from his notebook and looks at me. He is, as always, sitting on his brown leather sofa, the colour of honey, with his arms resting on his lap, holding the pen and notebook. "You always have to prove something, don't you?" he calmly utters, not letting on whether it is a statement or a question. "Your fear is proportional to the risk you think you are taking, and you only take that risk because you have imposed goals on yourself that I cannot understand. Do you want to show that you are capable of facing one of the largest hospitals in the city and restructuring it, if necessary, against everything and everyone? Do you want to show this to yourself? Or, and forgive me for what I am about to say because I know you won't like it, do you simply want to fill a void that has taken hold of you in recent times?"

I feel a lump in my throat; he is not wrong. The last two years have been particularly tough.

"And how is Ursula?" he asks, continuing before giving me time to answer, "Olivia, let's stop here for today. You are trying to open doors, heavy and difficult doors to cross. Don't put restrictions on yourself from the start; give yourself the possibility to dream, you have nothing to lose."

I get up feeling more confused than when I entered, and yet, I smile, I smile at the possibilities of the future, my future.

Maggy McAndrew

Chapter 2

January 10th - A Kiss Resolves All

Camila

Today, unlike usual, I wait for long minutes in the small waiting room. Strange, Fili is rarely late. I choose the sofa at the back, perhaps because it is the one, of the three, that is farthest from the door. The room is empty, but still, it causes me some discomfort.

"Sorry for the delay Camila, the previous appointment ran late. Sorry. How are you?" Fili comes to get me at the door with a smile. I enter the office, and almost without realizing it, I am already sitting in what is "my" place.

"How are you?" he repeats, prompting me to speak. "How is Julia?" he insists in the face of my silence. Fili knows me well, well enough to know that most of the time my sadness and my joy have a name, Julia Garcia.

"She's acting strange again. She's irritated, you can't say anything or she yells back. Things at her hospital are complicated. I don't know if you know, but they have a new clinical director, from what I understand an unpleasant person. An Olivia something or other, she was put there by interests and connections, or at least that's what they say."

"And is Julia irritated because of that?"

"I don't know Fili, we've been married for years and I still can't understand Julia. You know what happened, and I know I told you I could move forward. I believed that, but now, now I don't know anymore," I suspend for a moment what I was going to say.

"Why?"

Without letting him ask more questions, I embark on an account of yesterday.

§§

I leave home early and catch the usual train. Sitting on the bench in front of me is a woman. My eyes fix on her hands. She holds the book tightly, as if her life depends on it, and turns the pages at a steady pace. I don't move my head or look away. It must be a romance novel, I think, unable to see the cover, hidden by another one made of red leather.

It's six-thirty, through the window I can see the lights of the approaching city. In less than two hours I will enter the operating room, I think, while continuing to follow the turning of the pages. She has surprisingly long fingers, she could be a surgeon.

--

I arrive at the hospital and head straight for the locker room. As usual, there is a lot of hustle and bustle, with everyone talking over each other. I think of Julia and her problems at Central Hospital. I'm glad I chose to work here, at the University Hospital, if it weren't for my mother also working here it would be perfect, I think to myself. Next to me, several doctors and nurses change clothes. Already dressed, I sit on one of the benches, my back to the wall, with my elbows resting on my knees.

"You're getting thinner and thinner... How about we have dinner today? How long has it been since we went out together," says one of the nurses, a long-time friend.

"I can't. Julia and I have plans to have dinner at home."

"How is she?"

"Great, always operating. But today, she promised to leave the chaos of Central and have dinner with me at home. At least, our hospital is always calmer," I say laughing.

"That calmness remains to be seen. Did you know that Doctor Esther Gonzalez is going to join our team? We're going to have another star. It seems she starts in a month."

--

It's almost ten o'clock at night when I finally hear the key turn in the lock and the noise of the door opening. Julia enters as if everything is normal. Without taking off her coat, she crosses the room towards me and bends down to give me a kiss.

I reciprocate in a mechanical, almost unpleasant gesture. "What happened? Didn't we have plans for dinner?" I ask, without much expectation that the answer will calm my irritation.

"I'm sorry, you know how it is, the earlier we want to leave the more complications. First the arrival of the new clinical director, you can't imagine! I have to tell you. And when I was already ready to leave, I had to go back." As she speaks, she hands me her cell phone with truly impressive images. "Look, see how well the adhesions show up. The resolution is great, look at the aortic outlet, the valve had already been operated on, you know how it is, complications everywhere."

I listen as I look at the photographs. Exposed heart, clamps and retractors, I recognize Julia's fingers, despite the gloves. In one of the images, the field is flooded with blood. I can imagine the difficulty of what she describes.

In my hand, the phone vibrates to warn that a message has arrived. Then another and yet another. The notifications appear on the screen, and it is inevitable not to see. The sender, or perhaps I should say "the" sender is not identified and I can only read: 'Darling, I can't...' I contain the desire to see the rest of the sentence, I don't say a single word, and return the phone to her. Without looking, she grabs it and puts it in her back pocket.

"Come on, let's have dinner," she says, extending her hand.

I make no effort to get up. With a body movement I turn the chair, and my back is to her. She doesn't give up, she never gives up. She stands behind me, puts her hands on my shoulders and kisses me. I spin the chair again. I stretch my arms and push her, with more force than necessary. With the surprise of the movement, she takes a step back and almost loses her balance.

"What's wrong? Aren't you hungry? Let's eat," she insists.

"Who is it this time?"

"No one! Please, Camila, stop! I don't know why you insist on thinking that every time I'm late I'm with someone."

"Maybe because it's happened before!" I can't hide my exasperation. I try to speak softly so as not to wake Mateo, but it's impossible, I feel like exploding. Julia manages to be both the best and the worst person in the world at the same time. I fell in love with her irreverence, her intelligence, with that came the arrogance and selfishness of someone who feels far above others. I understand that dealing with life and death on a daily basis forces her to create protections, but she has distanced herself, as if the banality of everyday life is totally uninteresting.

"There are days when you don't stop looking at that damn phone. Wherever you are, you're always holding it. You didn't even realize it, but the other day, you went so far as to get out of the shower, all wet, because you had left it on the nightstand. Who is it? Why does she call you 'darling'?"

She doesn't answer and squats in front of my chair. I get up. I don't want apologies. I don't want empty conversations. In reality I have no idea what I want.

"Mommy, the bed was falling..." says Mateo softly, appearing at the door of the living room, with his curly hair dishevelled and his brown plush cat under his arm.

Julia looks at me as if it were my fault he woke up. She gets up, takes his hand and leaves towards the bedroom. "It was just a nightmare, love," I hear her say, already in the hallway.

I remain standing, motionless in the middle of the room. I look at the table, where dinner remains untouched. Suddenly, a phone rings. It's hers. I look around trying to figure out where the sound is coming from. It's on the floor, under the desk. It must have fallen out of her pocket when she bent down. From a distance I see the light flashing. Who calls at this hour? I control the urge to go get it, I stand still, take a deep breath and finally the sound stops. Not even a minute later, a sign of another message.

"Mateo has already fallen asleep, we have to speak more softly," she whispers as she re-enters.

I shiver at her hoarse tone of voice, and for a moment I remember back to the times when we lived in Boston.

I sit on the couch before resuming the conversation. "I'm not managing to deal with this. You're always out, between surgeries, emergencies, congresses and who knows what else. The feeling I have is that you're never here, and when you are, the phone doesn't stop." I realize I'm giving in, I feel my muscles relax and my voice has regained its usual tone.

"Listen...", she says, sitting next to me, "I know what happened left scars. Mateo was so little, you weren't well, one thing led to another."

"We're not going to have this conversation again, are we? You betrayed me, that's a fact, and I don't think there can be any mitigating factors." Whenever we return to this subject, I remember how I felt after Mateo was born, everything that happened, and I feel an anger I'm unable to hide.

"It wasn't planned, it didn't mean anything."

"You could be honest..." She remains seated next to me with her coat on, just as she entered almost an hour ago. Her hands rest on her lap, shoulders slumped, eyes fixed on the window, staring into infinity. "Was it good? Was it better?"

"It wasn't bad, it wasn't good, it was different", she finally averts her eyes from the window and looks at me, placing her hands over mine.

The phone, which has meanwhile recovered from the floor, rings again. She ignores it, as if unaware. I lean back on the pillows, yielding to the weight of fatigue. I'm exhausted, I close my eyes for a moment and when I reopen them, her face is almost glued to mine. She leans in and kisses me.

As if propelled by a spring, I stand up and push her away with my hand, "Stop that. It's not going to happen! You can't think everything is resolved like this, you arrive and believe a kiss fixes everything."

"Don't underestimate me, I wasn't thinking of just a kiss", she states with a laugh. Her laughter is contagious and I can't help but smile, despite everything. "Don't be angry, my day wasn't easy. Before the surgery there was a huge meeting. They gathered us all in the auditorium, and you know what for? To introduce the new clinical director! They went and got a woman no one knows. Imagine, an anaesthesiologist with the air of a housewife and ideas to reform the system."

She gets up and paces back and forth as she speaks. Finally she takes off her coat, leaving it draped over the back of a chair. "And, you don't know the worst part, Assunción, always wanting to be the good Samaritan, put me in a working group with this woman. I couldn't refuse, but it can only go wrong!"

"I don't want to know. I'm going to bed. You can check your messages and reply, it seems there's someone urgently needing to talk to you." I raise my voice again and remember Mateo.

She completely ignores what I just said, approaches and puts her arms around me. She runs her thumb over my mouth and traces the contours of my face. The journey ends again on my lips, which are parted, allowing her passage. I linger for a few moments, before turning my back and leaving her alone.

I climb the stairs to the bedroom. I enter the bathroom, turn on the water and wait until I feel the steam. I undress, looking at the mirror reflecting the image of my naked body. I step into the stall, and let the hot jet fall on my head. Immersed in the noise of the water, I'm startled when the doors open and she enters. I open my eyes, wiping them with the back of my hand. The menthol scent of the gel invades the air, her hands slide down my back. The force of the water removes the foam almost immediately, but that's not important.

Her hands have something unique, a delicacy and at the same time an energy, capable of driving me crazy with a simple touch. And, at this moment, she seems determined to do much more than just a touch. She grabs me and brings her face close to mine, until there's no space between us. With the water running over our heads, she kisses me. She kisses my cheeks, the tip of my nose, my closed eyelids, and back on my lips.

Under the water it's not possible to argue and she takes advantage to move forward. Without me realizing, she pushes me until I'm against the transparent glass of the stall. I close my eyes again. I feel my knees weaken and I wrap my arms around her neck for support. Aware that I've surrendered, she intensifies the movements. I search for strength to stay standing, rest my head on her neck and, even under the water, I smell her perfume. She kisses me again, a soft kiss that contrasts with the impetus of her movements.

I know I won't last much longer and I know she knows it too.

§§

"When I said I could move on I believed it was true, and it has been... I won't say I don't think about it from time to time. But, in the last days, weeks, the symptoms repeat themselves, the same words, the same looks, in short the same signs. They teach us that, until proven otherwise, equal symptoms suggest equal diseases. Yesterday I had the clear feeling that she's seeing someone. That could justify much of what has been happening lately. The instability, the mood swings, the phone obsession, and even..."

"Even what?", Fili asks in the face of my hesitation.

"...even the way she makes love."

I look him in the eyes, before concluding, "This morning I felt furious with myself. When I woke up she was no longer home. I let it happen again."

I say goodbye and head out into the street with the firm decision to try to change something.

Maggy McAndrew

Chapter 3

January 24th – The Wedding Anniversary

Olivia

"You have no idea how much I wanted this day to come. These have been some of the most confusing weeks of the last many months. I feel more and more lost..."

Fili looks at me, still standing, as he carefully closes the office door. "Sit down, take off your coat and breathe," he says smiling, as he himself settles on the couch by the window.

§§

The house is full, friends I haven't seen in years greet me with kisses and hugs, flashing smiles. In the midst of the confusion, I see Leonor walk in. I cross the room almost running, apologizing for the inevitable bumps along the way.

"Calm down, mom..., let me breathe! I adore you too!", she comments with a laugh, taking a step back to free herself from my embrace.

"How are you? You're thin! Let me look at you..., I thought you weren't coming..., with the strikes and the confusion at the airports... How did you manage to get here? You're pale!" I pull her into the hallway, escaping from all those chatting happily in the living room.

"Stop that, I'm great! To be honest, even I thought I wouldn't be able to make it..., the airports are chaos. I ended up making the whole trip by train. The only advantage is that I slept like I hadn't in a long time. And you? How are you? You're going on about how thin I am, but you're the one who lost weight. The other day, on the phone, you seemed worried, is it the new job? Are you okay?"

We're the same when we meet. There are so many questions that there's no room left for answers. When I woke up today I felt sad, maybe sad isn't the right word, nostalgic. Anniversaries are occasions for taking stock and the analysis of these twenty-eight years is not at all straightforward. Looking at Leonor erases the not-so-good and fills my chest with happiness. If there are things to celebrate on this anniversary, Leonor is certainly one of them.

"The job is great. But it has many challenges and a lot of people wanting to get in the way, you know how it is. A new hospital, I come from outside, they see me as the enemy. It will improve, I'm sure it will! And the University?"

"They're agitated, the atmosphere was never great, and now it's worse, it's tense. I'm fine, you grit your teeth and keep going," she says, clenching her jaw in a physical demonstration of her words. "I don't give a damn about those who only know how to badmouth everything and everyone. In the middle, there are many good people and the work is fantastic. I won't give up..."

She doesn't get to finish what she was going to say because Javier appears behind me.

"What are you doing here hiding?" he asks, giving her two kisses. "Leonor, leave your things in the room and come to the living room. Everyone wants to know news from Her Majesty's kingdom..." he jokes.

"Come on dad, don't tease, the world is not in the mood for jokes! And how are you? Getting richer and richer?"

It's incredible how much we've grown apart. I met Javier one night at a mutual friend's party. We were both about to finish medical school, although we studied at different universities. One thing led to another, and we ended up getting married three years later, a conventional marriage that made both my family and his happy. If my parents were conservative, his were even more so, country people with several properties and a lot of money. A doctor son was everything they could wish for, and they didn't hide it. Javier did his internship in public health and immediately started working in the pharmaceutical industry. Little by little, he became a businessman in every sense of the word. Half a dozen years ago he accepted an international position and started traveling most of the time. At first I found it strange, then I got used to it and honestly, I started to like it. My life without him is more honest, more "mine."

"Some things never change, I don't know how you put up with it?!" comments Leonor, staring at her father who, already in his shirtsleeves, returns to the living room, speaking loudly, among strident laughter in a group made up entirely of men.

I turn in the opposite direction and start walking towards the room, "I don't put up with it, I ignore it! Forget about your father. How are you, really?"

"I met someone..." she puts the bag on the floor, next to the window, and suddenly falls silent as if she had said something she doesn't want to share.

I sit on the edge of the bed and pat the mattress with the palm of my hand for her to sit next to me. "You met 'someone'?" I don't say anything else, although I'm dying of curiosity. I know that with her, the best strategy is not to insist and wait patiently.

"I met a girl..." she begins, without looking at me.

"Yes..."

"She's a college classmate. She sings in a band."

"Leonor, please continue, you're making me nervous," I end up saying, half serious, half joking, putting my glasses on my head, holding back the hair that falls on my forehead.

"I don't know what to say. She's fantastic! I don't know how to explain it to you, she's... she's a free person, a real person. The other day she invited me to go and hear her. She's wonderful!"

"Fantastic, wonderful... those are heavy adjectives. Leonor, you're not one for easy compliments. Come on, say what you have to say. What's going on?" I swallow hard, anticipating the answer.

She doesn't say anything, picks up the phone and hands it to me. "She's beautiful!" I state, looking at the photograph.

"She worked in Havana for an NGO for over ten years, but last year she decided she wanted to finish her Ph.D. and went to London. We have some classes together."

"Right. But, sweetie, if you can... and of course, if you want to, explain to me a little better what's going on, I'll be very grateful!" I joke, putting my hand on my chest and sighing in a theatrical gesture.

"I went to dinner at her place."

"And?"

"And we talked a lot..." Leonor bites her finger, in a nervous tic.

"And?" I repeat, trying to unblock what stubbornly refuses to come out.

"We ended up getting involved." She looks me in the eyes, trying to read my reaction before I can even express it. "Do you think it's wrong? Are you shocked?"

"Shocked? Why would I be?"

"I don't know?! We've never talked about these things. You and Dad are so conventional. I don't know, I thought you'd think it was wrong," she leans towards me, hugs me and kisses me on both cheeks.

I hug her tightly, remembering when she was a child. It's hard to see stamped on Leonor's face that, in fact, she thought I wouldn't accept that she had a relationship with a girl.

"If you're happy, that's what matters," I say from the bottom of my heart. "You'll have to tell me everything, in detail, in every detail, but we have plenty of time," I joke.

"Oh, Mom..." she starts in an annoyed tone, "What do you want me to tell you? There's nothing to tell!"

We return to the living room, I pick up a glass of champagne and circle among the guests, chatting with some and others, without saying anything relevant.

Javier, who has had more to drink than he should have, taps the glass with

29

his fork, making it tinkle, which causes a moment of silence.

"Friends..." he begins, in a speech tone, ."..thank you for coming. Twenty-eight years of marriage..." Before continuing, he holds my shoulder and pulls me closer. He gives me a kiss on the lips, with a strong taste of alcohol, and in the same solemn tone he says again: "Friends... a round of applause for Olivia, who a few days ago took over as clinical director of our largest hospital."

Without delay, a chorus of applause is heard, which soon fades away to give the floor back to Javier: "These are days of new opportunities..."

Nobody says anything, because no one knows what to expect.

"On a special day like today, I wanted to share with you that, this week, I was invited to take the position of commercial director for all of Europe, in a year's time..." Immediately, an ovation sounds again, this time much louder than the one heard a few moments ago.

Someone asks a question that I can't hear and Javier hastens to answer, "I'll be based in Switzerland..." I ignore the rest of the answer, he's going to live in Switzerland next year?

Becoming oblivious to everything around me, I lose myself in memories and am transported to a party from years ago, a fundraising dinner.

My mission was to get guests to contribute donations to the cancer center. As much as I disliked that kind of event, there was no way to avoid it.

I put on makeup like I rarely did, pinned my hair up with gel and put on a long dress, elegant in its simplicity of a black dress. I remember thinking how thin I was. It was a difficult time and at the same time full of new possibilities.

The night was cold, it was October, but it already felt like winter. When I entered, the room, in one of the most chic hotels in the city, was packed. For minutes that seemed like hours, I chatted and sipped champagne, unable to eat anything. I went out to the balcony, next to me, alone in the most absolute silence, a woman in an immaculate black tuxedo with a lilac satin sash, made herself present by her elegance. I pretended not to notice and leaned against the railing, looking at the garden many floors below. The scent of her perfume sent a shiver through me, which I wanted to attribute to the cold night.

It was time to go up on stage and give the long-prepared speech. The conversations stopped and the room paused to hear what I had to say. After the usual thanks, without ambiguities or improvisations, I described our vision in detail, a plan centred on people and their needs. I left the stage to a strong ovation. Despite everything, that was an easy audience to win over.

The mission was accomplished. I accepted another glass of champagne and returned to the balcony, looking for some fresh air. Be careful what you wish for. I don't know how much time passed until I felt a hand rest on my shoulder.

"Lost? Congratulations on the speech. I hope I don't need it, but if one day I get sick I'd like to be treated in an institution like that." She extended her hand to me and shook mine, "Ursula."

"Thank you!" I replied, feeling myself blush. "Olivia."

Beside me was none other than the woman I had shared the balcony with moments before.

She set the champagne flute on the parapet, not seeming to care about the risk of it falling down below. "Do you want a cigarette?" she offers me a black and gold case.

"No thanks, I don't smoke."

"Neither do I." She clicks open a gold lighter, lit a cigarette and inhales deeply. "I came to this thing out of obligation, but I confess that your speech piqued my curiosity. Do you think you'll be able to do it? You want to join services, do you know how many powers you'll be affecting?"

She listened to my answers and for each one of them she had at least three more questions. I realized that she works in the financial sector, and that her company was one of the usual donors. The conversation flowed as if we had known each other forever, but the cold was unrelenting and I found myself shivering. Without saying a word, she took off her jacket and placed it on my back, taking the opportunity to let her arm rest on my shoulders for much longer than necessary.

"It's cold," she stated, "How about we go downstairs to the bar? We can continue talking without catching pneumonia. I know you're a doctor, but I'd still prefer not to have to play the role of the patient," she said with a laugh. Her laughter was contagious and her smile so engaging that it was hard to look away.

"Sure, let's go! But put your jacket back on, I have mine inside."

We entered the room, and left right after, through the other door, retrieving our coats.

At that hour the bar was practically empty. A piano could be heard and the light was so dim that it was hard to see beyond our table. She ordered a gin and tonic and I a whiskey. By the time the drinks arrived we were already immersed in conversation again. The topics kept turning, turning, until I found myself talking about Javier and our life.

"You talk about your daughter going abroad as a terrible thing." She had already finished her gin and signalled the waiter to bring another one.

"You're mistaken. To me it seems like the opening of new opportunities."

"How so?"

"You can think about yourself, how long has it been since you've done that? Twenty years?" As she spoke, she put her hands on mine and fixed her eyes on mine. "What do 'you' need?"

I pulled my hands away under the pretext of bringing the glass to my mouth and looked away.

"You have the discreet charm of someone who hides, but you only have to listen and observe carefully to know that you are special." She was seducing me, or so it seemed. How long had it been...

I couldn't allow myself. I changed the subject: "And you? Are you married? Do you have children?"

"No, neither one nor the other. Time is too precious to hand it over to just one person."

"What does that mean?"

"Maybe one day..." She leaned in, leaving her face inches from mine. I closed my eyes, and imagined a kiss. When I reopened them, she had leaned back in her chair and was slowly drinking the liquid that remained in her glass.

For a month everything was reduced to two or three ambiguous messages. I didn't reply to any of them. One day, close to midnight, the phone vibrated. My first thought was for Leonor, had something happened? I looked, anticipating the worst, and immediately felt my heart race. 'Ursula'! 'I'll wait for you tomorrow at four, at the bar where we were,' 'Since you didn't tell me, let's see if I can guess what you need...'

It was ten minutes to four when I walked through the hotel doors. She was sitting by the piano drinking a glass of white wine. We chatted for a few minutes, with no common thread.

"I'm in room 1043, do you want to come up?"

The invitation was so direct that I shuddered. I didn't say anything, but I didn't move. She got up serenely, took my hand and pulled me. She put her arm around me, and with the intimacy of someone who has known you for years, led me to the elevator.

When the room door closed I was invaded by a feeling I didn't know. She noticed and wrapped me in an embrace. I felt her lips on mine. The softness of the kiss was indescribable. Without ever detaching her lips, she touched me gently, measuring the consequences of each gesture. I realized that she was proceeding with a calmness that, most likely, was not her own. I felt her fingers on my back and was swept by a wave of heat. She unzipped my blouse, in surprise, I took a step back.

"Did I do something I shouldn't have?" she asked, looking me in the eyes.

"I can't... I never..." My heart was beating erratically. The words stubbornly refused to come out. My mouth was dry.

"I know."

I never quite understood what she meant by that "I know", but she hugged me again and kissed me as if neither of us had said anything. Little by little, the urgency overrode the fear and desire won out over guilt. I surrendered to the obvious, I wanted that woman more than anything else at that moment.

"Do you want to stop?" she asked when I pulled away from her kiss, out of an urgent need to breathe.

"No," I replied, without the slightest doubt. With a courage I don't know where it came from, I let myself fall on the bed. I think I surprised her. For a few seconds she did and said nothing, then she smiled, and took off her shirt. She walked around the bed, letting me see her body and desire her with increasing intensity. Before lying down next to me, she took off the rest of her clothes, and was naked.

The afternoons in room 1043 were what allowed me to survive.

§§

Fili intervenes with her delicate voice as always, "Refuges, real or imagined, are as essential to survival as water or food," she picks up her agenda, "See you next week?" The question is rhetorical.

Maggy McAndrew

Chapter 4

January 24th - Every Story has a Beginning

Camila

"Hello, Camila, good afternoon. You're looking better. How are things?" Fili gestures for me to sit, moving one of the pillows on the couch.

"I'm happy. This morning, I received an unexpected call from my brother. I thought something had happened..., and in fact, it did! Actually, it was good news. Why is it that when the phone suddenly rings, I always think it's bad news?"

I recall the phone call and what happened in the last few days, my mind drifting to the captivating stranger I encountered on the train.

§§

Outside, the day begins to dawn, and the trees rush past the window. Without looking away, I continue to follow the turning of the pages as she reads. I can't tell if she's beautiful or how old she is. Maybe fifty, maybe less. She sits in a relaxed yet self-assured pose. Her long hair, tied in a ponytail, has a loose strand that falls over her face from time to time, forcing her to tuck it behind her ear. As our gazes meet, I notice her eyes are a deep, mesmerizing blue. Her face is pale, and her slightly parted lips reveal a line of white teeth. There's an undeniable allure about her that I can't quite place.

I'm tired, barely slept last night. Julia, on the other hand, slept soundly as always, blissfully unaware of the thoughts racing through my mind.

When the train stops at my station, I stand up and grab my backpack from under the seat. Seven-thirty, I have half an hour to get to the hospital. Outside, the sun shines in a completely clear sky, though not enough to ease the cold. People jostle and go their own ways. In the midst of the rush, I freeze, and without knowing why, I look back. The woman with the book slowly descends the step separating the carriage from the platform, wearing a white coat I hadn't noticed before. She walks away until she disappears into the crowd, leaving me with a lingering sense of intrigue.

I quicken my pace and try to focus on the surgery that awaits me. I stop at the usual café and leave a few minutes later with a steaming cup of coffee. The sweetness of the two packets of sugar I poured in makes me feel better, and I smile. I'm so distracted that when the phone rings, I jump, spilling much of the coffee. Fortunately, I don't burn or even stain myself.

"Sis, you won't believe what happened!"

"It's so good to hear from you. What time is it there? Did something happen?" From his voice, I know that whatever happened can only be good.

"I got the position on the Pediatrics team..., I'm going to Boston!"

"Really? Congratulations!" I reply, surprised. "I didn't know you had applied. And...?"

"We broke up. I know..., don't be mad. I should have told you, but I couldn't bear to hear 'I told you so.'"

I interrupt him, "How could you think I would say that? And worse, how could you not tell me something like that?" I'm used to him telling me everything, and this is no small matter.

"You were right. You were always right. It was right in front of my eyes, and I didn't want to see it," he sighs and continues, "He cheated on me again and again, and deep down, I always knew. I told myself it was nothing. You know how it is, we only see what we're prepared to see."

I don't say anything. He has no idea, but I understand much better than he can imagine, my thoughts drifting back to the mysterious woman on the train and the unspoken connection we seemed to share.

If my parents weren't lenient with me, they were a thousand times worse with him. When my brother came out, they went to the trouble of crossing the ocean to berate him. My mother said horrible things to him. My father did no better, and as always, he hid behind a complicit silence. After what happened, I don't think he'll ever return.

"Come on, sis, be happy for me. I have a contract, a six-figure salary, and five weeks of vacation. Sounds good, doesn't it? I'll be very close to where you used to live, ready for a new life!"

As the surprise fades, I bombard him with questions about the new house and the new job. He responds enthusiastically, not seeming like my shy, reserved brother at all.

When I hang up, I remember the times I lived in Boston, and I can't help but wonder if fate has something unexpected in store for me too, my mind wandering back to the captivating stranger on the train.

It was one of the biggest conferences the University organized. That year, I was presenting a lecture on virtual images and three-dimensional reconstruction, and she was speaking right after me about robotic surgery. I didn't know her personally, but I had heard a lot about her work. By coincidence, at dinner, we ended up sitting side by side. Julia was a fascinating woman, exuding intelligence and confidence, punctuated by a biting sense of humour. After much conversation and a few glasses of wine, she lost her discretion and openly flirted with me.

"I don't understand how we've never crossed paths before. It's true, I'm much older than you, but this world is small. I'm sure we've been together before," she said, her eyes lingering on mine with a suggestive glint.

"If we had been, I think I would remember," I replied, fuelling the conversation in the tone she had set. "The world isn't that small. When I was doing my internship in neuro, you were already making a name for yourself in cardiothoracic surgery. I've read a lot about you, many of your articles."

"You know everything about me, and I know nothing about you." She rested her elbow on the table and her head on her hand, batting her eyelashes purposefully, signalling that she wasn't going to give up.

"There's not much to know. I finished my internship and came here to do my Ph.D. If all goes as planned, I'm less than six months away from defending my thesis," I concluded with a grimace of panic.

"And then? Will you go back?"

"No... I'm with someone...," I left the sentence hanging, not knowing exactly what to say.

"Ahhh, I see..., it was too good to be true," she muttered under her breath. "And who is he, someone in the field?" Julia stared at me with her green eyes, biting her lower lip with her front teeth.

I brought the glass to my mouth and took a sip before answering, noticing that she followed my every movement with her gaze. "She..."

"Ahhh, I see," she repeated again, furrowing the corners of her lips.

As if nothing I had said mattered to her goals, she opened a provocative smile and leaned towards me, her body getting too close to mine. In the small space between us, she placed her hand on my knee.

"Do you want to get out of here?" she asked me, as if it were the obvious thing to do for two people who had just met.

If the question was direct, my answer was even more so, "Yes."

She was staying in an apartment hotel near the centre. She explained to me that she had come for the conference but was going to stay for three months to take a course on a new laparoscopic technique. The night was warm, and the streets were almost deserted. We ended up stopping at the door of her building.

"Shall we go up?" she questioned, letting go of my hand for the first time.

"I don't think so..., I mean, I have to go back home." Without giving me time for indecision, she took me in her arms and kissed me, right there on the street, at the door of the building, stealing the last drop of my sensibility.

In the single room that made up the apartment, everything seemed to be meticulously in the right place.

"I'm tidy, but not this much! I have daily cleaning service, that's why everything is like this," she declared, laughing at my expression when we entered.

There wasn't much choice of where to sit - either on the wooden chairs at the kitchenette table or on the bed. I opted for the former.

"I have nothing to offer you, only tea... It's a bit out of context, isn't it? Do you want to go out?" she inquired, frowning when she opened the small refrigerator.

I hastened to accept the tea. The soft, warm taste, combined with the aroma emanating from each of the mugs, gave the atmosphere a sense of intimacy and cosiness. The chairs were too uncomfortable, so we took off our shoes and sat cross-legged on the duvet. Beside me, she talked in her husky voice, making me laugh with a humour laced with sarcasm that pierced every moment.

I remember thinking that I shouldn't, but it was stronger than me. I had never cheated on anyone and thought it could never happen, not with me. It seems I was wrong! Julia, for her part, showed complete disregard for the fact that I had told her I was living with someone. She finished her tea, set the mug on the bedside table, and slid down on the bed until she was lying down. She asked me question after question about my Ph.D., wanting to know details about the project. It didn't take much effort for me to get lost in techniques and images, our bodies inching closer with each passing moment, the anticipation building between us.

Her hands touched my knee again, reminding me of the dinner table. But this time, there was no one around us. It was a caress, a touch made with full intention. I couldn't keep my thoughts organized, and gradually, I stopped talking.

Immediately, she withdrew her hand and looked at me, "No, don't stop. I want to know everything about your project. Who knows, maybe we can work together."

How could she keep talking when she was driving me crazy? "I don't know if I can. Do you really want me to continue?"

"Yes! And you? Do you want me to continue?" Sarcasm was the keynote, but I knew she wouldn't come closer until she heard my answer.

Her fingers had a magical touch. The words came out of me in fits and starts, probably making little sense. I couldn't do any better. I closed my eyes and eventually fell silent. Fortunately, she didn't demand what she had asked of me, and this time, she continued.

I realized what it was like to be in love, unable to think, breathe, sleep, or wake up without her image, without her scent. After she left, I realized how little I knew about her life. Julia had a special way of seeming to talk a lot and, in the end, saying almost nothing, at least when the conversation was about her.

Finally, the day of my thesis defence arrived. A phone call from my mother, a distant congratulations muttered through clenched teeth, showed just how important the achievement was.

Three weeks! Three weeks was how long it took me to make the decision that marked my life. I was going to go back home.

I arrived at the airport, and there she was, waiting for me. Roses! No one had ever given me roses before! If I had any doubts, her kiss would have erased them immediately.

Things are never what we imagine, and even less so when we've imagined them for a long time. Of course, Julia wasn't alone. The situation left me disarmed. Why had she never told me anything? She gave me hope for a relationship, or so I understood. She made vows of love, showed up at the airport - what did I misunderstand?

In the following weeks, I immersed myself in work, looked for an apartment, and in less than a month, I regained my space and my mental health.

My autonomy, or at least the pursuit of it, provoked her. She showed up every day, and on many nights, she ended up staying over. One Sunday, after a night where we hardly slept, she invited me for a walk in the park. It wasn't a usual destination. Sitting on an iron bench, in a bucolic setting of families with children and dogs running and laughing, she informed me that she had separated from her partner.

§§

Fili makes himself heard, indicating that it's time for us to finish, "Julia will never stop being who she is. What you have to try to understand is if the magic she creates, and she does create it, is enough to make you happy. Think about that. Shall we schedule the next appointment?"

Chapter 5

February 7th - Once Again

Olivia

For the first time in so many years, I arrive late. More than late, I'm irritated! "Calm down, Olivia, it's only been ten minutes. We'll stay a little longer at the end. Breathe, sit down, and calm yourself," Fili tries, in vain, to reassure me, but what I'm feeling is stronger.

He hands me a glass of water and, instead of sitting on his usual couch, he sits next to me. It's rare to have Fili's presence so close.

I drink the water in one gulp and take a deep breath. "Sorry! I came directly from the hospital. Things are complicated... It's been almost a month, and it's an accumulation of problems."

"Are you talking about the hospital?" he asks, picking up his pen.

§§

The meeting of our working group is scheduled for five o'clock. Just before two, Assunción knocks on the door and opens it even before I respond. "May I come in? Are you very busy?" she asks, sticking her head through the crack. I get up, leaving the presentation I've been preparing for days on the screen.

45

It seems never-ending, never good enough. "Of course, come in."

"I came to challenge you to lunch. Don't you eat? That's why I'm like this, and you maintain that elegance," she jokes in a pleasant tone, revealing a row of very white teeth. "I wanted to talk to you before the meeting."

I eat the soup slowly, taking the opportunity to warm my hands around the bowl, while she takes on the expense of the conversation. "I haven't told you yet, I'm glad you came here. Your work at the oncology centre was phenomenal," she states between two spoonful of soup, which she eats voraciously. "I'm hungry, you can tell, right?" she laughs at herself, patting her belly.

"You're making me uncomfortable. What's coming?" I ask, laughing too.

"Accept the compliments, they're heartfelt..." she interrupts the sentence to drink water, "But you have to be careful."

"Careful with what?" I look at her and shrug my shoulders.

"Your email was a bit hasty, don't you think? People were already worried, and now..." She wipes her mouth with the napkin and leaves the sentence hanging.

"Now what? I don't understand!" I exclaim, surprised. "The only thing I did was share my ideas about process remodelling. I only sent the document to our group, the way you talk, it seems like I shared it with the whole hospital." From her expression, I realize the situation is more serious than I imagined.

"Not you, but Antonio did!" the answer is short and laconic.

"Antonio what?"

"He took the email and sent it to the department directors, nurses, and others of his friends, making a point of adding very inappropriate comments."

"Seriously?! But why? I thought we were going to start discussing ideas today."

"He will never accept your arrival. He spent years beside Arthur, and when that fatality happened, he never considered any other possibility than being the successor. But the bigger problem is named Julia Garcia. She's one of the most intelligent people I know, but also one of the most stubborn. She took over as head of the department recently, and she's the first woman to achieve it. Suddenly, you show up and, from one day to the next, you put that in jeopardy. What did you expect?" Assunción still has all the food on her plate and an empty fork in her hand.

"Changes cause discomfort."

"Do you realize what you're saying? It's a fight of David against Goliath."

I enter the room exactly at the appointed time. Strangely, everyone is already seated as if they had arranged a different time than mine.

As soon as I project the second slide, Antonio and Julia exchange glances. I try to ignore it, but the murmured comments are too much, even for me.

"Excuse me, but is there something you'd like to share?"

Before he can speak, Julia interposes, "I don't know how you think that can work. They're just theories. It's clear you don't get your hands on. When have you ever run a department?"

"Never. I was an anaesthesiologist for many years, but I didn't run the department."

Antonio takes advantage of my pause, "Do you realize that those private hospitals are very different from us? Here, we have obligations, you know? I understand, you want to show off, but please, put your feet on the ground before doing something with irreversible consequences."

"I understand that you don't like seeing me here..." I say with a sigh that I wish I had managed to avoid.

He doesn't give me a chance and interrupts again, "Why wouldn't I like it? You're a pleasant person and surely a great anaesthesiologist, but... I'd like to believe that people are hired on merit."

Assunción, silent until now, intervenes, "You're going too far, Antonio!"

"Let's cut the crap and talk about concrete things. Who knows, maybe we're the ones who don't understand Doctor. Olivia Lopez's fantastic plan. After all, what's the idea for the surgical specialties?" asks Julia with a sarcasm she doesn't even try to disguise.

I pretend to accept her good intentions and explain my idea about integrated units.

"You can't believe what you're saying... it doesn't work, not here, not anywhere. I don't know if you're naive, or if you have other interests behind your 'proposals'," she says, flushed, with an altered voice.

"Do you want to explain yourself? Stop with the insinuations and say what you have to say! Come on, say it to my face!" It's the last straw that makes me lose my composure.

"Do you think we don't know you are where you are because of your husband? But OK, I can live with that if you don't interfere in my way. Now, as if that wasn't enough, you want to persecute people again..."

"Julia, control yourself. Go outside." Once again, Assunción tries to put some order in the room, but it's too late.

I don't really understand where she's going with this. Automatically, I close the computer and turn off the screen. I sit down, take off my glasses, and lean back in my chair, fixing my gaze on Julia's face. Her phone keeps ringing non-stop.

"What do you mean by 'persecute people'?" I finally ask.

"Poor innocent! That role doesn't suit you. Why did the head nurse of the oncology centre leave? And the director of radiotherapy?"

"There are always those who leave."

"Of course, and you didn't even know they're gay..."

"What are you insinuating?!" I ask, incredulous at the accusation.

She rises, her face flushed and hair dishevelled from repeatedly running her hand through it, a gesture that demonstrates, if not her nervousness, her irritation. "Stop this farce and admit why you're here. It will make everything easier. It's obvious that you want Antonio and me to leave, but I'm telling you, as far as I'm concerned, you won't succeed. Everyone knows I'm married to a woman and that Antonio lives with the head nurse of the operating room. Quite a coincidence, isn't it?!"

Before she finishes her sentence, the phone rings again. She finally decides to answer. Shrugging her shoulders, she steps out into the corridor, letting the door slam behind her. Despite the circumstances, one thing is undeniable—she's as seductive as few women I've ever known.

"You have no idea how much I had to fight to get here. Artur was very important; I owe him the position I'm in. He always fought so that no one would be discriminated against," Antonio affirms, now in a much more moderate tone.

I had no idea he was living with a man. I understand his frustration, but he's

49

being manipulated by her.

"You don't know me... You don't know. I'm friends with the head nurse who left the oncology centre. Her departure had nothing to do with me." If I were to expose a bit of my own life, I could easily destroy these pathetic arguments, but I won't allow myself to do that. It wouldn't be fair.

--

As soon as I open the door to the house, I hear Javier's voice: "Did you know that Leonor is living with some woman?" His face is angry, and his voice trembles with exasperation. "You knew, didn't you?" Without giving me time to respond, he continues, "It's immoral! I told her, either she comes back immediately, or she can't count on my money. She can do what she wants, but she has to support herself... The last thing I need is to pay for these deviations..."

I interrupt that string of nonsense, having to raise my voice to be heard: "Yes, it's true! She told me when she was here." I didn't know they were living together, but right now, that's the least important thing, I think. I stand, leaning against the living room doorframe, still wearing my coat with my bag on my shoulder. "She didn't tell you because she already knew the scandal you would make."

"You're on her side, aren't you?" Javier approaches and grabs my arm while speaking, "Is that it?! You're making a fool of me! I'm the last to know, but you both live at my expense."

I can't contain a grimace of pain. His hand squeezes me and hurts me. I realize that before I arrived, he had been drinking; the smell of alcohol is unbearable. Unfortunately, the scene is not unfamiliar to me. It's been a long time since it happened, but I know exactly how it will end if I can't cut him off.

"Stop it. Calm down, please. There's no point in shouting. There's no point in accusing everyone. Leonor is an adult and can do what she wants with her life. None of us can stop her. We have to support her." I walk over to the sofa, set down my bag, and take off my coat, trying to bring some normalcy to all of this.

"Support? Is that what you say when your daughter lives with a woman? You're too naive about certain things... Have you thought about what might be going on in that house?"

I weigh my options; at this moment, it's essential to have a strategy to contain greater harm. "They're friends, colleagues. If they share an apartment, they reduce expenses. It could be a good idea," I evaluate each word and swallow hard.

"A whore! A depraved woman, that's what she is! And your daughter follows her. How can you be so gullible!"

I interrupt him: "So, what did you find out? Who told you? Leonor?"

"Of course not. She's a coward."

I have to restrain myself from saying anything.

"I received a notification from the bank about a payment in foreign currency. You know I'm a holder of her account... I was worried it might be a theft. I called her, and she didn't answer. I insisted two or three times and was surprised by that tramp, who had her phone. She must not be from here; she didn't understand anything I was saying. Then she finally understood and told me that Leonor had gone to the supermarket and left her phone at home.

'At home'! Which home? A few hours later, your daughter called me with some story about sharing an apartment with a friend. I told her, either she comes back immediately, or I won't give her another cent!"

I look at him; he seems a little calmer. "I also contribute to paying the expenses. Leonor can't come back. She can't drop everything just because you want her to."

Contrary to what I intended, my words act like gasoline on fire. He gets up and advances in my direction. His eyes are bloodshot, his jaws clenched, and his eyebrows arched. Sitting on the edge of the sofa, I rethink my possibilities. Without warning, he raises his arm in the air and slaps me. I stifle a scream.

He gets very close, too close, and grabs me hard by the arms, shaking me: "You think? You think we live on what you earn?" he shouts. "I don't know where you're going with this, but you're getting there."

My face and arms hurt, but I know doing nothing is the best option. He continues, totally out of control, "Pleasure?! Not even that anymore! Sometimes I wonder if you've found someone else... Nonsense, right?! Look at you... Who would want..."

I don't know if from exhaustion or lack of arguments, but he gives me a shove that makes me fall to the floor and walks away. He grabs his coat and keys and leaves, slamming the door.

I can't stand up. I stay like this, bent over, curled up, lying on the floor. I cry inside, but I don't shed a single tear. I know I should have put an end to all of this a long time ago. But in one thing, Javier is right—it's his money that pays most of the bills.

I wish I could talk to Ursula...

I wake up in the morning lying on the sofa, aching all over my body with several bruises on my arms. I have no choice but to get up, take a shower, and head to the hospital.

§§

"Again, Olivia?!" says Fili, stopping his writing and looking at me. "Do you feel better? You're a little rosier; when you came in, you were so pale I thought you might faint at any moment."

Fili gets up as he speaks and heads for his sofa. I realize now that he sat next to me, fearing I might feel ill.

"I know! Every time it happens, I'm ashamed of myself. Then I try to forget and convince myself it was the last time. Leonor called me today."

"What did you tell her?" asks Fili, not hiding his curiosity.

"I was a coward. I didn't say anything relevant. I told her not to rush, that maybe it would be good to maintain her independence while giving herself more time to evaluate her feelings. Time is not the best advisor in these kinds of things; it brings us the weight of conscience and the bonds of society. Actually, I hope she doesn't do anything I told her and simply follows her heart."

It's well past my time. I leave through the office door that leads directly to the stairs and wait for the elevator, wiping away a tear I can't hold back with the back of my hand.

Maggy McAndrew

Chapter 6

February 7th – Running

Camila

I'm starting to think that changing my appointment time wasn't a good idea. Fili is late again. There's no one else in the waiting room. In the distance, I can hear the murmur of voices, although what they're saying isn't clear.

I pick up my phone, check my messages, then my emails. Nothing new. Julia says she's going to be late, as if that's a surprise. We should start doing the opposite, and she would only let me know if she was on time. We'd save a lot of messages that way, I think, still feeling irritated.

Finally, the sound of a door closing, and right after, Fili's voice: "Camila, good afternoon. Shall we go in? How are you?"

§§

"I can't believe I convinced you to come today," Paloma has a big smile on her face as she kisses me affectionately on both cheeks. We decided to meet at the park. It's easier than running on the streets, and I haven't run in so long that I'm going to need to get back in shape. She looks fantastic, her curls tied back with a ribbon, wearing black suit that highlights the muscular body of someone who runs several miles every day.

We met about two years ago at a mutual friend's 40th birthday party and discovered that we shared a love for running. Since then, we've been meeting regularly. We can't always manage to get together, the three of us, so often it's just Paloma and me. We've developed a friendship that has become deeper and deeper over time. She is extraordinarily calm, an excellent listener, one of those people who always seems to have the right thing to say at the right time.

"Sorry I'm late. Julia called me and I had to answer. She was out of control. There was a meeting at the hospital and I don't think things went particularly well. I told you, they're in the process of restructuring at Central. They have a new person in charge of clinical management. Back to Julia, she was agitated, screaming. She thinks the new director is homophobic," I pause just to breathe and continue, "As if Julia's changes weren't already enough, the famous Doctor Esther Gonzalez is joining my hospital next week. Do you know who she is? Her reputation precedes her. I can't help but feel a mixture of nervousness and curiosity."

"Seriously?"

"What? Are you talking about Esther?"

"No, about Julia's director. Homophobic?" Paloma asks, frowning. "How awful. Who is it?"

"I don't know, Olivia something. Julia is obsessed with getting the woman out. If I know her, she'll end up succeeding!" I sigh and slowly start running. As we speed up, every muscle hurts. "Today, you're going to have to be gentle with me. Do you know how long it's been since I ran?"

"Seven kilometres and a strawberry smoothie, how does that sound? Olivia Lopez? She was at the Oncology Centre. My company handled their legal representation for a while. I remember her."

"She's been unbearable!", I say, unable to stop thinking about Julia.

"Who, that Olivia?"

"No, Julia. She's in a bad mood every day. If it's not one thing, it's another. She's spending less and less time at home. I don't know..."

"What?"

"She must be seeing someone, again," I say bluntly.

"Why?"

"Is that all you're going to say? Just 'what?', 'why?' Have you gone back to the age of whys? I already told you, she's spending less and less time at home. But what really gets me is that she's obsessed with her phone again."

"And you?"

"Me? Nothing. I've seen this movie before. Most of the time, I try to pretend I don't notice. The other day, Mateo heard us arguing and got scared. Besides, you know how she is. She accuses me, yells, apologizes and in the end... in the end, she resolves everything in bed. I try to resist, I swear it will be different and... and it always ends the same way, a moment of pleasure and a morning filled with frustration."

"Not everything is bad," she says ironically.

"You don't look so good either. Is there something going on that I don't know about?"

Paloma shares with me that she has a new court case. It's a subject that fascinates me, and she knows it. Most of the details are confidential and the ones that aren't are so intricate that I have a hard time understanding the technical details. Just the idea of our fates being shaped by the decisions of strangers gives me the chills. It's a family law case, involving inheritance and custody of two children. She tells me what she can, and I let myself get carried away by her words as if I were in a movie. Gradually, Paloma increases the pace of our run. It's amazing how she can run and talk at the same time without getting even a little bit tired.

Five minutes after we sit down, the much-desired strawberry smoothies are in front of us. I bring the glass close and drink half of it in one go. I let the sugar do its thing and lean back.

Paloma drinks more reservedly, sipping the liquid in small gulps. She fiddles with the cardboard straw between her fingers and adjusts a few strands of hair.

"I have to tell you something," she says in a worried tone, making me sit up straight and stare. "The night before last I ran into Julia..."

I'm surprised, and even more surprised that Julia didn't tell me anything. I make an effort to remember what happened two nights ago. I was at home with Mateo, Julia had to cover for a colleague and spent the night at the hospital. I don't understand how Paloma could have seen Julia.

"I was with a friend at a bar downtown, it must have been midnight or later, when I looked at the bar and saw Julia..."

"Friend?" I can't resist asking, realizing that my comment is uncalled for.

Without answering me, she continues: "She didn't see me. There's no easy way to tell you this, but I also can't not tell you. Julia was with someone, very much with someone. I had never seen the other woman before. She was a blonde with long hair, about 30 years old. They were laughing and drinking. They stayed for half an hour and left together."

I lean back again, although the plastic of the chair isn't comfortable. I feel like I need the support.

"Camila! Camila! Are you okay? Say something," Paloma moves closer and puts her hands around mine in a protective gesture.

"What do you want me to say? That I already knew this was going to happen? I don't know what you want me to say!" I exclaim, a mixture of fury and anger bubbling up inside me. "I'm sorry, it's not you I'm angry with. I'm sorry." I lift myself slightly, just enough to give her a kiss on the cheek, and then let myself fall back onto the chair, my body heavy with the weight of my emotions.

"I had to tell you. You don't deserve this. She's bad for you, she makes you submissive, it's like you're always in debt to her." Her words echo in my mind as I make my way home, the truth of them stinging like a fresh wound.

--

When I arrive home, Mateo is sitting on the couch. He's already taken a bath and looks adorable in his red flannel pyjama, sitting cross-legged, laughing at the cartoons. I don't want to, and I'm not going to, argue with Julia about what I just learned.

The three of us have dinner together, which lately has been a rare occurrence. Mateo makes us laugh with his stories and funny faces. "Mommy, we have a party..., for Carnival, I want to go as a doctor like you..., I want to operate on hearts. When I told Pep, he asked if you can make people fall in love.

Can you? He needs your help..., his parents aren't in love anymore, he says they're going to separate..., can you fix their hearts? Can you? Can you operate on them?"

Not even Julia has an immediate answer. Fortunately, he doesn't stop and continues uninterrupted, "You're going to the party, aren't you? There's going to be a parade..., and prizes!"

I answer affirmatively and look at her, waiting for her agreement. Instead, she responds, "Mommy is at the hospital, maybe she can't go to your school, but you can tell me all about it later, and show me the pictures..., you can film it, that's even better!"

--

I have to run if I don't want to miss the train. I sit down, panting, and put my backpack under the seat. Out of the corner of my eye, I can see a boy sleeping soundly, his head drooping, his mouth slightly open. I focus again on the landscape. The train stops and a few more sleepy-looking people get on. It picks up speed again and I let myself get lost in thought once more. I raise my head and look at the seat across the aisle, previously empty. A woman has sat down, the same woman as the other day, with the same red-covered book. I observe her, not that there's much to see. She runs her hand through her hair, brushes away some strands that fall over her forehead, and remains fixed on her reading. Outside, the day begins to dawn. The train stops again, the movement makes her shudder and, for a moment, she fixes her eyes on mine.

When I arrive at the hospital, the atmosphere in the locker room is livelier than usual for a Monday morning. As soon as I approach, I hear voices of crossed conversations.

"Is something going on?" I interrupt as I get dressed, waving to the group chatting on the other side of the room.

"You don't know?" asks one of the nurses, shaking her head.

"Know what?"

"Esther, Doctor Esther Gonzalez, the star of neurosurgery, is already here, and you're the one operating with her today. I don't know if it's an honour or a punishment," she comments, with a comical expression. "Come on, hurry up if you don't want to be late for the first meeting."

I walk over to the sinks and start disinfecting my hands. A red-haired woman turns on the faucet next to me and, without saying anything, also begins to meticulously scrub her fingers, nails, and palms in rhythmic, repetitive motions. I recognize her, she's the new chief, Esther Gonzalez.

"Good morning," I say in a low voice. The figure has an intimidating air about her, very white skin, closed features, and a set of freckles on her cheekbones that soften the rigidity of her expression. "I'm Camila..."

Without letting me finish, she replies, "I know who you are, Doctor Rossi, the protected intern, the daughter of Amelia Velasquez."

For a brief moment I pause what I'm doing and look at her. Her eyes don't waver and remain fixed on the water running in the sink, reddened by the disinfecting liquid.

It doesn't take many minutes to see that she's great at what she does. She takes command and proceeds at a fast and confident pace. It's a spinal surgery, not very complicated, but requiring meticulousness and patience. To my amazement, as soon as we started, she requested music. From time to time, she nods her head to the beat and smiles to the sound of a popular band. She chats with the anaesthesiologist as if she knows her, and yet, apart from a few monosyllables, she hasn't addressed me yet.

"Does Amelia still operate?" she asks suddenly, out of nowhere.

"My mother?" I utter clumsily. Of course she's referring to my mother, who else?!

"She's good, she's great..., one of the best."

Not knowing what to say, I choose to remain silent, pretending to be absorbed in the suture I'm doing.

"I met her in Italy..."

I still have no clue what I'm supposed to answer.

As she speaks, Esther positions herself behind me, placing her right hand next to mine inside the surgical field, letting her body touch mine in the movement.

"You see this tissue here?" she asks, pointing to a wrinkled, yellowish fragment just over five millimetres, lodged next to the vertebral body. "It's tissue that tore when you pulled. It got stuck here. It may not matter at all, but it could also lead to fibrosis."

I'm stunned by the change of subject and the physical contact. I stop what I'm doing, immobilizing myself. She goes on in a long monologue about fibrosis, infection, and the need to ensure completely clean processes. With the forceps in her hand, she grabs the thin piece of tissue and removes it. The movement is swift and precise. I can't help but be impressed by the fact that she saw this tiny fragment move.

"You can continue," she says, "Prepare to close, calmly, layer by layer." She removes her hand and sets down the forceps, but doesn't move away. She stays glued to my back, observing every movement. I try to concentrate. Through the gowns I feel the warmth of her body against mine. The situation is uncomfortable, but I sense that if I move, it will be even worse.

§§

I look at Fili, trying to interpret his expression and continue, "I didn't know what to think, much less what to do. Those were ten or fifteen endless minutes. Until now, I haven't figured out if she had any intention, I hope it was just my imagination..."

Unlike usual, Fili interrupts me: "And what did you imagine?"

Maggy McAndrew

Chapter 7

February 21st - David vs. Goliath

Olivia

Today I arrived too early. There are still fifteen minutes until the scheduled time. I hesitated between going up or getting a coffee, but it's too cold to walk around from one place to another. I sit on one of the sofas in the waiting room, take off my coat, and place it over my legs. Gradually, I let myself get lost in thought, and I almost startle when I see Fili standing at the door, waiting for me.

"How are you, how have these two weeks been? Calmer?" Fili asks questions while searching for the pen that rolled under his sofa.

"Calmer, I think so..." I reflect, my voice tinged with uncertainty.

"You don't seem very convinced..." Fili notes, studying me intently.

§§

Sitting in the office with headphones on and music blasting, I keep putting off the moment to go home. My heart feels heavy, weighed down by the events of the day.

Before leaving, I decide to come to the bar for a coffee, just to pass a few more minutes. Standing in line, I follow the conversation of two interns right behind me. From what they say, I understand they are from anaesthesia, and the topic centre's around the operating room schedules and the privileges of some, explicitly criticizing the head of service. I hear the ring of a phone, and instinctively I look back.

"It's the call code for the resuscitation team... I have to go," is all I hear him say to his colleague before he rushes off.

"You? You're on call?" the other asks, not hiding his surprise. I'm also amazed.

"I am. There's no one else... Do you know how many of us are here tonight? I hope I don't have to be the one..." The end of the sentence is barely audible as he hurries away.

On impulse, I leave the line and follow him. I catch up to him in the emergency department corridor. "I'm going with you, I'm an anaesthesiologist," I say, my voice steady despite the adrenaline pumping through my veins.

He sketches a smile, nods, and doesn't reply.

From the commotion, I understand that whatever happened took place in the waiting room. The security guards try to prevent the confusion from increasing and inform me that the patient has already been transported inside, to the resuscitation room.

"No pulse," someone says, urgency lacing their words.

"Keep bagging. Start compressions. Defibrillator. Let's intubate. Put in another line." I know the voice giving the orders. I look around and see Julia next to the defibrillator. For a moment our eyes meet, an unspoken understanding passing between us.

"I'll intubate," I say without hesitation. "He must have a difficult airway." My hands are shaking slightly, but I force them to steady.

"Fibrillation! Prepare to shock. Clear!" We all take our hands off as our eyes remain fixed on the monitor. Nothing, still no pulse. My heart sinks.

"Compressions. Another dose of adrenaline." Julia commands, her voice unwavering.

"I can't see anything! It's all obstructed. It won't pass! Restart bagging," I say after a failed intubation attempt. The patient is very obese and no matter how hard I try, I can't see the vocal cords to pass the tube. It's been a long time since I've done this. Momentarily, I freeze, paralyzed by doubt and fear.

It must not have been more than a few seconds, but they feel like long minutes when I hear the young intern's voice next to me: "Doctor Lopez! Doctor Lopez, do you need help?"

"No! Stop bagging." I place the laryngoscope again and continue to see practically nothing. Somewhat blindly, I very slowly introduce the tube. "I visualize the cords! Epiglottis!" I rotate a little to the right and there it is, it passed. "I'm in! Inflate the cuff."

I raise my head and look around. I ask the young man who remains by my side for the stethoscope, "It's in. Symmetrical sounds," I confirm, relieved.

"No pulse. Still in fibrillation. Prepare to shock. Clear!" Julia's voice is heard again, and a few seconds later, "We have a rhythm!" A collective sigh of relief sweeps through the room.

The cardiology team has arrived in the meantime and takes over command of the situation. From what I can gather, the patient had just been admitted when he lost consciousness still in the waiting room; no one knows exactly what happened.

"Thank you, Doctor Lopez, I don't know how to thank you, I wouldn't have known what to do," the young man thanks me as he accompanies me to the work room, wringing his hands.

I feel myself trembling from head to toe, it's been so long... "Go rest," I say, "You shouldn't have been put in this position. I'm glad I could help."

When I'm alone, I sit in a chair and take a deep breath. Without strength or spirit, I do what I always do on these occasions - I call Ursula.

"How are you? How are things?" Ursula asks immediately, as if expecting my call. Her warm voice is a balm to my frayed nerves.

"What things? Right now there's so much going on, you have to be more specific," I reply, letting a thousand images flash before my eyes. "What things?" I repeat again.

"Everything! Are you sad?" Ursula probes gently.

"I don't know, I'm irritated..." In a detailed description, I relate not only what just happened, but also the incidents of the last few days. Tears prick at my eyes as the weight of it all crashes down on me.

"Be happy that you made a difference in someone's life. That's what you have to hold on to, not what the idiots who work there say and think... One of these days I'm going to come there and give you the biggest kiss they've ever seen, it will be a pleasure!" She laughs, and it's contagious. We both laugh, imagining the scene. For a moment, the heaviness lifts.

"Seriously, you don't know how hard it's been to resist the pressure. Complaints and threats are pouring in. Three people left the anaesthesia team. Yesterday, two more presented justifications for not doing nights, and now this." I sigh, rubbing my temples.

"Enough about the hospital. Changing the subject, how is Leonor? By the way, happy birthday! I forgot to tell you on the actual day." The words are uttered with the irony of someone who knows my marriage from the inside.

"She's fine... confused, but fine." I'm going to share Leonor's dilemmas, I have to talk to someone. Ursula doesn't say anything, waiting for me to continue. "She told me she's in love with a woman."

"Wow! That's surprising! I don't know what amazes me more, that she's in love with a woman or that she told you," Ursula jokes, but her voice is gentle. "But that leaves her confused?"

"It seems the other woman wants an open relationship. Her life experience is light-years ahead of Leonor's." I confess, worry creeping into my tone.

"You're assuming..." Ursula points out.

"What do you mean by that?" I ask, unsatisfied with the comment.

"Don't be offended."

"Right, you're correct. I still see her as 8 years old, a braid on each side, running to school with a backpack." I admit, nostalgia mixing with maternal concern.

"What else did she say? I love stories. Knowing your daughter, I promise I won't let my imagination run wild, because unlike you, I don't imagine her as 8 years old."

I pretend to be indignant, but Ursula continues, "Poor little Leonor, so helpless and defenceless, do you really think so? Look at us!"

"What does this have to do with us? There you go again... We're at a different age, with different experiences." I counter, frustrated.

"Really?! It's an age issue?" Ursula says sarcastically, challenging my perspective.

I sigh, knowing deep down she's right. Leonor is an adult now, capable of making her own choices. But it doesn't stop the worry from gnawing at me. I just want to protect her, shield her from potential heartbreak. Though as Ursula reminds me, we've all been there - stumbling through love and life, making mistakes, getting back up. It's part of the journey.

For now, I push aside thoughts of Leonor and focus on the incredible save.

--

When I arrive home, to my astonishment, Javier is in the kitchen preparing dinner. What could be the occasion, I ask myself, my heart fluttering with a mix of surprise and cautious anticipation.

We sit at the table, savouring the aroma of mushrooms and the taste of a very chilled sparkling wine. I place another forkful of rice in my mouth; it melts between my teeth in a flavourful cream. "It's fantastic! It's been so long since you've made this, I almost forgot. It's one of my favourite dishes," I exclaim, genuine appreciation warming my voice.

While we eat, we chat about trivial topics, never addressing what happened or even bringing up Leonor again. It's always like this. The subject is never touched upon again, as if it had never existed. A familiar dance of avoidance, steps ingrained over the years.

We're having coffee when he finally broaches the reason for this dinner: "Olivia, I wanted to talk to you about the proposal I have to go to Switzerland."

About time, I think to myself, saying nothing, a twinge of resentment simmering beneath the surface.

"We haven't talked about this yet. It's also true that, until yesterday, I didn't know much. The current director is leaving the Company at the end of the year, and if I accept, the position is mine. It's the opportunity of a lifetime!" he says exuberantly, eyes shining with ambition. "It's more, much more, than I could have dreamed of."

Work is what makes him vibrate - the money, the power, the small and big victories. It's the true love of his life, I realize with a pang of bitterness.

"It's fifteen countries, a thirty percent increase, not even counting the bonuses. What do you think? It's a great opportunity for you! For Leonor, it's the same, it doesn't matter if she comes to visit us in Switzerland or comes here."

I stop listening to him. How can he think that going to Switzerland is an opportunity for me and completely ignore the fact that I just started a new project? Anger rises in my chest, hot and sharp.

"If you want, you can even stop working. Money isn't a problem. You can just do the things you like. You're always complaining that you don't have time," he continues, oblivious to my growing fury.

"Are you kidding?! How can you think my work is worth nothing?! How can you think I'm going to drop everything to follow you, who knows where? You're going to do what you want. And me? Have you ever asked what I want?" I blurt out, agitated, my voice trembling with suppressed emotion.

"Don't shout, we're just talking," he states in a falsely measured tone. The red spots on his face and neck don't let him hide how irritated he is. "Do you think I shouldn't accept? Is that it?"

It's a poisoned question. He knows I'll never tell him not to accept. "Of course not! You should go, if that's what you want. But you can't think we're going to follow you on this path, which is increasingly only yours and no one else's," I retort, standing my ground even as my heart cracks a little more.

"What do you mean by that? I'm still the one paying the bills. Travel, houses, schools, everything! You've never heard me complain, have you?" he fires back, victimhood dripping from his words.

"That's what you're doing," I say, taking a deep breath to regain the energy I know I'll need, steeling myself for the battle ahead.

Javier can't contain himself and continues shouting, "What do you want? Do you want me to go alone? That's easy, but then don't complain." He slams his fist on the table and storms out, slamming the door, leaving me alone with the shattered remains of our evening, our marriage, our life.

§§

"It must have been a difficult conversation," Fili says gently, compassion softening his features. "You have to think about what you really want. If he goes alone, it will most likely be the end of your marriage."

"You think so? We're already so distant, even living in the same house," I reflect, the observation more for myself than for him. "I can't leave everything..." My voice wavers, torn between duty and desire, fear and possibility.

"Everything? What is 'everything'?" Fili asks, looking me in the eyes, his gaze both probing and understanding.

I pause, considering his question, really considering it for perhaps the first time. What is everything? "I don't know," I admit, voice small but determined. "But I think it's time I figured it out."

Maggy McAndrew

Chapter 8

February 21st – Panic Attacks

Camila

I arrive at the office in the late afternoon; it's already dusk outside. Fili comes to the door to get me and invites me in. I notice that he has the small desk lamp on, flooding the space with a pleasant, intimate yellowish light. When he sits down, he makes his usual movement of crossing his leg, resting his ankle on the knee of the other leg, leaving his sock visible. Over the years, I've seen dozens of his socks with their more or less discreet patterns, and observing them has become almost a ritual in each session. Today, the black socks are covered with small green frogs, resting on leaves, lounging in an immense lake.

Fili looks at me, waiting for me to start the conversation. I don't keep him waiting and begin recounting the last few days.

§§

Today, nothing is happening the way I want it to, I reflect as I rub my hands too hard, running my fingers over each other, letting the water run almost up to my elbow. A young woman was admitted during the night, and the team decided to wait until morning to operate, but I have the notion that every minute counts. This morning, the woman with the red book wasn't in the carriage, or at least I didn't see her. It's a shame; I was starting to get used to her presence, finding comfort in our silent connection.

I enter the room with the patient already anesthetized and everyone in their places. The music today has a classic rhythm, slow and solemn, a contrast to the tension thrumming through my veins.

"Ready to start, dear?" Esther asks, making me uncomfortable with the endearment.

"Of course, Doctor Gonzalez, whenever you want," I reply without lifting my eyes, trying to mask my unease.

It's a procedure I've done countless times. The screens are on, the nurse beside me hands me the catheter, and I start the process. During the first few minutes, everything goes as planned, and I slowly advance the wire, assessing the risks at every moment.

"Tachycardic rhythm! Blood pressure rising!" the anaesthesiologist exclaims, alarm colouring her voice.

"Stop! Pull back!" Esther directs, her eyes fixed on the screen.

I do exactly what she asks. We're still far from the target. I pull the wire back a little, and the rhythm stabilizes again.

"We can proceed," she says, nodding at me to continue.

I take a deep breath and move my hand again. My heart is pounding, and sweat is running under my cap, anxiety prickling across my skin.

"Tachycardia!" echoes loudly in the room.

"Stop!" Esther says in a low voice, leaving no doubt that it's an order. "The catheter pressured the vessel wall; there must be a rupture... There! See that thin line of contrast? It's outside the limit. Pull back carefully. We'll insert another microcatheter and try to continue. The bleeding is minimal."

"The rhythm is still high," the anaesthesiologist states, concern etched on her face.

"Doctor Rossi! Camila!" I hear from far away, my mind foggy with panic.

"Switch places with me!" Esther has positioned herself by my side without me noticing. She looks at the anaesthesiologist and continues, "Control the blood pressure. Protamine to reverse the anticoagulation. She may decompensate at any moment."

I can't feel my body, and I'm unable to move. I want to get out of here, but my muscles won't obey me, paralyzed by fear.

"Camila, calm down... everything is under control. I'm going to put my hands over yours, and you'll pass me the wire when I say so. Then you'll step aside and stay here to assist me, okay?" Her voice is calm and sounds extraordinarily slow, like someone talking to a child. Little by little, I recover and do what she asks, shame and relief warring within me.

With unparalleled skill, she keeps the first microcatheter still and manages to insert the second. The movements are meticulous, and time seems to stand still. The rhythm has stabilized, and from the silence on the anaesthesia side, there are no more complications, at least not in this minute. More than an hour passes until she gives a laugh and says, "Can we change the music, please?" The tension breaks, and I can breathe again.

I spent the entire afternoon in neuro-critical care monitoring the patient. Fortunately, she's doing well. As I walk to the train station, I recall Esther's words when we left the operating room. She closed the door, and we were alone in the workroom. I trembled at the possibilities, dreading her judgment.

"You froze! Why?" she asked directly, her gaze piercing.

"I'm sorry!" I blurted out, shame heating my cheeks.

"I'm not looking for apologies. I know you're a great surgeon, but I also know that lately, you've been hiding from more complex procedures. I've been looking at your cases, and you haven't had a single recent cutting-edge surgery, in contrast to before you were away when you had several. It seems counterintuitive," she observed, curiosity and concern mingling in her voice.

"It's true," I reply, sitting down and holding my head in my hands, elbows on the table. She maintains the silence, forcing me to continue. "I have panic attacks," I murmur. It's hard to admit, vulnerability clawing at my throat. "They started when Mateo was born, and a year later, they got so bad that I had to stay home. It was horrible. But it never happened in the operating room before today."

"It's common... and how are you now?" she asks gently, compassion softening her features.

"I'm better. The sessions with Doctor Riviera..."

"Fili? He's excellent!" She nods approvingly.

"Today, I don't know what happened... if you think it's better, I won't operate," I offer, defeat weighing heavy on my shoulders.

"Don't be ridiculous. You were one of the best, and you're going to be again. Enough talk. You're going to see our patient, and I'm going home," she declares, her tone brooking no argument.

Without saying anything else, she approaches me, caresses my face, turns around, and leaves, leaving me alone with my thoughts and a glimmer of hope amidst the lingering fear.

--

I make my way back on an almost empty train. I put on my headphones, rest my head against the window, and close my eyes, seeking a moment of solitude to process the day's events.

When I see my mother's name on the screen, my first thought is that it can only be another problem. I consider not answering, but I know that later, it will cost me having to call her back and listen to her unpleasant comments, a price I'm not willing to pay.

"How are you? Well?" The question leaves no room for any answer other than to agree. I don't think she really wants to know how I am; it's just a formality before getting directly to the reason for her call, a perfunctory gesture devoid of genuine care.

"Yes, all good. And you?" With the distance, I've lost the habit of asking about her or my father individually. There was never great closeness between us, but despite everything, before I went to the United States, I had the feeling that I could count on him. He was distant, formal, but we talked. I asked for his opinions, and he genuinely tried to be part of my life. My sister is the favourite daughter, and there was never any doubt about that. The brilliant student, gifted in music, a lawyer, married, with two daughters, just like herself. My brother was always excluded; he didn't date, didn't play sports, and didn't even like going out or drinking. The things and people he liked were kept far away, in the utmost secrecy, a part of himself he had to hide.

"We're fine," she replies laconically. "I imagine you don't know, but your niece is turning 10..." Of course I know, why wouldn't I?! "Your father and I decided to throw a party for a group of close friends and family. It's an important date and deserves to be celebrated. I want to know if I can count on you and Mateo?"

The question catches me off guard. The degree of nervousness that takes hold of me during these phone calls is beyond anything minimally reasonable, an irrational fear that grips my heart. Not letting the silence settle, I respond automatically, "Yes, of course. Tell me the time, and we'll be there."

How could I have answered 'yes, of course'? The invitation was explicit, 'you and Mateo'. We've been together for years, and they continue to pretend that Julia doesn't exist, erasing her from our lives as if she were a mere inconvenience.

I arrive home to find Mateo angry, unable to explain what Mommy is doing, but she hasn't finished the game they had started, leaving him frustrated and upset. I gather from the conversation that Julia has been home for over two hours, lost in her work.

I knock and enter without waiting for a response. She's wearing headphones, immersed in images and articles, with both computer screens full of documents while she takes handwritten notes in one of her notebooks. She looks up, glances at me, and removes one of her headphones.

"Everything okay?" she asks. "I'm almost done. Do you need anything?"

I can't help but notice the distance between us. Not a kiss, not a caress, nothing. Worse, I don't even feel the lack anymore, numbness replacing the ache of longing. I end up not mentioning the phone call and decide to wait until dinner. At the table, I broach the subject: "You know, my mother called me today..."

"Why, did someone die?" she jokes sarcastically, her tone biting.

"No. She wanted to invite us to my niece's birthday. Shall we go? Or should I make up some excuse and say no?"

"Let's go, please Mommy, let's go!" Mateo says, bouncing in his chair. "I love parties!"

"I'm not going! But I think it's great that you go with him," Julia replies immediately, her voice firm and unyielding.

The conversation continues, divided between questions about the party and sarcastic remarks about my parents. I achieved my goal; she'll never know she wasn't invited, spared the pain of their rejection once more.

I wake up to the shrill sound of the alarm clock, not remembering having fallen asleep. Six in the morning, I have to hurry if I intend to catch the train. As I step into the shower, I feel the hot water running down my body, and I remember the look of the woman with the red cover book. Will I see her today? The thought brings a flicker of warmth amidst the morning chill.

§§

"You shared the panic attacks with Esther Gonzalez?" Fili asks, lifting his head and looking at me, curiosity mingling with concern in his gaze.

"Yes, why? Do you think I did something wrong?" I ask, surprised, brushing away the hair that insists on falling over my eyes, a nervous habit I can't seem to shake.

"I'm afraid she might use it against you," he confesses, worry etched on his features.

"I don't believe that. She seemed concerned, implying that she's going to support me. Besides, I feel much better," I reassure him, conviction colouring my words.

"Of course, you're right. There's no reason not to share," he agrees, offering a supportive smile that eases the knot in my stomach, a silent understanding passing between us.

Chapter 9

March 6th - Aortic Aneurysm

Olivia

The windows seem to shake with the force of the rain. The already dark sky is sliced by lightning, appearing from all sides like rays of light. The beauty of the storm is immense, but it doesn't disguise the power of nature, which always gives me a chill in my stomach. Although I left the car very close, I got completely soaked just crossing the street and getting here.

I enter the waiting room, as always empty, take off my jacket and place it open on one of the couches, hoping it might dry. Before I even have time to sit down, Fili appears at the door and signals for me to follow him. We enter the office together and sit down.

"How are you?" he asks, as he always does, while preparing things, picking up the notebook and pen, at the same time leaning back and crossing his leg. "Confused!" is the only thing I say. Then, on purpose, I smile and let a prolonged silence settle.

"How laconic, you don't seem like yourself. What have you been up to? Playing with fire?" Fili is ironic, looking at me with a mordant smile.

"So many things have happened, I don't know where to start," I confess, my mind reeling with the events of the past few days.

"Perhaps at the beginning, it's always a good option," he suggests, his eyes glinting with curiosity.

§§

It's almost seven o'clock, I should go home. Alone, I won't prepare dinner, I'll have to survive with yesterday's leftovers. Nothing that worries me. I save the document I'm working on, turn off the computer, and stand up. I take off my lab coat and grab the jacket hanging on the coat rack. I already have one sleeve on when there's a knock at the door.

The head nurse of the operating room opens a crack and peeks in.

"Carlos?" I'm surprised by the unexpected visit. "Come in, I was just leaving. What's going on, can I help?" It's not at all usual for him to come to my office, and even less so at this hour. I take off the half-worn jacket again and put it on the table.

He looks worried. He sits down and nervously rubs his hands together. "We have an urgent surgery in a little while. When I found out, about two hours ago, I talked to the team leader, and everything was fine. He's on call, with the two youngest interns, plus the anaesthesiologist who supports obstetrics. It wasn't ideal, but it worked! But now he just came to me, says he's running a high fever and is leaving. Only the two interns will be left during the night..., it's impossible. They can't..., they don't have the training, it's too complex a surgery." As he speaks, colour returns to his face, and I notice he relaxes the tension in his jaws a bit.

84

"I see..." I say, trying to integrate the information. "Can't we really postpone until tomorrow morning?"

"It's a descending aortic aneurysm, in a young man in his twenties..." I immediately understand the severity and urgency of the situation. Carlos continues, "We can transfer the patient to the University Hospital."

"No! It's risky." I consider the consequences of a transfer, and of not doing it.

"I'll call and see if any of the colleagues who are off duty can come," I say, as I head to the secretary's desk to consult the schedules. I call each of the theoretically available doctors one by one, "...yes, I know I'm calling you at very short notice, but if it wasn't urgent, I wouldn't be bothering you...", "I understand, I completely understand that you have other commitments..." After several conversations all the same, there's no one else I can call. Carlos remains seated, his gaze lowered, staring at the tabletop.

"What do we do? Do we transfer the patient?" he asks, without raising his eyes.

I remain silent for a moment, flooded by a feeling of anguish and at the same time an uncontrollable urge to act, "No!"

"What do you mean, no? We don't have anyone to anesthetize..., we can't put one of the youngest..."

"Of course not! I'll go!"

Carlos raises his head and looks at me, frowning slightly. "What do you mean, you'll go?"

"You have a surgery and need an anaesthesiologist, well then, you have me." I stand up and smile. Adrenaline takes over my body, and I'm flooded with unexpected energy. I put the lab coat back on, "Let's go, let's go to the operating room. You have an hour to explain everything I need to know so I don't look completely 'out of place'." I cross my fingers in a gesture of faith, which makes him laugh. His face has cleared and he's back to his usual smile. We walk together through the corridors. At this hour there are few people, and our journey is peaceful. We pass one of the colleagues from cardiology, and two of the emergency doctors who greet me. Since the day of the resuscitation, I've gained points with some colleagues. In the doctors' room of the operating room, one of the interns is already waiting for me.

"Doctor Lopez, can I summarize what I know about the case for you," she declares almost fearfully.

"That would be great. Please, call me Olivia. Let's do this. Tell me what we know, and from there we'll make the plan," I reply, flashing the most captivating of my smiles.

At my words, she smiles too. She puts her hands on the keyboard and goes through the clinical record: "This is a 28-year-old man with a family history of aneurysms, an uncle and a cousin, but without an established etiological diagnosis. Marfan Syndrome was suspected, but never confirmed. It's an aneurysm of the beginning of the descending aorta, already known for two years, but seemed controlled." She interrupts the explanation and looks at me, checking if I'm following. I stop writing and make a gesture of agreement. "He had severe chest pain and came to the hospital. They evaluated him and on the MRI they found rapid and unexpected growth since the last evaluation..."

In this context, the decision to operate seems indisputable. The risk of rupture imposes the urgency of the procedure.

Carlos re-enters the room carrying three cups of coffee in his hand. He hands one to each of us. "We're going to need it," he comments.

"I'm sure we will, thank you!" I exclaim, surprised by the gesture. "Is there a surgical plan already defined?" I ask.

"The surgery team says they'll be down in a few minutes. From what I've heard, they're going to try an endoscopic approach."

"Are you sure? It seems too big for that to me..., but I'm not a specialist," I add right after, not wanting to seem like I'm interfering. "For us, it would be much easier. Anyway, let's prepare the room for all eventualities. If it's endoscopic, so much the better, but we'll arrange everything as if it were open surgery. Cerebral monitoring, hemodynamic, and material for extracorporeal circulation," I articulate short, quick sentences, almost swallowing the words.

"I like your determination," says Carlos. "Rest assured, I'll leave everything ready, if necessary, you just have to ask, if not, all the better."

The surgery will take hours, and then I have to do the recovery follow-up. I take a deep breath and mentally review all the steps. The agitation is such that until the moment they open the door, I don't stop to think about who is going to operate. Julia Garcia! She looks at me and then around the room: "Where is the anaesthesia team?" she asks.

"I'm the one who's going to anesthetize," I reply.

Her countenance momentarily changes, showing perplexity. Raul, for his part, doesn't seem to find anything extraordinary and explains the surgical plan to me in detail.

I put on the cap and adjust the elastic bands of the mask. I have the same feeling as the day I arrived at this hospital and passed through the entrance doors for the first time, a mixture of anxiety and euphoria. My heart races with anticipation, but I take a deep breath to steady myself.

I pull up a stool to the head of the patient and begin a brief exchange of words to calm him down. I learn that he is an architect and has a 2-year-old daughter. As would be expected, he is nervous, but at the same time, very aware of everything that is going to happen. I place a reassuring hand on his shoulder and promise him we'll take good care of him.

I call the younger colleague, one of the nurses, and in a few moments he is anesthetized. I watch his features relax as he drifts off into a deep, medicated sleep.

Julia enters the room and puts on a second pair of gloves. Everything is ready for us to start. She looks at me and asks in a tone I hadn't heard from her before, "Do you mind if I put on music? It helps me concentrate."

"It's no problem for me," I reply, appreciating anything that will help this challenging surgery go smoothly.

The room fills with the sound of a piano, Mozart, most likely performed by Kissin. The beautiful notes seem to dance through the sterile air. Julia begins, and as planned, she makes the endoscopic approach. Everything seems to be going well. I keep checking the tracings, verifying the values, and making an adjustment or two to the medication running in the perfusion.

"Damn it! Shit! Look! It's much bigger than it looked on the MRI!" Her voice is altered and denotes her concern. My stomach clenches at her words.

The other surgeon by her side leans in, not letting go of the material he has in his hand: "No doubt, it's bigger! We're not going to be able to do this like this! What do you want to do? We can't abort..." Although he keeps his hands steady, he also shows his nervousness. Drops of sweat trickle down his forehead, which one of the nurses takes care of wiping with a compress.

"There's no other choice, we have to convert!" The phrase is said with assertiveness and irritation. Julia drops the instruments she has in her hand, leaving her colleague to finish. She walks to one corner of the room, and looks me in the eye: "Can you come here for a moment, Olivia." I can't help but notice that it's the first time she's called me by my name, forsaking the irony.

"Of course!"

"We have to go open..."

"Okay." I nod, trying to project a calm I don't quite feel.

"Have you done this before?" the question comes out fearfully. What options does she have if I say no?

"Yes, Julia, yes! I worked for many years as an anaesthesiologist in cardiothoracic. I haven't done an intervention like this in a while, but there are things you don't forget," I say, trying to convince myself that what I'm saying is true. I draw on my years of experience to steady my nerves.

"We have to ask for monitoring and get everything ready for the possibility of extracorporeal circulation, we're going to need it..."

I interrupt her before she calls the nurses. "Look, I don't know if I did the right thing, but I thought about the possibility of this happening and asked Carlos to prepare everything, in case we needed it. So, you don't have to do anything, I'll talk to him and you can start in five minutes. If you want, go outside, prepare yourself, because the night is going to be long."

Julia doesn't say anything, her eyes speak for her. She turns and walks towards the door. She stops a few steps ahead, turns back, and says, "Thank you!" Despite the mask I can see that she smiles. A wave of relief washes over me.

Almost five hours later we leave the operating room. The young man resisted well and made my job easier. The surgery went without serious complications and they managed to repair the aneurysm. Now it's a matter of waiting for the next few hours, the next few days, to be able to breathe a sigh of relief.

I accompany him to the Intensive Care Unit. In a small waiting room, his mother and wife await news, clinging to each other with desperate hope. I look around and see that Julia is not present, Raul opens the door and addresses them, and shortly after, they hug him emotionally, tears streaming down their faces.

Without difficulty I convince my colleagues in the Unit that I'm going to spend the night in the empty doctor's support room. They usually rest in the larger room on the other side of the floor.

I turn on the light and observe the space. I've never been here before. It's a small room with two beds, one on each side. On the wall opposite the door, there's a window, now completely closed. Right by the entrance, there's a bathroom, also tiny.

I find the strength to take a quick shower and put on a clean scrub suit. I kick off my shoes and lie down, fully dressed, on one of the beds. When I close my eyes, I remember Julia, her green eyes, her distress when she called me. My heart flutters at the memory of her vulnerability, a side of her I've never seen before.

I don't know how much time has passed when I wake up to the sound of someone gently opening the door to the room. I don't move and pretend to be asleep, my pulse quickening. The bathroom light comes on and as my eyes adjust to the dim light, I can make out that it's a woman. She closes the door and the room plunges back into darkness. A few minutes later, the bathroom door opens again. This time I'm attentive and I realize that it's Julia, she took off her scrub pants and is wearing only her underwear and a t-shirt. My breath catches in my throat at the sight of her long, toned legs. She turns off the light and lies down on the bed against the other wall.

I roll over, but I can't fall asleep. Does she know it's me here? The fatigue has disappeared, and I'm completely awake. I feel my heart race and desire take hold of me. I try, in vain, to calm myself, but the effort is completely fruitless. It's as if my body has dissociated from my brain and is acting on its own. My muscles contract, my skin tingles, and I'm flooded with a wave of heat.

In an unthinking act, without measuring the consequences, or even thinking about them, I push back the sheet, get up and approach the other bed. She remains motionless with her back to me, her regular breathing seems to indicate she's asleep. I pull back the edge of the blanket and lie down next to her, trying not to wake her. I don't know what I'm doing, but it's stronger than me.

I don't touch her, leaving a space between us, but gradually, I gain confidence. She moves one of her legs, placing it over mine. I freeze. Her breathing seems to indicate a deep sleep. I bring my face close to her hair and inhale deeply. Despite the day we've had, the slightly acidic smell of her perfume can still be detected. I place my hand on her and run it over the soft fabric, exploring. I kiss her hair, sure that my gesture will not wake her. My mistake!

She turns over suddenly, startling me. I pull back. Without letting me say anything, she grabs me with both hands, pulls me to her and kisses me with the same impetuosity she used to criticize me.

She doesn't say anything and doesn't ask anything either. She frees herself from her t-shirt making her intentions explicit. I feel her and, unable to contain myself, I sigh. Her hands have something extraordinary about them. I visualize her putting on gloves, long fingers, firm hands. Now it's skin against skin. I let her continue, I feel her touch, playing and teasing me.

I regain the minimum of lucidity to allow myself to take back control. I can't see anything in the dark of the room. But, without needing light, I kiss her, a hot kiss which only ends due to the urgency to breathe. When she tries to touch me, I stop her, and place my hand around her. The gesture is simple and direct, immediately having the desired effect.

She's nestled in my body, I don't have time or space for more.

"Liv! Now!"

Fortunately, the young man recovered without complications and my colleagues in the Unit did not call me. When I opened my eyes, she was no longer in the room. I don't know how she managed to leave without waking me, but the fact is she did. Not a word, not a note, nothing.

I can't stop thinking...

--

Already at home, I wake up startled by the ringing of the phone. I answer. It's Assunción. "How are you? Did I wake you up? I've heard the news!... It's all anyone is talking about..."

"Good morning..., I mean, I don't even know if it's still morning..., I only got in this morning and fell asleep. What news? I don't know what you're talking about..." Half groggy, I sit up in bed trying to wake up enough to continue the conversation.

"I want to know everything about last night..."

"What do you mean?" In my head the film of the night plays at accelerated speed. What does she know? And what does she want to know?

"Don't be modest. Julia told everyone what happened..."

I freeze, my heart almost jumping out of my mouth. What could Julia have told? Even she wouldn't be capable of such a thing? Or would she?

I don't say anything and Assunción goes on, "She told everyone how brilliant you were in the OR. Coming from her, you couldn't have higher praise. Don't think it's all roses, she praised your performance, but she didn't fail to blame you for the lack of staff, after all she's still 'Julia'."

§§

Before going out into the street I realize that I left my coat forgotten in the waiting room. While I wait for the elevator I think about what I just told Fili, and also about how much I didn't tell him.

When I go back in, a woman is sitting on the couch at the back, who greets me with a smile, turning her head towards the couch where my coat remains unflinching. I can't help but notice how the smile causes two dimples in her face.

Chapter 10

March 6th – Contexts

Camila

Sitting in the waiting room, I look out the window. Outside, it seems like the sky is about to fall, such is the force of the rain. I hate storms. Strangely, there's a jacket stretched out over the back of one of the sofas. It was certainly put there to dry.

I'm surprised by the voice of a woman who enters the room. She greets me, and I reciprocate with a smile. She looks at the jacket and shakes her head, as if scolding herself. She picks it up, puts it on, and leaves. Almost immediately, Fili's voice is heard. They nearly cross paths.

I enter the office and almost without preamble, I start talking. "Look, Fili, the other day I was telling you about Esther. I was amazed that you thought I shouldn't have talked to her about the panic attacks, but I'm starting to think you're right. She's not someone you can trust." It wasn't until many days after being here with Fili that I remembered that when I told Esther I was in therapy, she immediately recognized his name. Could it be that they know each other?

§§

Two hamburgers and two lemonades. After the first few bites, I recover a bit from the inherent fatigue of having been in the OR all morning.

"Is something wrong? You don't seem like yourself today. You're usually so lively." I'm having lunch at the hospital bar with Vitoria, one of my favorite nurses, surrounded by the hustle and bustle of conversations and laughter. She looks at me and smiles, but her gaze seems sad.

"I don't know, I don't think I can..."

"Can't what?"

"Operate in the same room as Esther? She's..."

"No?!"

"Yes."

"You mean Esther is the woman you've been seeing for over two years?" My astonishment is such that the words come out in a jumble. I knew she had a complicated relationship with a surgeon from another hospital, but for it to be Esther, I never could have even dreamed.

"We're not together anymore. Actually, we never really were. To be honest, we hadn't seen each other for quite a while. Yesterday she invited me to dinner. I, like an idiot, accepted. I don't know why I keep doing this. It always ends badly."

"What happened?" I ask, unable to contain my curiosity.

"You know, one thing led to another, a kiss, a caress. You know. It's like she's a magnet. I know I can't, that I don't want to, but when she's near me, it's stronger than me. We were together, and at the end of the night we ended up arguing. I lost my head and told her how hypocritical she is. She plays with my feelings, as if I were a puppet she uses at her whim. That's what she's used to doing with people. Uses, abuses, and throws away. I've known this for so long, I think since the first time we were together and the next day she treated me as if we hardly knew each other. We can't work together. We really can't!"

"But what did she say yesterday?" I ask, unable to continue eating the hamburger that remains almost untouched. I don't think either of us will have lunch today.

"After everything, she told me I'm crazy, that she 'doesn't have the patience'. I couldn't believe it. She got dressed, put on the haughtiest air you can imagine, and slammed the door on her way out." She shrugs and runs a hand through her hair. "She can't! She can't just leave like that, as if it were nothing."

"Were you at your place?"

"We were. I've never been to her house," she answers softly.

"Maybe it's better this way."

"She has a failed relationship and she's the only one who doesn't see it. It's all a big lie, really. She pretends all the time. She supposedly has a long-distance relationship, but I don't even know if that's really true." Her tone turned bitter. "I got involved... I got seriously involved, and she plays with that." She falls silent and empties the glass in front of her and smiles, "Enough about me. After all, you're the one who's been operating with her, what do you think?"

"Our interactions have been strange to say the least. She seems to know a lot about me, she's always making jokes and comments. The other day she made insinuations about my internship, saying I was favored. At one point it seemed to me that she was implying that I had a thing with my tutor."

"Are you kidding?!" she murmurs, with an incredulous look.

"No! She did it, and not just once or twice. I don't know what she might know, but she clearly has some intention. I don't feel comfortable in the OR with her."

"But what do you think she might want?"

"I don't know, I don't understand. Today, we were alone in the doctors' lounge, I was finishing up some notes and she sat down next to me. She was even nice, but suddenly she had her hand on my leg. I don't know what her intention was, but it made me uncomfortable." I shiver at the memory, my skin crawling where she touched me.

"Unbelievable! Unbelievable, how people are!"

"Maybe it's just me imagining things," I say in a vain attempt to downplay it.

"Unfortunately, I don't think so. Esther is like that, it's not just with you. She likes that game of seduction, of power. It's part of her style."

Enough talking and thinking about Esther, I think to myself, changing the subject, "I didn't tell you the latest about my mother." She knows my mother well, the great Amelia Velasquez. After all, they worked together a few years ago. She looks at me and doesn't say anything. I tell her everything about the party invitation and how she continues to ignore Julia "...and I said yes. I'm so stupid, such a coward."

"Your mother may have a difficult temperament, but you have to agree that she's a genius."

"Brilliant, arrogant..." I can't resist adding, "And homophobic."

--

I get home early, in time to play with Mateo and prepare dinner, a rare occurrence these days. My heart swells with joy as I hear Mateo's laughter echoing through the house, a sound I've been missing too much lately.

We're already in bed when Julia says, "I forgot to tell you, but next weekend I have to stay at the hospital. Several colleagues are sick, you know how it is?! Now, with this woman, I can't take it easy. I feel like she's watching my every move."

"You don't need to make up excuses," I snap, a tinge of bitterness in my voice.

"What's gotten into you? Why the aggression?" Julia asks, taken aback by my tone.

"You tell me... Are you going to do another on-call shift, or does your 'on-call' have a name?" The phrases jump out of my mouth with a sarcasm I don't usually have. I hear Paloma's words in my head, repeating that Julia diminishes me. The anger bubbles up inside me, threatening to spill over.

"I don't know what you're talking about, or why we're even having this conversation, if you can call it that?! Jealousy? Again?" She's clearly regained control of the situation. She changes her tone and is going to turn the tables, a move that's characteristic of her. I know exactly what she intends to do.

"You're not well, what's going on?" she ends by reminding me of this same phrase in so many other arguments. The patronizing tone makes my blood boil.

There were moments when these same words made me cry, wondering if she was right, if it was me who wasn't well, who wasn't good enough. "No, I'm not well, but that matters little for the case. You're losing your touch. You used to be discreet. This time, you went to public places and were seen..." A colossal silence falls. She looks away and remains motionless. I take a breath and muster the courage to continue, "Do you want me to describe? I didn't see it, but from what I heard, I can well imagine, down to the smallest details. Who is it? Do I know her?" As I speak, I recall every detail of the description and grow more and more enraged. The betrayal stings like a slap across the face.

Julia gets up and, without saying a word, goes to the bathroom and closes the door behind her. When she returns, she sits next to me on the bed, "You're right! I'm sorry! But nothing happened."

She says these words and again lets a moment of silence settle. The truth is, the strategy works. I'm getting anxious and uncomfortable.

I've already lost. It wouldn't even be necessary to continue to know how the night will end. I can't hold back my emotions and I interrogate her screaming, my eyes full of tears, torn between anger and hurt. She lets me talk and scream, without even trying to answer, until I exhaust my arguments and strength. I collapse back onto the pillows, spent.

"Things aren't easy at the hospital," is her comment minutes later.

"And when your life isn't easy, you go out conquering the first woman you can take to bed?" I ask, leaning back against the pillows, utterly defeated.

"I went out for a drink, to clear my head, that's all. And that's all anyone could have told you, because that's what happened."

Without saying anything else, she gets up again. She turns off the lights and leaves the room immersed in darkness. I close my eyes and snuggle into the duvet. I feel her body approach, and her breath on my ear. When she presses against me, I realize she's naked. Before giving me time to react, she whispers: "I'm sorry!"

§§

"I'm not going to tell you anything else, because you know this story well, and you know how it ends."

Fili puts down his pen and pad and looks at me without saying anything.

Maggy McAndrew

Chapter 11
March 20th – Apologies

Olivia

In contrast to the last time I was here, today there's a radiant spring sun. I ran into Fili as soon as I arrived. He invited me to come into the office, but asked me to wait a bit while he made a phone call. It's unusual for me to be here alone. I take the opportunity to look around the room, my gaze drawn to the countless books neatly arranged on the shelf that covers one of the walls near the corner. Arranged by colour, it seems like a random mix of themes, ranging from photography albums to technical books, and an impressive set of novels. I don't know if Fili is passionate about reading or if, like me, he simply likes having books around.

A few minutes later, he re-enters, apologizing. He sits down and immediately asks the usual question, "How are you, Olivia? How have these days been?" He smiles and picks up his pen.

With a mechanical gesture, I glance at his socks - I'm a fan. Today, breaking the predictability of his usual position, he hasn't crossed his legs, which means I can't see what surprise they bring.

"I don't know, to be honest, I really don't know. Everything is happening at the same time..." I look out the window, trying to find a common thread, my thoughts swirling like a tempest.

"Everything like what? Can you be more specific?"

§§

I've just been called to the administration office. During all these days, Julia and I haven't spoken again, we haven't even crossed paths in the hallway. At home, Javier also seems to avoid encounters, arriving late and always leaving before I even wake up. I have no idea what this meeting is about, but it's surely not good news. Maybe she's there, I think, smiling wryly. On the way, I meet Assunción and António, who come together. Apparently, we were all summoned. They greet me affably, even António, who gives me a smile, "I've heard about your performance in the operating room, congratulations! It's a good thing you were available."

I thank him, unable to discern the exact meaning of his words. Is it a compliment, or just a sarcastic way of saying I was available because I have nothing to do? I try not to dwell too much on the subject and ignore it. I must be seeing ghosts where they don't exist.

We're all here, except Julia. Assunción talks about some loose topics, making small talk while we wait. After fifteen minutes, the administrator enters the room, and if there were any doubts, they would have ceased to exist just by looking at her face. Without ceremony or introductions, she begins to speak even before sitting down.

"We are very, very concerned. What is your plan, Olivia?" she says, looking directly at me, waiting for an answer. "We can't risk losing so many people, it jeopardizes the functioning of the operating room... and even the hospital!" My amazement is total, I have no idea what she's talking about. I consider asking, but where does that leave me? Fortunately, Assunción comes to my rescue, it's becoming a habit.

"I'm also worried," she looks at me, discreetly raises an eyebrow, and continues, "That email from yesterday was very unpleasant. The anaesthesia team may not agree with the changes, but threatening a mass resignation is too much. It's blackmail. There isn't even a definitive plan yet, I don't know what got into their heads?!"

So that's it, the anaesthesia department is showing what they think of my presence in the operating room. I'm sure this attitude isn't just due to the restructuring, it's more personal. That also explains why I didn't receive the email.

"I agree, it sounds like blackmail, but right now they have the power, we can't stop the operating room due to lack of staff," the administrator replies, maintaining her rigid pose, without taking her eyes off me.

I finally speak, trying not to let it show that, until minutes ago, I knew nothing. "I was going to call them for a meeting this afternoon. Let's hear what they have to propose, maybe I can get at least some of them to understand how ridiculous this all is. The situation doesn't benefit anyone. In the meantime, we could think about hiring external doctors for some shifts."

"That will make them even more furious!" Assunción counters instantly, showing that this time she's not on my side.

"I also think so," the administrator hastens to agree. "Olivia, talk to them. It's important that they're committed. We don't want an unmotivated team, a discontented team."

I don't know what she thinks, but she's far from reality. They were already discontented long before I arrived, I'm just a pretext.

"I don't know... and I don't want to make this a personal issue," she continues, "Maybe they didn't like you going to the operating room without talking to anyone. The head of department only found out the next day. I think an apology could help."

An apology?! There was no one from the team, we had an urgent situation, I stayed here, I solved the issue, and in the end, I should apologize?! It's very bad! I look around, but everyone seems to support what was just said. Assunción lowers her head and doesn't face me.

"Of course, if you think so, I'll talk to her today," I say calmly, while seething with anger inside, putting my mastery of hiding emotions to the test. I put my hand in my pocket again, and this time I take out my phone.

During the meeting, it vibrated several times. What could it be? 'I didn't think it was wise for us to meet in such bright light..., but if you'll accept a drink tonight, I'll be waiting for you at Dune's at ten.' The number isn't identified, but I have no doubt about who's writing. My mind wanders and I stop following what's going on in the room, the words blurring together.

What is the objective? Will she start missing all the meetings? Does she want to meet me? For what? What kind of game is this? As I list unanswered questions, I remember that it was me who took the initiative that night. But this is an unsustainable situation, it can never lead to anything good. I'm married and so is she. Moreover, she's unbearable. She's arrogant and selfish, treating others with a superiority that I can't swallow. With all this very clear in my head, I make a definitive decision. I don't want to talk about this subject anymore, I'm going to ignore the messages and pretend it never happened.

--

At five in the afternoon, the head of anaesthesiology knocks on my office door and enters before I even answer. Sitting in front of me, I can't help but see the cynicism in her eyes. She's an intimidating figure, very thin, with completely white hair and an austere countenance. I admit that part of it may just be the result of my own discomfort.

"Sorry to ask you to come here, so suddenly. I think it's important to clarify what happened the other day when I went to the operating room. I don't know what they told you, but my intention was never, at any time, to do anything without your knowledge. The surgery was really urgent. I couldn't get anyone to come. I tried to call you several times, but I couldn't reach you either..."

"Really, you tried to call me? How strange, I didn't have any calls from you! No one could come? Who did you talk to?" The questions are rhetorical and follow one another laced with derision.

"I wanted to apologize. Listen, I'll tell you again, in no way did I want to question your leadership," I state without deviating an inch from the script I just rehearsed.

"My dear, you don't need to apologize to me. After all, if you really wanted to apologize, it wouldn't be now. You got what you wanted, I suppose..." The words are as harsh as her appearance.

I take a deep breath and restrain the urge to take her apart, "What do you mean, what I wanted?"

"You wanted people to talk about you. You succeeded! My interns are very impressed with what they saw, they keep commenting 'Doctor Lopez was sublime!'. We were all called into question! As if we weren't here every day, for years, to solve the hospital's problems... We were here before you arrived and we'll be here after you leave!" she shouts, not hiding her fury. I'm not made of iron and my level of irritation increases. She continues, without slowing down, bordering on offensive.

Why did you leave San Joan Hospital? I never quite understood... They said you lost a patient in the operating room..., but they say so many things..."

Her words pierce through me like shards of glass, reopening old wounds I thought had long since healed. The memories of that fateful night come flooding back, threatening to drown me in a sea of guilt and regret. My heart races as I struggle to maintain my composure, to not let her see how deeply her cruel insinuations have affected me.

I burst out, my voice rising above hers, "You're going to stop! And you're going to stop right now!" I know they can probably hear me down the corridor, but it's too late now. "There was no qualified anaesthesiologist available to enter the operating room that night. You may not know this, but a man's life was at stake. Thanks to the efforts of everyone who spent the night here, he's been discharged and is recovering at home. He'll be able to play with his daughter and be with his wife. Not thanks to you or your team. And it's not the first time - the other day there was a resuscitation and there was no one here either, only interns. So if you have any criticism to make,

make it! But don't hide behind a false offense that never happened. I'm not the one who has apologies to make, you're the one who owes me a thank you!" I stop, exhausted, take off my glasses and lean back, waiting for what's to come.

She applauds mockingly, "I hope you have fun managing the service and the operating room." Without giving me time to respond, she turns her back and leaves.

I hear her words echoing in my head again, "...they said you lost a patient in the room..., but they say so many things..." I remember that day. Why? I'll never stop asking myself, "Why?"

I get up and go to get a coffee from the machine in the hallway, maybe that way I can think about something else. My phone signals a message. I take it out of my lab coat pocket and look at the screen 'I can't stop smelling your scent!'.

--

I have dinner alone at home in front of the television. I just spoke with Leonor, and I'm worried. I could tell right away from her voice that something was wrong. She tried to hide it and talk to me about college, but she ended up saying that she was at home, or rather at her girlfriend's house, alone. From what I understood, they have an open relationship, where each one can be with whoever they want. In her words, romantic relationships are like friendships - we can have several friends at the same time, and that doesn't mean we love each one of them any less. They fill different spaces. I understand and accept the concept, I think it makes perfect sense, but for some reason, I couldn't help but feel anguished.

I think of Ursula and then of Julia. To be honest, how is that different from what Leonor just told me? The lack of transparency!

When I look at the clock it's twenty past ten. I take a deep breath and try not to think about Julia sitting at a table, waiting for me at Dune's. A message makes my phone on the table vibrate. 'You don't know what you're missing, because we only miss what we know, and what I have for you, I'm sure you've never experienced before!' I read it over and over more than ten times as if the text would change with time. The words stir something in me, in a way I hadn't anticipated. I felt the same thing in the meeting.

I can't just sit here. The drive to Dune's takes no more than fifteen minutes. I park and hurry to the door, pausing for a moment before entering to catch my breath. The room is dimly lit and I have trouble seeing who is sitting at the tables. After adjusting to the semi-darkness, I see a woman sitting alone at a table in the back, her back to the door. I go over there, my heart pounding. When I'm ready to greet her, the woman turns around, and to my surprise, it's not Julia. I back away embarrassed, and in the midst of many apologies for the confusion, I sit on one of the high stools at the bar.

A curly-haired waiter asks me what I want to drink. "A whiskey," I reply without thinking. I look around again, trying to find Julia.

As he sets the glass down in front of me, the waiter pauses for a moment and asks, "You wouldn't happen to be looking for a dark-haired woman with short hair and green eyes, would you? Sorry to ask, but I see you looking around..., so I thought..."

"Yes, she's a friend... we arranged to meet, but I'm very late..."

"She was sitting at that table," says the boy, pointing to one side of the room,

"She had two gins and left about ten, fifteen minutes ago. You just missed each other. If you call her, maybe she's still nearby."

I consider the suggestion, but decide not to. I'll let fate decide. I pick up the glass and take a sip of whiskey, making a face.

§§

I look at Fili, smile and comment "It was better this way. It doesn't make sense to think that there could be something between us."

"Your mouth and your eyes are saying different things," he replies.

"What do you mean? Do you think I should let it go further?"

"I don't know! What do you want? Do you want it to go further?"

"No! I want to regain my peace of mind, besides, it would never be possible."

"It is possible!" Fili puts his notebook on the table and places the pen on top. He uncrosses his leg and crosses it again, this time in the opposite direction.

"I would be betraying Javier..." I say softly.

"Don't you betray Javier every time you're with Ursula?" he asks with a smile.

"No! They're different things," the sentence comes out abruptly, as if it were urgent to justify myself. Fortunately, time is up and Fili can't continue with more questions. I go out into the street and breathe deeply, inhaling an air that tastes like spring. I'm going to move on with my life and forget about that night.

Maggy McAndrew

Chapter 12

March 20th - The Party

Camila

"How are you, Camila? And Julia?" Fili glances at his notebook, flipping through a few pages, re-reading his previous notes.

"She's been calmer. After our last argument, things have settled down. Even her phone has become less of a presence. Things at her hospital are still very tense, but from what I've heard, there haven't been any more direct confrontations. She's still obsessed with the new clinical director. From everything I've learned, she really does seem to be a detestable person." As I recount the events, I think about Julia's face as she described the situation. Fili interjects, asking, "Do you really think this person can be as horrible as they're describing her?"

"I do! There are terrible people out there. Worse, there are deceitful people with power, and in my opinion, those are the most dangerous. The only comparison I can make is with my mother, but she's not deceitful, she's blatant about it!" I say with a lump in my throat.

"Did you see her?"

"I did," I reply, my mind racing with thoughts of everything that happened at the party.

§§

We arrive at my mother's house, the party already in full swing. Children who are spitting images of their parents or grandparents run around outside, filling the air with their loud, shrill voices. My sister and brother-in-law are in a group at the back, she looks at me and nods, not moving an inch.

My father approaches, "I'm glad you came. I missed my grandson. Come, Mateo, come to Grandpa," he says, pulling him in for a hug, enveloping him in his embrace. I can't remember him ever hugging me.

My role here is done.

I leave the room and sit on the terrace, a glass of white wine in my hand. One of the best things about these parties is that they always have spectacular wine. The weather is fantastic, and I take the opportunity to relax on one of the loungers, fiddling with my cell phone in my hand.

"Hello Camila, how are you?" I jump when I hear my mother's voice right next to me, her hand on my shoulder. Without thinking, I discreetly slip my phone into my pocket. She sits down beside me and for a minute, engages in small talk. She's an expert at this, discussing everything with a studied superficiality, letting the topics flow. Finally, she broaches the subject she really came to talk to me about, "Your father and I intend to set up a trust fund for the kids. For when they start their adult lives, when the time is right."

"Thank you!" I say, trying to figure out where the conversation is heading.

"I'm glad you think it's a good idea. The funds can only be accessed when they come of age. In case something happens to us, to your father and me, administrators will be appointed. In this case, it would be your sister and her husband, for your nieces and nephews. And for Mateo, you and your cousin."

"What do you mean?!" I'm a bit stunned by the suggestion. My mother's nephew is a snob I used to play with as a kid, and even then, he was unbearable.

"Since Mateo doesn't have a father, your cousin is the right person to be the administrator. Of course, this only comes into play if something happens to us. Don't answer now, think about it, and we'll talk next week. Now, if you don't mind, I have to get back inside." Without letting me retort, she gets up and turns her back, walking away quickly. I think that was the whole point - drop the bomb and exit the scene. Impressive! She always manages to do it! I feel a tear and hurry to wipe it away with the back of my hand. Even though I'm alone, you never know who might show up.

In my pocket, I feel my phone vibrate with a call. Who could it be? Doctor Esther Gonzalez! There couldn't be a worse day, worse circumstances... I'm not going to answer. The phone makes itself felt again, this time with a message. What could be so urgent? It's Saturday!

'Hi...', it simply says. I almost drop it, as if the message burned my hands. What does she want? What game is this? I read the next message: 'What are you doing?', it pops up unexpectedly. And now?

'Nothing, I'm sitting on the terrace at my parents' house, drinking a glass of wine...'

I could almost swear I didn't give her time to read before a new question appears on the screen. 'Alone?'

'Yes, alone!'

'Want some company?'

What does she mean by "company"?! This time I'm stunned and don't respond. A few minutes later a new message appears, 'Maybe you found some better company...'

'No, I'm still alone.'

No reply comes. So much the better.

The phone rings and I jump, startled. My heart races and I feel my hands sweat, 'Julia'.

"Hello! How's the cream of society in this city? Do you still know how to converse with them?" She hit the nail on the head, in fact, I don't anymore.

"Everything's fine. Mateo is with my father, they won't let go of each other. I'm out here on the terrace drinking a glass of wine."

"Alone?"

How strange, exactly the same question.

"Yes, alone. As soon as they sing happy birthday, we're heading home."

"That's what I wanted to tell you. I'm going to the hospital, I have procedures to review and others to do, I don't even know... It's all so crazy, so senseless, that I don't even know where to begin. But I'm going there to show that I'm not 'against' it, I just think it's all completely idiotic, starting with the person proposing the changes without knowing what they're talking about." She's back to her habit of badmouthing. After hearing so much about this character, I'd love to meet her.

"No problem. When we leave here, we'll head home. Mateo has eaten so many sweets that he won't want dinner, he'll go straight to bed, if he doesn't fall asleep in the car." I hang up with a feeling of relief, knowing that I'll get home and won't have to give explanations or talk about anything that happened here.

Even during the call, I feel my phone vibrate with the arrival of another message. 'Look behind you!'

I jump, turn around, and look at the balcony door. Standing there with a glass in her hand is none other than Esther herself. Without giving me time to process, she smiles and walks towards me. "Hi Camila, are you okay? You look pale. I've already had the chance to meet your son. Charming!"

I can't hide my surprise, and she lets out a laugh.

"Doctor Gonzalez?!"

"Your mother found out I had started working at the hospital and invited me. I see she didn't tell you. It's been a while since we last saw each other. It's good to reunite with old friends... She's one of the best."

I'm not exactly sure what she's referring to, but I'm still unable to say absolutely anything. I grab my glass and empty it in one go. She takes advantage of the free space on my chair and sits down next to me. Once again, too close. The scent of her perfume, which I've learned to recognize, is more intense today.

"Julia didn't come? I didn't see her."

With each second, I'm a little more surprised. She knows Julia too? Come to think of it, of course she must know her. After all, Julia is one of the best in the country, even in Europe. "No, she didn't come. She's working," I add.

"Better for me," she says under her breath. "Want another drink?" she asks, pointing to my empty glass. She walks away and returns with two glasses of champagne. "Next week, we have a removal of a cerebellar tumour. A dramatic case, in a kid. You're going to operate with me," she says, continuing her explanation while slowly sipping her champagne.

When I hear her, my heart races, my hands get sweaty, and I feel my legs tremble. None of this goes unnoticed by her. "You're going to operate with me, and you're going to be the best. We're going to save that kid's life and career. Don't doubt it."

As she speaks, she sets down her glass and puts her hand on my leg. I feel as uncomfortable as the last time at the hospital, but at the same time, I feel the fear that had gripped me fade away.

Before I have a chance to respond, I hear my father's voice announcing that it's time to blow out the candles. Inside the room, I see Esther chatting animatedly with my mother.

I leave with Mateo about half an hour later. I look around, but she seems to have vanished. We get in the car, and he falls fast asleep. I slowly drive the short road that leads to the beach. I park, open the window, and let the music play, careful not to wake him, hoping it will make me stop hearing my own thoughts.

--

A week has passed since the day of the party. My mother called me again to talk about the fund. I can't listen to her anymore. She knows how to be insistent. I maintained my composure and didn't give in, but it was enough to keep me from concentrating for the rest of the day. I have to find the right moment to talk to Julia and get this out of my head once and for all. Maybe at dinner, I think as I enter the house.

But, of course, her plan is different. She eats in less than five minutes, not paying any attention to what Mateo is saying, and gets up from the table, making an excuse. The phone rings once, then again, and I count more than five times before she finally decides to answer. In the distance, I hear her irritated voice, "Stop calling. I already told you..." I can't make out the end of the sentence. She must have closed the office door.

I take Mateo to bed and tell him a story. The same one, for over two weeks. Before turning off the light, already hidden under the duvet, with only his eyes and little nose peeking out, he asks, "Mom, why is Mommy so angry? Was it me? I left my toys in the living room, but... I was going to clean up."

"Of course not, love," I reply, feeling immense anger towards her for making him think that way. I remember when I was little, my father would yell, my mother would slam the door and lock herself in the bedroom. My brother and I would hide under my bed, trying not to hear the sound of the argument. Many times, I fell asleep thinking it was our fault, that they would be better off if we didn't exist. It wasn't just once or twice that I heard my father say they shouldn't have had more children after my sister.

"You're never home, and when you are, you lock yourself in the office with the excuse of a difficult surgery... Since when, Julia? Since when did all surgeries become difficult?" I say, opening the office door without knocking. "Is it your friend again?"

I end up saying everything I didn't want to and in a tone that takes away any reason I might have had.

"What are you talking about? Who?"

"Don't play dumb." Julia frowns, but before she can argue, I continue, "Don't worry, I didn't read the messages."

She finally looks up from the article she's reading and stares at me without hiding her surprise. I don't know if it's from my sudden entrance or from what I just said. "You want to argue, huh? I've had enough arguments at the hospital. I don't need you for one more. You talk about my messages, what about yours?" she counterattacks, lashing out in all directions. I don't think she's looking for anything specific, just trying to turn the argument around. "Did you install a dating app? You say I'm not here, but I could ask you the same thing. Where have you been? You've been coming home later and later each day."

Before I'm fully aware of what's happening, I'm already trying to find excuses. She remains impassive, not justifying herself or feeling the need to do so. In my back pocket, I feel my phone vibrate, and my heart instantly beats faster.

"Are you sure it's my attention you want, Camila?" The question leaves me stunned.

"What do you mean by that? I don't understand."

"You tell me... If I were the suspicious type, I might think something is going on," she pauses for a moment and concludes, "...but I'm not!"

I'm not going to let the conversation, or whatever this is, end without me saying what I need to. "Listen, I didn't come here to argue. I have something to tell you since the day of the party."

"Go ahead, it can only be good news! What was Professor Velasquez's fantastic feat? Or was it your father? She, despite everything, usually has more intelligent ideas..." She lets out a laugh and stands up, standing still in front of me. For a moment, I think she's going to kiss me, but no, she stops halfway, leaning on the edge of the desk.

"I don't know how you can find it funny. Only you and your sense of humour!" I say, irritated. "My mother talked to me about something, and she's called several times insisting on it. In short, they want to set up a trust fund for each of the grandchildren. The issue is that the fund needs administrators. For now, it's them, but if something happens to them, they have to appoint other people."

"And?" she asks, without moving. "Let me guess, they don't want me!"

"No, they don't. They're proposing my cousin."

She remains impassive, leaning against the table with her hands on either side, as if she needed to hold on. "Okay!"

"What do you mean, 'okay'?" I say, exasperated. "Did you hear what I said?"

"I heard you! Fortunately, my hearing is just fine!" She stands up and walks back around to the other side of the desk, settling into the swivel chair once more. "I couldn't care less about who's going to administer that damn fund. What are the options? Not having a fund at all? It's unlikely that your parents will both die in the next thirteen years, so if we play the statistics game, it doesn't matter one bit who gets appointed. In the most catastrophic, most dramatic scenario..." She lets out another small laugh, her dark sense of humour shining through. "In that scenario, which I was going to call the 'worst,' but I'm not sure if that name fits, your parents die, and you become one of the heirs. You'll be rich, very rich. Who's going to give a damn about that fund then?!"

Her pragmatism and quick thinking never cease to amaze me. She's right, but that doesn't make my parents' attitude okay. "So, you don't want me to say anything?"

"Of course I want you to say something. I want you to say, 'Yes, thank you, dear Mom!'" she says with a laugh.

I take a deep breath, trying to calm the storm of emotions raging inside me. "Fine. If that's what you want, I'll tell them yes. But don't expect me to be happy about it."

She shrugs, seemingly unfazed by my distress. "Happiness is overrated. What matters is that we're practical. Your parents will be satisfied, the fund will be set up, and life will go on. No need to make a fuss over something so trivial."

§§

"It was one of the strangest parties I've ever been to, Fili. My mother, Esther..."

Chapter 13

April 3rd – The Final Act

Olivia

I'm sitting on the couch in Fili's office, crossing and uncrossing my legs, trying to alleviate the pain I feel in them. "I'm sorry, Fili, today is one of those days when I should have gone to clear my head before talking to anyone, even you," despite my efforts, my voice betrays irritation. I feel all my muscles contracted. I open and close my mouth trying, in vain, to relax my jaws.

"Breathe, you seem to need it!" Fili says jokingly, trying to ease the tension.

"Is it the hospital?"

"Not exactly," I reply.

§§

At the front door, I barely have the strength to search for my keys, which seem to have a special gift for disappearing at the bottom of my purse. I won't be able to resist much longer. I know this, and so do my adversaries. Finally, I feel the metal between my fingers and open the door. Without even taking off my coat, I sit on the couch and breathe deeply.

My phone has a light on and an envelope. 'From what happened, I'd say it wasn't your first time, am I wrong?' I'm still reading when the light flashes, 'Liv, I need to see you again,' 'Maybe this time with a little more light...' I smile.

It's so dissonant when she sees me at the hospital, she attacks me as if I were the enemy, and at the same time... I don't understand the rules of this game, but it's becoming increasingly evident that I'm going to have to enter it.

My thoughts are interrupted by Javier's shouting. I thought I was alone in the house, but apparently, I was wrong. He must be locked in the office, furiously arguing with someone on the phone. "You think this ends like this? You're very wrong! Don't count on me! You won't get another cent! Forget I exist..., have you thought about if this gets out?! So, girl, stay away from me, it's the least decency you have left!... Your mother? Your mother, I don't know..., but one thing is certain, she's not going to keep deceiving me and making a fool of me either. You both live off me, living the good life..., she's the next one I need to have a conversation with!"

My whole body trembles. I'm sure he's talking to Leonor, I can't even imagine what she must have told him. I grab the keys again and, without thinking twice, I head out the door.

I get in the car and drive aimlessly. Almost an hour later, I stop in a parking lot and sit there, lights off, contemplating the few people passing by. I know it's inevitable to go back home, especially since, in my haste to leave, I left my phone on the couch.

When I enter, the living room is dark, and there's no sound. For a second, I feel relieved at the prospect of Javier having left. It's only for a second, as soon as I turn on the light, I see that he's sitting on the couch in the back with an empty glass in his hand and a bottle of whiskey on the floor.

"It's a good thing you're here, we need to talk!"

I put the keys on the table, take off my coat, and sit on the other end. "Sure, go ahead..." I try to seem calm, the more I show what's going on in my soul, the worse it will be.

"Don't play stupid!" he shouts. "Do you think I'm an idiot?! Did you think I wouldn't find out that you're supporting your daughter's immorality?!" His voice rises in pitch and, at the same time, his face is covered in red spots. He grabs the bottle, shakes it in the air, and fills the glass again, drinking it all in one gulp. I remain silent. I look at the keys on the table, I know that if I try to get up to get them, he will stop me.

"Come on, speak up! You have nothing to say?! Did you know that she's messing around with that friend she lives with? And do you know how I found out? Do you?! Of course not! You've neglected your duties for a long time. You spend all day holed up in that hospital, and your daughter..., your daughter...." He clenches his fist and punches the table violently, making it shake. "Today at lunch, a colleague of mine came to me with a grave face. At first, I didn't understand..., obviously! I'm always the idiot who doesn't know anything, right?!" He paces the room from side to side, like an enraged animal. "He took out his phone and showed me a photo they shared around... Look! Take a good look!" He comes over to me and grabs my hand, forcing me to hold the phone. The smell of alcohol can be felt even before he approaches. On the screen, a photo of Leonor and her girlfriend kissing.

Without giving me time to speak, or even to really see the image, he gives me a shove that makes the phone fall to the floor. "You knew, didn't you? Bitch!" I remain silent. He grabs me by the shoulders, holding my arms with both hands. It hurts when he squeezes, Javier is very strong. I know that, once again, there will be marks, but I try to keep a minimum of rationality, and I know that for now the best thing to do is not to move. If it's possible, he raises his voice even more, "Answer me! You knew, didn't you?" he says, shaking me and pushing me to the floor.

With a courage and strength derived from the fear I feel, I stand up. He grabs me again and I pull back, freeing myself from his arms. I lose my balance, I stagger, until I end up falling again. Everything hurts, but I know I can't stay here, completely vulnerable to whatever goes through his head. I grab the couch and manage to get up again. "I knew! Yes! I knew! And I support her! I support her unconditionally!" I shout. Javier comes at me, his fist clenched and his gaze fixed, taken over by an uncontrollable rage. Before he can hit me, I raise my arm and give him a violent slap. The gesture doesn't surprise him more than it does me. In silence, under the muffled echo of my action, we stand for a moment looking at each other.

"It's over! Javier, it's over!" I say in an icy voice. "This time, it's over! We've reached our limit."

Without adding anything, he turns around and leaves, without slamming the door, he simply leaves, as if it were the final act of a play.

I let myself fall on the couch, motionless, eyes closed, feeling my heart beat. I don't know how long I stay like this. I feel the distant vibration of my phone, which must have gotten lost among the cushions when I left hours ago. I stand up with some difficulty, run my hands over my face, pick up my glasses that had fallen to the floor, and tuck my hair behind my ears. I grab the remote and turn on the TV to some channel, just to have the company of human voices. I get up and get a glass of water before starting the search for my phone.

--

I find myself with António in the work room of the internal medicine ward. A few weeks ago, I decided to start visiting the services, not as a gesture of control, but in an attempt to be closer to the staff. He's seated with two interns, debating a difficult diagnosis of a patient with a fever of unknown origin. I sit with them and, little by little, I forget what I came to do and get caught up in their hypotheses and questions. António's dedication is impressive, as is his analytical ability. In fact, people change a lot depending on the context, I think to myself.

"Doctor Fuentes... António! Hurry! Bed 14..." I hear a nurse's voice coming from the corridor. António jumps up, and I run after him.

The patient is pale and breathing with difficulty. Immediately, he places the stethoscope on the woman's chest, trying to calm her with words I can't make out.

"Muffled sounds on the left. Increase oxygen. The effusion must be worsening. Call cardiothoracic. I want their opinion before putting in the drain." The sentences are short and affirmative, causing the team around him to move. With nothing I can do, I stay and observe.

When Raul arrives, I realize I was hoping it could be Julia. He and António talk for several minutes, and the decision is to transfer the patient to the intermediate care unit and put the drain there.

"Olivia, I'm glad you came. Sorry for the confusion..." António says when he finally sits back down with me in the work room.

"Don't apologize, I'm the one who came to disturb you."

"Not at all! Besides, I wanted to show you something," he says, handing me a cup of coffee. "I talked to Assunción last week, and I have a plan to show you. Maybe we can do some of what you propose... not everything, but some things," he says, blushing as he pulls a pen from his coat pocket and starts making a diagram full of boxes and arrows on one of the sheets on the table. When he finishes, I can't believe what I just heard came out of his mouth. Congratulations to Assunción, she has a diplomatic ability far beyond what I could have imagined.

--

I arrive at the meeting purposely late. Everyone is already seated, and through the glass, I see Julia, and to my amazement, she's not wearing a lab coat. She's wearing very dark blue jeans and a white shirt with the sleeves rolled up to the elbows, revealing a metal watch on her left wrist.

I quickly greet everyone and take one of the empty chairs. Julia looks me in the eye, with the exuberant intensity of her green eyes, as if she wants to see inside me. The last time I saw her eyes, they were covered by the protective goggles in the operating room, and the green seemed even deeper, the result of the gravity of the moment and the force she puts into each look.

"Good afternoon, Doctor Olivia Lopez," she says as I sit down.

"Hello, Olivia, good afternoon. In the meantime, we've started," Assunción continues. "António told us that he was with you this morning and summarized your conversation."

"Is the patient okay?" I ask, looking at him.

"Fortunately, she's recovering, thank you!"

Julia's hoarse voice makes itself heard, not allowing the conversation to proceed. "António may have done a great job, but it's not realistic. No one talked to us, no one asked the surgical teams how they fit into this 'modern' model." The word 'modern' is used in a deliberately sarcastic way, which she emphasizes with a dry laugh. "Don't you think that if you want to create a 'heart' unit, the least you should have done was ask my department how it would integrate?" She's irritated and won't make our work any easier.

Assunción intervenes, "Sure, Julia, you have a point..."

"Some? You can just say I'm right, I don't think there's any doubt..." Julia shakes her head and arches her eyebrows.

"As you wish! You're right! You weren't present at the last meeting, and we assumed that the opinion of the various services had been integrated... maybe you could help instead of just criticizing..."

I stop following Assunción's words when my phone vibrates in my white coat pocket. Usually, I wouldn't check a message during a meeting, but something makes me uneasy. Discreetly, under the table, I look at the screen. 'What do you have under your coat?' How does she do it? She yells and argues against everything and everyone, and in the same minute, she sends this message.

I focus back on Assunción. "Maybe we could organize surgical units by major areas and, instead of integrating them into the functional units."

This time, Julia seems to agree minimally. "And anaesthesia?"

The harmless question is anything but. It's an arrow aimed directly at me. What does she know that I don't? The phone vibrates again. I look at Julia, who remains motionless, with an angelic face. I ostentatiously put my hands visible on the table so she understands I don't intend to pick up the phone, and I try to focus on what António is saying.

The phone vibrates again and again. What's going on? Has she made this a game?! But it takes two to play.

Julia doesn't seem willing to let go of the anaesthesia topic. "I'm amazed to see you here discussing functional units when there may not be a team to operate next week... What do we do? Do we call you, Doctor Olivia Lopez?" She hardens her tone as she goes on, and I feel increasingly lost in the dissonance of the moment. The phone also seems to be against me and rings with a call, forcing me to take it out of my pocket to turn it off. It's inevitable to see the messages. 'A kiss...', 'Your taste.'

§§

"It's over, Fili. It was the final act. The last scene. I know I've told you this more times than I should have and many more than I'd like."

"One thing is certain, Olivia, there will be a time that is the last. I hope you're right and that it was this one."

I go out to the stairs and wait for the elevator. I look in the small mirror and can't help but notice that I'm smiling. This was really the last time, I think to myself.

Chapter 14
April 3rd – The Storm

Camila

"How's the hospital? How's Esther?" Fili asks after we sit down and exchange the usual greetings.

"Esther is much worse than I thought. It's true that my friend Vitoria talked to me many times about the woman she was in a relationship with, and it's also true that I told her many times to stay away, but I never truly imagined what was going on. Esther is horrible."

"Horrible is a very reductive word," Fili responds slowly as if it takes some time to assimilate the word. "But, are you talking about your friend or yourself, Camila?" Fili asks, prompting me to continue.

§§

Finally, the day seems to have ended. Tonight, I arranged to have dinner with Vitoria, my nurse friend. She was off duty, so we didn't see each other at the hospital. The waiter greets me and places the beer in front of me. She walks through the door, and even from afar, I can't help but notice that she's drenched. Outside, the rain shows no mercy.

"Everything okay?" she greets me almost mechanically, which is unusual for her, shaking her wet hair.

"Tired," I let slip, pursing my lips. I lean my head against the bench's upholstery and take several gulps of beer in a row. The liquid has a positive effect, I sit up straighter and continue, "The days don't have the necessary hours, and the weeks always have too few days..." I complete, pretending to cry before opening a smile. "And you? You have a case face, what did she do this time?" I take a deep breath, finish the liquid at the bottom of the glass, rest my elbow on the table and my head in my hand, staring at her. "Hadn't you ended things for good?" I ask, knowing the answer perfectly well.

"No, I mean, after the argument the other day, she apologized, and we started seeing each other again."

"And?"

"And nothing new. Today is Friday, she went to spend the weekend with the other one," she replies, shrugging her shoulders. I don't ask anything, but I also don't look away. "I'm tired of this situation, but..."

This time, I don't let her finish and interrupt abruptly, startling her. "That's not love, it's obsession! What else does she have to do for you to see how much she hurts you? It's a sick relationship. It's everything you've always criticized, everything you've always despised," I say in an aggressive tone that mirrors my deepest irritation.

"Maybe you're right, maybe it is obsession," she responds, giving in. "But I like her."

I intervene again, "Esther is a woman in a man's world, and she behaves like

132

one of them in the worst possible way. I understand that she has another side. It's been months since I've felt so secure in the operating room. She conveys a confidence I've never felt before. But at the same time, she's the same person who passes by me and gropes me, who calls me 'darling'..."

"I know you're right. I know I should have walked away a long time ago."

"You never told me how you met her," I say, thinking about how little I really know about this story.

"Do you want to know?"

"I do!"

She takes a deep breath and orders another beer before starting, "For a few months, I worked shifts at Central. She worked there. We were together in the operating room, and one thing led to another. A look, a coffee after a complex surgery. Nothing obvious, but a different atmosphere settled in. Esther never talks about her personal life. At the hospital, some thought she was married, others that she had a secret lover, but I think almost no one knew the true story. There was an afternoon when we operated together, and I found her different. She was sad, quiet, not herself. That night, I unusually sent her a message asking if she was okay. She replied minutes later with an invitation to dinner. Dinner ended up turning into a drink at my place. That night, I wanted to make a move, but at the last moment, she refused. I didn't understand. I was frustrated. I thought it was because I was a nurse, because I was black, I don't know, everything went through my head that day. The next day she called me, apologized, and begged me to have dinner with her. I found out that she had been in a relationship with a woman for over ten years. They didn't live together, the other one lives outside the city. In reality, it seemed to me that it was more a way for neither of them to have to commit to anything. She always tells me that she wants to separate from the other one. She's promised me dozens of times, but there's always something, it's never the right time. Phone calls, messages, and I watch in silence."

"You're one of the bravest and smartest people I know, and suddenly, suddenly this woman enters your life, and you transform."

"Every month, the other one comes here to spend a weekend, and on the other, Esther goes to her. It will never be different. In her life, I'm the 'other' one," she says, letting out a forced laugh and running her hand over her face. "Enough talk about Esther," she raises her glass and says, "New people, less complications, and more love!"

--

I leave the restaurant in time to catch the last train. When I finally sit down, I'm soaked to the bone. The carriage is empty, as would be expected on a stormy night, except for a couple sitting several seats ahead. I put my bag on the floor and my coat on the bench. Outside, lightning slices through the sky. I lean my head back and close my eyes, letting the music play loudly in my headphones. Minutes later, I feel the carriage start to move. It's only half an hour, I think.

I don't know how much time has passed, but the train has been moving for a while when the carriage suddenly jolts to a halt. It's not the normal braking of a station, it's something drier, more sudden. I open my eyes and take a few moments to understand what's going on. We're in the dark, the only light coming from the windows and the emergency signals, but as we cross an area already outside the city, the darkness is almost complete.

As I sit across the aisle, I catch a glimpse of a woman's silhouette. As far as I can see, the remaining seats remain empty. I fix my gaze on her, and notice that she's trembling. I stand up and approach her, sitting in the seat next to her. I can now see tears running down her face. She's pale and has her eyes closed, grasping her backpack with one hand as if protecting it.

"It's okay. Everything is fine. Can I help?" I say softly. "Sorry, I didn't mean to startle you. I was over there," I affirm, pointing to the seat on the other side when she shudders and opens her eyes. "You're shivering. Can I help?" I continue, placing my hand on her arm.

"Are we stopped? I don't feel very well," she says, breathing heavily and closing her eyes again.

"It must be a power outage, but it shouldn't take long to resume. Breathe deeply. I'll help! Let go of the backpack, put it here." I take the backpack from her lap and place it on the seat in front of us. "Breathe with me." I grasp both of her hands in mine and begin to breathe slowly and deeply.

Gradually, she manages to follow the rhythm. We stay like this until we're interrupted by a thunderclap that literally shakes the train. My efforts vanish instantly, her body trembles, and tears start to fall again. She releases my hands and curls up, hiding her face between her fingers.

The sound of the next thunderclap coincides with the touch of her arms, which take me in an embrace. I run my hand through her hair in a caress. Without realizing it, I'm hugging her too. My arms are around her body, and my hands rest on her back. My fingers move slowly and touch her neck under the collar of her wool sweater. For a few moments, there's no space between us. She moves her face away, and with the light coming through the window,

I can now clearly distinguish her. It's the woman with the red cover book.

"Sorry," she murmurs, moving back. "I don't feel well, and besides, I hate thunderstorms."

"Me too," I reply with a smile.

"Thank you!"

"For what?"

"For being here," she puts her hand back on my arm. "I don't know what's wrong with me. I haven't been well for a few weeks now. Suddenly, I start shaking all over, or I feel dizzy as if I'm about to faint."

"Haven't you seen a doctor? You should find out what it is."

"It's probably nothing... Besides, I don't have time for doctors."

"What do you do for work?"

"I'm a lawyer," she says, smiling for the first time.

Her skin is still pale, and despite the dim light, she seems sweaty, which contrasts with the cold that can be felt. Before she can continue, her breathing becomes irregular, her hand on my arm becomes limp, she blinks her eyes, and loses consciousness. Within seconds, I place my fingers on her pulse. Her heart is racing, and she's sweating. Almost immediately, she comes to.

"I'm dizzy... I can't see well, everything is blurry. What happened?"

"You fainted, but it was only for a moment. Have you eaten?" I remember to ask.

"Not since lunch."

I look at my watch. It's almost eleven o'clock. I go to my bag and take out a carton of chocolate milk. "Here, drink this. It will help."

Without questioning, she does as I say. After a few minutes, she seems much better.

"It must be the accumulated fatigue." I don't say anything, and she runs her hand over her face, wiping away a tear that has fallen again. Without me asking, she continues, giving me an explanation, "A few months ago, I had an ultrasound because I had some colic. They didn't find any stones, but instead, they saw an image on the pancreas. They said they couldn't say anything because the ultrasound has low sensitivity in these things..."

"What things?"

"Pancreatic tumours," she replies abruptly.

"You don't have a pancreatic tumour," I state, as if not even wanting to consider the possibility.

"I must have one. But I don't want to know. My father died..." she says, looking at me as I stare at her, stunned. "...He died when I was little. We never knew what it was, but when I asked my mother, I became convinced that it could have been pancreatic cancer."

"You're letting your imagination run wild. The diagnosis of pancreatic cancer is difficult. It's impossible to know. It could have been that or anything else. You fixated on that idea because they told you that you have a suspicious image, and you're afraid."

The carriage shakes again, a dry noise is heard, and the lights flicker, turning off again.

In the dark, she hugs me again. The touch of her lips on mine is as unexpected as it is predictable. I don't pull away and let it happen. I want it to happen. I part my lips and taste the sweetness of hers. An exploratory touch turns into a kiss. I don't know if it's still thundering outside, if the train has stopped or started moving again. I reciprocate the kiss. I hold her tightly and pull her closer. Despite the clothes, I can feel her chest pressed against mine and the hurried beating of our hearts.

The lights come on, the carriage shakes again, and the train resumes its pace. It's as if an alarm has sounded. I jump up and stand, forcing her to move away so as not to lose her balance with the movement. "Sorry, I have to go." I hastily grab my bag and run through the carriage, crossing one after the other until I sit in a seat far away.

When I put my bag down, I realize that the hospital card ribbon is not attached in its usual place. It must have fallen off. Patience. I lean my head against the seat, close my eyes, and relive what just happened. It's been years since I felt anything like it.

§§

I hear Fili's voice, reminding me that I'm sitting in his office. "Anything like what?" He adjusts his glasses and sets down his notebook.

"What do you mean?"

"You say you haven't felt anything like it... Like what, Camila?"

I understand the question, but I don't have an answer. "Like what I felt in Boston," I end up saying.

Chapter 15

April 17th – Bruises

Olivia

Today, when I ring the doorbell, it's Fili himself who opens the door for me.

"Olivia, please come on in."

"Thanks" I said, stepping into his office.

Fili took his seat across from me, leaning back and crossing his legs.

"You have an air of mystery about you. Is everything alright?" Fili asks.

"A lot is happening all at once."

§§

I enter apartment 1043 and immediately feel lighter. Ursula opens the door, envelops me in an embrace, and kisses me intensely with a sweet taste and the tranquillity of familiar pleasure. I relax, letting her control the moment as I always have. She, aware of the situation, manages it masterfully.

"I missed you," she says, her voice husky with desire.

"I missed you too! I needed you..." I don't dare say how much.

Ursula is wearing only a silk robe, and I'd bet she has nothing on underneath.

I'm still in the brown pants and blouse I wore to work. We sit on the bed. Beside me, she talks animatedly about her trip to Paris, the meetings, how much she longed for me. She turns to me and grabs my arm, pulling me in for a kiss. I can't suppress a yelp of pain. She immediately stops, perplexed, furrowing her brow. She says nothing, asks nothing. She resumes talking, then leans in and kisses me delicately, gliding it over my lips and hers.

She unbuttons my blouse and pulls it off. Her gaze immediately falls on my arms. Without a word, she resumes her barrage of kisses, trailing down. Shedding her robe to reveal what I suspected, she restarts her journey of caresses and kisses. I'm lost to her.

" Don't think about anything," she murmurs.

"What are you doing?" Without warning, while still talking, she repositions her hand.

"Nothing! I'm talking to you... did you get lost? We were discussing Paris." A mischievous smile betrays that she knows exactly what she's doing as she continues exploring paths she knows well.

"Stop, don't do that..."

"Why? " she asks, grinding against me more intensely.

I can't see her face but I know she's grinning. I try desperately to delay the inevitable, but I know it won't be long.

She pulls away for a moment, but I soon feel her again. I feel a cool touch. An object slides along. I can't tell what it is.

In a flash it all becomes clear. "Ursula, no! Not today!!" But my words aren't meant to be taken seriously and we both know it.

"Let it happen."

We catch our breath in silence. She can never lie still for long before the call of a cigarette. She goes to sit in the ocher velvet armchair by the window, unconcerned about her nudity. I take the opportunity to get up for a glass of water.

I lie back down as she takes her last drags and stubs out the cigarette in the ashtray on the table. I wrap my arms around her, trying to warm her cooled body. Our mouths meet again and despite our exhausted bodies, the kiss is irresistible. "That was just the first," she whispers against my ear.

Her hands don't seem to register what just transpired. Not a minute passes before I feel another wave of pleasure.

"What happened this time? Why didn't you call me?" Her gaze is direct, her lips pursed into a thin line.

"You weren't here... there was nothing you could've done," I reply, feeling the sting of tears in my eyes. I lightly trace a finger over the large purple bruises marring my arms. They'll take weeks to fully disappear and months before I stop thinking about them.

"This can't continue. There are no excuses, no justifications. Tell me what you need, I'll help with anything, everything necessary for this to have been the last time." Ursula has tears in her eyes. In all our years together, I've rarely seen her cry. I know she's serious and has the means to help.

"I want a divorce!" I say through gritted teeth, then repeat it louder. "I want a divorce. I have to separate from him definitively."

"You need a lawyer? I know just the right person to help." Without waiting for my response, she picks up her phone. Before placing the call, she looks at me, waiting for my agreement. I hesitate for a moment but end up nodding. "Alexis will call you to set up a meeting. It's important you talk in person. You have to tell her everything, down to the last detail no matter how hard it is, and I know it will be." Ursula gets up and returns to the sofa at the foot of the bed.

"I don't know what I'd do without you," I whisper.

"Let's take a trip! I have a meeting in Brussels. We can take a few days off together, what do you think? Far from everything and everyone, good wine and food..." She lies back down next to me.

"I need to tell you something..."

She's described other women she's been with many times. And I, having nothing else to share, always talked about my relationship with Javier. We're together with the complete honesty only true freedom allows.

I put on the robe she keeps for me in the bathroom and return to bed, turning on the small lamp on the nightstand. She goes to the kitchen and comes back with two glasses of white wine. Sitting on the bed, she looks at me, waiting for what I have to say.

"Remember me telling you about a surgeon at the hospital who violently attacked all my proposals and accused me of being homophobic?" I ask, starting the conversation.

"Of course, Julia Garcia!" she responds without hesitation.

How strange that she remembers her name. I mentioned Julia the same way I talked about Antonio, Assunción and many others. Why did she latch onto the name?

"Exactly. Julia was one of the people who bothered me the most and has impeded the process of change. There was an emergency surgery and no anaesthesiologist available. I was still there, so I ended up going to the OR. When we finished, I decided to rest in one of the on-call rooms for what was left of the night. I was almost asleep when Julia entered, not realizing it was me, and lay down in the other bed. I don't know what came over me, but I was seized by a need to prove I'm not at all what she thinks, that I went over to her bed... one thing led to another... and you can imagine how it ended!" Ursula smiles, the corners of her mouth quirking in that characteristic way of hers.

"Yes, I can imagine..." she comments mysteriously, taking a sip from the glass in her hand.

I'm so caught up in my story that I ignore the obvious signs there's more going on here. "When I woke up in the morning, she was already gone."

"And then?" she asks.

"Then nothing. She continues to be aggressive and treat me with arrogance whenever we meet."

"Julia Garcia!"

"Yes, what about Julia Garcia?" I ask, getting a bit irritated.

"We know each other!" she exclaims with a little laugh, tilting her head back as if remembering something.

"What do you mean, you know Julia?" Suddenly nothing makes sense...

Ursula sits up straighter on the bed, crossing her legs. "Don't worry, we've never been together, not in the way you're thinking." She laughs again and looks at me, shaking her head. "Julia is highly respected, both for her professional qualities and her powers of seduction. You can be sure you weren't the first, or even the tenth, woman she's been with. That's just how she is... she lives for the conquest, whatever form it takes - prestige, power, women."

I'm stunned. No matter how much I had pondered the situation, I never could have imagined this revelation. My mind reels, trying to process this unexpected twist. Ursula's words echo in my head. Julia, the brilliant surgeon, the formidable adversary, the captivating seductress.

"Don't let her hurt you," she says softly, her eyes filled with concern and tenderness.

"No! We're not going to be together again, ever!" I declare vehemently. But even as I say it, I know the truth. "But she affects me with just a look... and she knows it!"

"That's the power of Julia Garcia! So be careful!" Ursula warns, her tone serious.

§§

As I talk with Fili, I carefully filter my words. Even though I want to share everything, there are obviously some things I can't tell him.

"Did you speak with the lawyer? Are you really going to go through with the divorce?" he asks during a pause in the conversation, as I take a deep breath to steady myself.

"I did. There's no other alternative. But from what Alexis said, it's not going to be easy." My voice is heavy with resignation and determination.

Chapter 16

April 17th – Perspectives

Camila

"Hi Camila, how are you? Have you heard back from the woman with the red book cover?" Today, Fili is very direct in his approach, not even giving time for the usual small talk that fills the first few minutes of our sessions.

§§

The air is humid and stuffy, and after a few minutes, I'm already panting and almost unable to speak. Paloma, on the other hand, seems unaffected by the heat or fatigue. She runs beside me with an exasperating tranquillity. I don't know how she does it; no matter how much I train, I'll never be able to keep up with her.

"I can't believe it," she says, surprise written all over her face. We cross the wooden bridge and slow down our pace to observe a group of children. "You kissed a stranger on the train?! Seriously?"

"She wasn't exactly a stranger; I had seen her several times before. She takes the 6:30 train... Or rather, she used to because I haven't seen her since."

"You're kidding; you don't even know her name."

"In the midst of the confusion, I didn't ask. She wasn't well..."

"She wasn't well, and she kissed you? Sounds like a lovely disease."

"Stop it. It was nothing; it was the circumstances. She was frightened, and we got carried away. She always comes to read a book, very quiet, very focused. On two or three occasions, our eyes met. When the lights came back on, I got scared, grabbed my things, and ran out. I crossed a bunch of carriages and sat at the other end. She must have stayed where she was; at least she didn't come after me."

"What an extraordinary story! What are the odds? We have to be careful what we wish for," she says, laughing, reminding me of the toast that night with my nurse friend.

"You want to talk about odds? I'm not finished yet. I had the hospital card ribbon attached to my bag, and in the confusion, the ribbon must have fallen off..."

"You can request another card," she says, looking like she doesn't understand.

"The card has my name and the hospital's name on it."

"Do you think she'll search for you? Try to find your email and stalk you?"

"I don't know..." When I answer, I realize that I'm disappointed if that doesn't happen.

"Your love life is becoming more confusing than mine. You, the quiet Camila, who would have thought!" Paloma lets out a shrill laugh and increases her pace, running at a faster rhythm.

"Don't make fun of me. I'm not like that."

"Like what?"

"Can you go slower? I'm exhausted," I state, stopping. My shirt is soaked, and drops of sweat are dripping from my forehead. "That night, fate played a trick on me," I state emphatically while sighing deeply, "Nothing is going to happen."

"You can't give up every time you get tired." I don't know if she's referring to the running or the context. For now, I'm content to have a few minutes to catch my breath.

"Enough about this. Let's talk about you; we never talk about you."

"What do you want to know? Do you want me to tell you that I've also had an adventure with a stranger?" she says, laughing, and starts running again, this time very slowly.

"What have you been up to? Tell me! I know that look," I say, laughing.

"I like those dimples on your cheeks," she states before continuing, "You know I've been getting massages for years."

"Yes, and so?"

"I had an Argentinian masseur, quite handsome, by the way; he was really excellent." She leans against one of the park benches and pretends to do stretches. I, on the other hand, simply sit down to rest.

"And then?"

"A few months ago, he left. They gave me another masseur. In the dimly lit room, if I didn't know it was someone else, I could believe that nothing had changed. The same silence, the same music, and strong, gentle hands."

"Isn't that good?"

"Wait... There was one time when I felt the hands go down more than usual.

I questioned whether it was part of the massage or if I was imagining things..."

"And?" I ask again, showing my curiosity. It's good to have the usual Paloma back, with her stories and fantasies, I think.

"Come on, let's go to the cafe. You pretend to run, but I run for real," she says, laughing, "With a smoothie in front of me, I promise I'll tell you the rest."

We sit outside, the tables are almost all occupied, and one of the waitresses signals that she's seen us but asks us to wait; the terrace is unusually busy. I know Paloma won't resume her story until they bring us our drinks.

"I've been thinking about whether I should separate." The words come out in a whisper as if I'm sharing a secret.

"Just like that, out of the blue?"

"How can you say 'out of the blue'?"

"Does it have to do with that stranger on the train?" she asks, frowning.

"No, not at all. Julia is becoming more and more distant, and I seem to care less and less..." I wipe my forehead with the back of my hand and brush my hair back. "Sometimes I think we could be happier if we went our separate ways; other times, I feel like I can't live without her," I answer with little conviction. "Leave my dramas and continue, please!"

"There's not much more to tell. Nothing overt ever happened, nothing that gives me the certainty that what's happening isn't just a massage, but from week to week, I grew more impatient for the next session. I started thinking about it in the most inappropriate situations."

"From what you're saying, it sounds like a good topic to think about!" I say with a laugh.

She slaps my arm: "Don't make fun of me! A few weeks ago, it started as always; I had never had a massage like that before, but the sensation was pleasant. What can I say...."

"Wow, Paloma! That's quite the story!" I exclaim, leaning forward eagerly. "So, what happened next? Did you ever confront him about it?"

Paloma grins mischievously, clearly enjoying my rapt attention. "Well, let's just say I didn't exactly discourage his wandering hands. But I'll spare you the steamy details." She winks at me playfully.

I sit back, processing this revelation. A part of me is scandalized by Paloma's brazenness, but another part admires her confidence and ability to seize the moment. I find myself wondering if I could ever be that daring, that uninhibited.

As if reading my thoughts, Paloma reaches out and squeezes my hand. "Hey, don't overthink it. Sometimes you just have to let yourself get swept away by the moment, you know? Life's too short not to take a few risks now and then."

I nod slowly, mulling over her words. Maybe she's right. Maybe it's time I stop playing it so safe all the time.

--

It doesn't happen often, but today, Julia offers to clean up the kitchen. I sit on a stool, watching her. She seems cheerful, talking about the two surgeries she performed in the morning and laughing at her own jokes. She stops loading the dishwasher, leans against the counter, and looks at me. "Your mother came to talk to me today..."

"What do you mean, my mother came to talk to you?" I repeat, trying to make sense of what she just said.

"It's true! She called me to ask if I was at the hospital and if she could stop by. I didn't even know she had my number."

Julia pauses, and I interrupt nervously, "Was it about a patient? Was it about the fund for Mateo?"

"Nothing like that. It was surreal. She started by giving a speech about my qualities. Then, as if she had rehearsed it, she began talking about her dissatisfaction with the new direction of my hospital, as if she had anything to do with it. She doesn't even work there! If you had heard her, 'These new models will destroy everything we've achieved in recent decades... Medicine is a science; we can't let them convince us with this emotional nonsense. Julia knows, and I do too, how hard she fought to reach the management position, and now that she's made it, some random person wants to question what we've achieved?! This week, I spoke to some board members, and I think there will be changes...' While your mother kept talking nonstop, I was trying to find a common thread. For several minutes, I didn't understand where she was going with this."

I remain seated, looking at her as she paces back and forth while recounting the conversation. "You stayed silent?"

"Yes, most of the time. Your mother kept talking and talking, and at some point, she started talking about her friends in Boston. 'You know, Julia, your name was mentioned several times. Professor Thompson called me a few days ago; they're opening a new research center. It's a cutting-edge project, a clinical laboratory dedicated to heart valve replacement, using three-dimensional models of the heart and the original valves, reconstructed from the patient's own undifferentiated cells. It's extraordinary.' I noticed that while she was talking, your mother was looking at me, gauging my interest. I must have had a dumbfounded look on my face, wondering where this was going. Until finally, she said the only thing that really mattered: 'I'm willing to support you in leading the laboratory in Boston. Your relationship with Camila has no future; let her have a 'normal life.' You're an independent woman, Julia; you'll be happier if you can fully enjoy your career.' I'm telling you, I couldn't believe it... And you know, I thought I could expect anything from your mother, but even I wouldn't have dared to imagine this conversation."

I don't know what to say; my mouth is dry, and there's a lump in my throat. She comes close to me and gives me a kiss on the lips.

"I was speechless too," she says, as if that could comfort me.

"This is too awful!"

"Why? Do you think Professor Thompson wouldn't hire me?" she says, letting out a laugh that holds all her sarcasm.

"Stop it!" Although her laughter makes me crack a smile, I can't go along with her irony. "It's unbelievable how far my mother's arrogance goes!"

"She'll never be able to get to us!" Julia's certainty is unshakable. She gives me a kiss and turns her attention back to the dishes, ending the conversation. For a few minutes, I sit and watch her put away plates, glasses, and cutlery in a truly impressive methodical sequence. She never stops being a surgeon, not even when loading the dishwasher.

§§

"Did you tell her that you thought about separation?" Fili asks, uncrossing his leg and crossing it in the opposite direction. "Would you like her to go to Boston?"

"No, of course not! That's ridiculous..."

"Are you sure?" Fili nods, but his expression is inscrutable. "Sometimes, Camila, the things we think we want and the things we actually need are two very different things. It's important to be honest with yourself about your true desires, even if they scare you."

Chapter 17

May 2nd – Desire

Olivia

I'm sitting across from Fili, the sun streaming through the partially open window, bringing with it a slight breeze that does little to cool the unusually warm day.

"You look worried, is everything okay?" Fili asks from his usual spot.

I sigh heavily. "Every day brings new problems and no solutions to yesterday's difficulties. The temporary solution for the anaesthesia shortage seems to have caused more harm than good. I've been thinking maybe I should consider changing jobs. Perhaps I could go back to clinical practice, join an operating room team, I'd even earn more. As if the hospital troubles weren't enough, there's also the divorce, and Javier. I'm so glad Ursula introduced me to Alexis..."

"What does she think as a lawyer? Are you feeling more confident?" Fili inquires, remembering I had mentioned Alexis initially thought it would be a difficult process.

§§

"Olivia, I'm sorry I couldn't see you earlier, but I had to go to the doctor," Alexis says as I sit across from her at the impressive conference table in her law firm. Two weeks ago she told me everything was ready and suggested we inform Javier about the divorce petition. When he realized what was happening, I thought he was going to explode, have a heart attack even. With rage etched on his face, he accused me of everything that crossed his mind, ending with a slew of threats. Faced with Alexis' cool arguments, he ended up agreeing to almost everything, reducing the issue to money. I felt afraid, there was so much anger in his eyes.

"Are you sick?" I ask with concern.

"No, nothing special. But you know how these doctor things are," she replies with a laugh. "What did you want to tell me?"

"I discovered something..." Just thinking about it again, I feel the anger take over me.

"...I went to the bank to get the codes for the new card, and the account manager asked to speak with me. We went to a room away from the prying eyes at the service counters. When we sat down, I realized the young man was uncomfortable. In a few words, he explained that Javier had made large withdrawals from our joint accounts. He took out practically all the available assets, including the stock portfolios."

"That's illegal, Olivia. I know you have joint accounts, but he can't do that."

"Maybe, but until it's resolved, he gets what he wants, leaving me in a delicate situation and unable to help Leonor." I pause, exhausted. Everything seems too heavy, too difficult, even talking.

"Are you okay, Olivia? Do you want some water?" Alexis stands up and goes to the door, saying something I can't hear. A few minutes later, she returns with a glass that she hands to me.

"Thank you," I say, taking small sips as I try to calm myself. "I don't understand how we can live with someone for so long and come to the conclusion that we don't know that person."

"You do know the person. You know exactly what Javier is capable of. Even after all this, you still don't want to press charges?"

"I can't."

--

The day was long and my mind jumps between Alexis' serious words, the confusion at the hospital, and the messages that kept coming. The phone vibrates for the umpteenth time, causing me to throw it to the other side of the couch without even seeing what it is. As if I didn't know. I stare at the TV, a romantic comedy showing a passionate kiss. I have no patience for this! I change the channel, flipping through without ever settling on anything, until finally turning it off. I get up, turn off the lights, and head to the bedroom. I can't resist reading the last message, 'At Dune's, at eleven, no lab coat...'. I slip between the sheets, I have to be at the hospital early. The phone vibrates again, 'Don't you dare not come! The alternative is looking for you tomorrow in the office.'

I jump out of bed and stand still in the middle of the room. How dare she?! Even by text she's overbearing! Very well, she wants a meeting, she'll have it!

I return to Dune's and choose one of the high stools leaning against the bar, in the same place I was a few nights ago. I bring the glass of whiskey in front of me to my mouth, taking a generous sip, as I watch her enter and make her way from the door to here. In jeans, a black shirt and sneakers, she looks much younger. Even from a distance, I notice that she smiles when she sees me. I'm wearing a dress that I haven't worn in a long, long time. It's rare for me to wear dresses, but I couldn't think of anything better. Without saying anything, not even greeting me, she sits down next to me and looks me in the eyes.

"I see you didn't miss each other today!" exclaims the young waiter. She points to my glass and orders the same.

"The night you invited me to meet you here, I came, only I arrived too late. He realized I was looking for someone, and concluded it must be you," I explain.

I'm the only one talking. She sips slowly, never taking her eyes off my mouth.

"Come!" she says, as if it were an order. She gets up and crosses the room, disappearing behind a door. I realize she has entered the bathroom. Tonight I have no intention of resisting. I get up and follow her.

As soon as I enter, she locks the door, turning the key. She pushes me against the wall and kisses me as if it were the last kiss of her life. But one kiss is not enough, she knows it and I know it too. I feel my legs weaken, she takes a step to the side, allowing me to lean on the sink, and pause for a moment. Nothing will stop this moment, it's a path of no return. I grip her hair, letting out a sigh and closing my eyes.

She regains control. She stands up, kisses me and, in an affectionate gesture, adjusts my dress. "Let's go."

We cross the room, this time holding hands, pick up the things that were left on the bar, and leave. Julia is not one for holding hands, and neither am I, but at this moment the urgency of touch imposes itself, even if it's in this simple gesture.

Neither of us have the slightest idea where to go. She is the first to speak, in fact, since she arrived she hasn't said more than two or three words. "I can't invite you to my house for obvious reasons. Let's go to the hospital!"

"What do you mean, to the hospital?" I ask, not understanding what's going through her head.

"There's a room in the service that only I use when I stay overnight. No one else ever goes there."

I don't like the idea, but I don't have a better one. The ride to the hospital takes less than ten minutes. Sitting behind the wheel, not thinking about the whiskey I drank, I feel my body shudder again with the memory of what happened. I want this woman! I don't care about going to a service room in the hospital, I don't care about the risk of someone seeing us, the desire is greater than anything else, so much greater that nothing else exists.

The garage is deserted, and most of the corridors are too. As the elevator doors close, Julia doesn't waste any time and kisses me passionately. She grabs me and presses her lips against mine, our bodies melting into each other's embrace. The lights are dimmed, and we travel the short distance to the room without any interruptions. She opens the door, lets me in, and then locks it from the inside. The sound of the lock reminds me of the bathroom, and I can't help but feel it again. We're safe and alone, at least until dawn. She sits on the only bed in the room and turns on the light next to the headboard. I remain standing, suddenly feeling intimidated. What will be the next move, the next sentence?

"I don't know what you do to me..." she says in her husky voice that I've learned to recognize anywhere. "I desire you like I don't remember ever desiring anyone." She keeps her eyes lowered and rubs her hands together in a nervous tic.

Seeing her sitting here like this gives me a sense of her fragility, and at the same time, it heightens my urgency to have her. I approach her and wrap her in an embrace. No ulterior motives, no wandering hands, no kisses, just a hug. The closeness brings me the scent of her perfume. I let my head rest on her shoulder and close my eyes. She reciprocates and hugs me tightly. I feel the warmth of her breath, and I know I wouldn't want to be anywhere else.

Many minutes pass before we pull apart. I smile, and she smiles too. She reaches out an arm and grabs mine, probably to pull me closer. I let out a small cry of pain, which, although discreet, doesn't go unnoticed by her. "What's wrong? Did I hurt you?" she asks, surprised.

"No, it's nothing... I bumped into a door," I lie.

She seems convinced by the answer and sits close to me. She kisses my neck and continues along my cleavage. The kisses are hot and soft. With skill, she pull my dress up, and removes it over my head. I notice she sees the marks still visible on my arms. She doesn't say anything and continues to kiss me. I could spend the night like this but I gently push her.

"What are you doing?" she asks as if she hasn't understood my intention.

"Stay still!" I look into her eyes and smile. The green is almost unreal. She tries to move, but is my turn to kiss her. With the eagerness of someone who has waited too long,

"Liv, please!" My name said like have a special effect on me.

I kiss her once more before getting up. She makes a move to get up, but I don't allow it. "Don't you dare! Stay down. You're going to wait for everything I have for you!" I didn't think it would work, but she falls back and closes her eyes. For a moment, I simply observe.

I kiss her again, this time lightly. I have other plans, and I know I can't delay much longer.

"Please, don't stop! Don't stop!" she begs.

I don't intend to stop.

A long time passes before either of us is able to say anything.

"Never... It's not that when I first looked at you, I didn't think it was possible," she says.

The light in the room, although dim, allows me to see her clearly. Her eyes are shining more than usual, and I swear I see a tear. I run my hand over her face and brush a small lock of hair back. "What?" I ask with the simplicity the occasion allows.

"It's me who..." The loftiness of the words contrasts with the surrender in her gaze. "You've opened a Pandora's box!"

I don't remember the conversation ending or turning off the light. I only know we fell asleep because I suddenly wake up to the sound of a phone. I look at the window; it's still night. It can't be the cell phones since they're turned off. In a mechanical gesture, she reaches for the landline on the bedside table: "Julia Garcia," she says immediately.

She talks to someone for a few moments and hangs up.
Who could have known she was in this room?

§§

I say goodbye to Fili, knowing that I told him a lot, but many more things remained only inside my head.

Chapter 18

May 2nd – She is the Best

Camila

"When I left here two weeks ago, you asked me to think. I never could have imagined what would happen in these weeks," I say, still standing, heading towards my couch. Fili holds the door and follows me with his eyes without saying anything.

"Are you okay? You look tired, like you haven't slept..."

I interrupt him, "And I haven't... I feel like I haven't slept for more than a week." I lean back and close my eyes. I need to talk, but at the same time, I feel so exhausted.

"Is your father okay?" The question pulls me out of my apathy. How can he know something happened to my father? I haven't told him anything yet.

§§

"Your father..." My mother's voice comes out broken.

"What happened? Where are you?" It must be four or five in the morning. I was sleeping, but from her tone, I realize something very serious is going on.

"We're at the hospital... Central. Yesterday, your father said he wasn't going to work because he didn't feel well. I thought it was strange but didn't give it much thought. He stayed home, and I left. In the early afternoon, he called me to say he wasn't feeling better and that maybe it would be good for me to come home. So I did. I cancelled the rest of my appointments and went to him. When I arrived, he was sitting in the living room, as white as the wall. He wouldn't let me do anything, but by dinnertime, he even seemed better. A little while ago, he woke me up. He couldn't sleep, was nauseous, sweating, and clutching his chest in pain. You know your father. He insisted I shouldn't call anyone, but I ended up calling the emergency. And it was a good thing I did because right after that, he lost consciousness... Fortunately, when the ambulance arrived, he had already regained consciousness... You know how stubborn he is... I'm scared..." She pauses for a moment and murmurs, "Please, come here..."

Not knowing exactly what to say, I utter, "Stay calm. What have they done for him so far?" I'm alone with Mateo. Julia is at the hospital. I can't just leave like this.

"Besides the electrocardiogram and blood tests, I didn't see them do much more. A while ago, a cardiologist friend of mine came here... He was at our party the other day. I could see on his face that he was worried. He told me the situation is serious and that a conservative approach may not be possible... We know what that means. They're considering surgery..."

"They're going to operate in the acute phase? Why not use an antithrombotic? Or a percutaneous approach? Surgery in this context has many risks." Several questions go through my head. There are so many other options. Why consider surgery, and who is going to operate on him?

I'm not the only one grappling with these questions. On the other end of the phone, my mother insists, "Do you think I don't know that? Please, come here. I need your help."

I agree, hang up, and try to think about what I'm going to do. I call Julia again and again, but the phone doesn't give a signal. I can't take Mateo with me, but I also can't leave him at home alone. I look at the time on the alarm clock, 4:40. Patience, it'll have to do. I call Paloma. Nothing. I insist two more times.

"I'm sorry, I know it's the middle of the night..." I say when she answers.

"What happened? Are you okay? Mateo?" she asks, frightened.

"We're fine. It's my father... He's been admitted to the hospital. I don't know the details, but I think they're going to operate on his heart. Julia must be at the hospital, and she's not answering..."

"Stay calm. I'm coming over. Give me fifteen minutes."

I arrive at the hospital about forty minutes later. I find my mother in the room, sitting in a chair, the bed empty. She's pale and looks haggard, not seeming like the Amelia Velasquez who dominates any environment. She's not crying, but her face, without makeup, is marked by the tears that have fallen in the last few hours.

"What happened? Where's Dad?" I ask, afraid.

"He went for more tests and then straight to the operating room. I was with him and the doctors. They're going to operate. I still insisted if we couldn't start with a pharmacological approach, but the general opinion is that surgery gives more guarantees."

"Who's going to operate?"

"I demanded it be Julia..."

"Julia?" I ask, stupefied. We went from not even mentioning her name to wanting Dad to be operated on by her!

"She's the best. That's the only thing that matters! I don't think she's on duty today, but they've already contacted her, and she'll be the one operating."

On the contrary, I think, she's here at the hospital. Or is she not?

After the initial conversation, we remain silent, mostly because we haven't had anything in common for a long time. Now I understand the insistence for me to come. She thought she might need me to convince Julia.

It's already morning when my sister literally bursts into the room. In a tearful tone, she embraces my mother and plays her expected role. After the drama, they engage in a conversation that, as one would expect, totally excludes me. I jump up when one of Julia's assistants appears at the door. "He's fine. He's in recovery. In a little while, you can go see him. He's going to the Intensive Care Unit, but if all goes well, he'll be transferred to a room tomorrow. Doctor Julia Garcia will be right with you." Without further explanation or room for questions, he withdraws, leaving us alone. He must really be Julia's disciple, at least when it comes to conversation.

Shortly after, my mother and sister go up, accompanied by one of the nurses, who kindly comes to get them, apparently at the request of the clinical director herself. I remain seated on the same couch where I spent the early morning, trying to understand what happened. Julia enters the room, still in surgical scrubs, and looks around, surprised to find me alone.

"I tried calling you countless times... I didn't know what to do. My mother called. I was alone with Mateo. I couldn't get ahold of you..." Without letting her speak, I continue in an accusatory tone, "It's ironic, to say the least! I confess I minimized your power, and of all people, me..."

"Calm down. You can stop. Stay calm. I know you're nervous, but everything went well. He's stable and will recover." She sits on the couch next to me, places her hand on my knee, and caresses me. "In a few days, he'll be as good as new, and everything will return to normal." Her voice remains calm, and her face doesn't betray the fatigue of operating for so many hours. "Your mother doesn't like me and will never like me, but that doesn't mean I won't operate on your father and do the best I know how."

"How did it go?" I ask.

"Well, considering everything... You know what's most extraordinary? We're still short on anaesthesiologists. Only juniors were on the schedule. I was surprised by Olivia again. She was here and offered to go to the operating room herself." Julia smiles, seeming satisfied with what happened.

"The clinical director? The one you hate?" I ask, astonished.

"Exactly! I hate her, but I can't deny she's a great anaesthesiologist." She stands up and extends her hand for me to accompany her.

We go upstairs, with me still thinking about what the clinical director would be doing at the hospital in the middle of the night. When we arrive, there's a small crowd around the bed. Julia approaches one of the doctors and taps her on the shoulder, making her turn to us.

"Olivia Lopez," she says, introducing her.

Olivia smiles and extends her hand to me. She seems like a nice person, far from what I had imagined after hearing the descriptions. I look at her again, and for a moment, I have the feeling I've seen her somewhere before.

"I'll leave you all. Julia, if you need anything, just call." She smiles and says goodbye.

I watch her leave, still having the same feeling that I've seen her in another context. But where?

My mother and Julia are talking as if it were the most normal thing in the world. I carefully keep my distance, enough to hear the conversation but not close enough for either of them to call me to participate.

--

I return to the hospital two days later. My father is recovering well, and as Julia said, soon everything will return to normal. It's just the three of us in the room, and my mother carries on the conversation.

"You know, I've been thinking, and I would be happy to support Julia's career. This hospital is terrible and will only get worse. A recommendation from me still holds a lot of value and can open doors for her. While she stays here, she may be good, but she'll never have the opportunity to be truly excellent. She has to go abroad. And there, I'm sure she'll have a brilliant future..." I still don't understand, but she continues, as cold as always. "If you convince her to go to Boston, I'll talk to Professor Thompson. I know she admires him greatly."

I pretend I don't understand what she's saying and ask, "You want her to go to Boston?"

"Yes. You stay here with Mateo and get on with your life," she adds, shrugging her shoulders and raising the corner of her lip in a grimace of displeasure that she tries to hide behind a fake smile. "Don't be selfish. If you love her, you have to let her fly. Only you don't see it. Julia is not a woman to live imprisoned, not by you or anyone."

After leaving, I can no longer do anything I had planned for this afternoon. Without a defined direction, I walk through the park from one side to the other. I look at the people running by and think of Paloma. I should spend more time with her.

Tired, I sit on a bench and cry. I cry as I haven't cried in a long, long time. I let contained tears come out in a whirlwind, knowing it will be the last time I allow myself to cry because of my mother. With my legs bent on the bench, I hide my face between my hands and knees and sob for pains I've never shared.

§§

"What would it take for things with your mother to be resolved?" Fili asks, interrupting my long narrative.

"Everything! Everything she can't do because she's simply not capable. Contrary to what I told you before about Julia's clinical director, my mother is homophobic and doesn't hide it. She was abominable to my brother, and with me... she's less harsh, but even that is for the wrong reasons. It bothers her much more that her son is gay than that I'm a lesbian."

I go out into the street thinking about Fili's question. Things between my mother and me can never be resolved. Life doesn't go backward. Maybe the solution is to distance myself enough to stop suffering from it, I think as I walk slowly along the sidewalk.

Maggy McAndrew

Chapter 19

June 5th – The Conference

Olivia

"How was the conference?" I ask. This is definitely the month of conferences. Fili was away for more than two weeks at the annual psychiatry conference.

"It was great as always. I met fantastic people and reconnected with some I missed. It's incredible how we lose touch with people we were once close to... Olivia, enough about me. It's been over a month since you were here. Tell me the news." He looks at me and smiles, adjusting his glasses with his index finger, then picking up his notebook and pen. He's ready to begin.

"I also went to a conference," I reply, leaving an air of mystery.

"Really? Alone?" If anyone else had asked, the question might not have made sense, but coming from him, it just shows how well he knows me.

§§

The room is packed. After a very brief opening speech, I sit in a chair in the front row and hand the floor over to Assunción. She will lead our presentation. In the audience, besides all the members of the administration, are the department heads and many of the hospital's professionals. I lean back and think about what we've already achieved and how much we still need to do if we really want to change anything. Five minutes later, my phone vibrates in my lab coat pocket. 'A whisky later?' I look back in search of Julia but don't see her anywhere. The phone vibrates again. 'Naked! Leaning over the top of a table...' I feel my heart race as I read the text. I must have blushed; my face feels hot. I put the phone back in my pocket as if someone could see what I'm reading. Once again, I look around but still don't see her. She has to be here, but where?

When Assunción finishes the presentation, several arms are raised to ask questions. The first comes from a colleague in anaesthesia, who returns to the topic of hiring and staff shortages. She doesn't waste much time on the answer, vehemently assuring that the matter will be resolved. When she seems about to change the subject, she pauses and announces, "For now, the department is under the direct responsibility of our Clinical Director." Her words cause a moment of silence.

'A victory! Congratulations!' 'Shall we celebrate?' I shouldn't be looking at my phone, but I can't help it. I'm still lost in thought when I hear her voice echo through the room. An unreasonable panic invades me, and I don't even hear her first words. "...we don't agree with what has been happening. Doctor Olivia Lopez may have good intentions, but the strategy is counterproductive if we lose our most qualified staff..." Julia continues speaking. I now realize why I couldn't see her. I was looking back in search of her, and she's sitting in the front row, right next to the chair of the Board of Directors. No matter how much I get to know her, she never ceases to surprise me.

I come to the office just to leave my lab coat. I put some documents inside my bag and leave. I think about Julia's invitation to have a drink, but I immediately put the idea aside. I want to take a hot bath and enjoy having the house to myself. Fortunately, Javier is away for two weeks.

In the garage, I have the feeling of being watched. I put my bag on the back seat and look around, but I don't see anyone. It must just be an impression. Lately, everything seems strange to me. Another message: 'Where are you going? Don't you want company?' I slam my hand on the steering wheel... How is this possible? Where is she? Why is she pursuing me like this? I get out of the car again and look around... There's no one in the garage.

'It depends on what you have to offer! Surprise me!' I reply. Immediately after, I start the engine and drive off, the tires screeching.

I arrive home about twenty minutes later. Too lazy to enter the building's garage, I park the car in a spot across the street. In fact, that's what I do most of the time. I slowly gather my things and head for the door. I cross the street absentmindedly and climb the five steps to the entrance, searching for the key inside my bag. As I'm looking down, I don't notice someone approaching, standing between me and the door.

"Hello, stranger!" I jump with fright. "You don't need to be scared!" Julia, standing in front of me, smiles.

"What are you doing here?"

"You asked for a surprise. I thought you wanted company! And besides, I want you! If you send me away, I'll go. If not, invite me in and offer me a whisky. I know you don't have anyone waiting for you at home."

How does she know where I live? And how can she know there's no one at home? I only mentioned it to Assunción.

"You want me to go with you to the cardiothoracic conference?" I ask, not believing the proposal she's making. "How can we go together to a conference full of people, where everyone knows you and some even know me?"

"That's exactly why. We'll go together because we work together. Nothing strange about it," she states exultantly. "Nothing strange. During the day, you'll go to your sessions, and I'll go to mine, and then we have the whole night... I'll tell you more. As the conference ends on a Thursday and there are several courses on the following days, I thought we could use that as an excuse and stay until Sunday. There's a nearby beach. I've heard it's fantastic, with transparent water and white sand. I can try to book something..." Her face mirrors the joy of someone who anticipates each step of the trip and enjoys it as if she were already there.

I reflect on the possible consequences. Javier won't want to know if I'm going to a conference, much less with whom. I've hardly seen him and spoken to him almost not at all. In other words, I have little to lose. And her? Julia never talks about her wife or son. It's like a totally separate world, another life. I respect that and don't ask.

My heart races at the thought of spending uninterrupted days with Julia, exploring a new place together, free from the constraints and watchful eyes of our daily lives. The prospect is both thrilling and terrifying. I know I'm stepping into uncharted territory, but the magnetic pull between us is undeniable.

"Okay," I hear myself saying, my voice barely above a whisper. "Let's do it. Let's go to the conference together."

Julia's face lights up with a radiant smile, and she pulls me into a passionate kiss. For a moment, the world falls away, and there's nothing but the softness of her lips, the warmth of her skin, and the intoxicating scent of her perfume. When we finally break apart, breathless and giddy, I can't help but laugh.

"You're going to be the death of me, you know that?"

"Oh, but what a way to go," she teases, her eyes sparkling with mischief. "Now, about that whisky..."

--

The first day is hectic, and I lose sight of her right after the opening session. Throughout the day, I move between the various rooms, and we don't cross paths again. There are thousands of people gathered in a huge space. It's been a long time since I attended a congress like this one. It feels good to be back in scientific sessions, but at the same time, I'm frightened by how much some areas have evolved. I need to try to stay more updated or pursue a career within a specific field, even if I want to.

It's almost nine in the evening when I enter the room. I undress and prepare a hot bath, not before ordering a salad and a good wine from room service. I sink into the bathtub, letting my body adjust to the water temperature until I'm completely submerged. I feel my muscles relax, and a sense of calm washes over me. It's good to be here! It's good to be here, even if right now, it means being alone in the room, without the slightest idea of where she is. There's a knock on the door. It must be room service; they were faster than

I imagined. "You can come in, please leave it on the table," I say loudly enough for the employee in the corridor to hear. I hear the sound of the door opening and, after a moment, the sound of it closing. I lean my head back and let myself get lost in dreams, closing my eyes. Classical music plays softly in the bathroom, transporting me to the memory of Kissin's piano sound... I nearly die of fright when I open my eyes and see Julia, completely naked, standing in front of me.

"Where were you? Or more importantly, who were you with?" she asks, laughing as she enters the bathtub.

"What are you doing here? How did you get in?" I question, my heart still pounding from the surprise.

"It wasn't easy. I had to convince the employee that I wasn't a burglar, that I knew you, and that I was going to surprise you. After some effort, he relented and let me in. You didn't answer me, you were smiling... who were you thinking about?" Before allowing me to respond, she kisses me.

I let her kiss and caress me for long minutes, but I will be the one dictating the rules of this game. She closes her eyes, and I know she's yielded. I turn on the handheld shower, letting a stream of water flow, neither too intense nor too gentle. I aim the water in her direction.

"Lív!... Please!"

I let her implore a little more, then turn off the shower and slide my hand to where the jet of water was before.

"Lív!" she murmurs.

I know she can't take it anymore.

"Lív!" The feeling I get when she whispers my name as we make love is so extraordinary that I'll never be able to describe it. It's as if everything falls into the right place, the world stops, and nothing else exists.

--

The days of the congress are filled with emotions. She seems to live every moment to seduce me. She gives herself to me in a way I never thought possible. During this week, I am someone else, with no past, no future, only the present. And the present is wonderful. She's not just an expert lover; she's an intelligent woman with a sense of humour laced with irony and a delicacy that peeks through in every gesture.

However, despite everything, I know that I can't fully surrender myself. I hope she's not aware of this. Every time we make love, I'm the one in control; there's always a point where I take charge. It's so different from what I have with Ursula.

§§

"Being with her made me realize the power she wields. Not so much over me, because I already knew that, but over everyone. People stop to listen to her and literally drink in her words. It's incredible," I confess, still in awe of the effect she has on others.

"Are you in love?" Fili asks as if it were a simple and trivial question.

"No! Of course not!" I reply, perhaps a little too quickly, trying to convince myself as much as him.

§§

Leonor just got home. We need to talk, and it's going to be a long and difficult conversation. It's time to come clean; Alexis is right, I need her on my side, and I can't have that if I don't tell her the whole story.

"I'm worried, Mom. I've never seen you like this... you look tired," she says, sitting down next to me.

I get straight to the point, briefly explaining what Alexis has been doing and what happened. She starts to say something, but I don't allow it and continue, "No, please don't interrupt me. I have to go all the way, or I won't be able to. When I asked for a divorce, your father was furious about everything, and besides, he realized that you live with a woman and thought I was complicit. In fact, it was just the straw that broke the camel's back. We haven't been okay for many years, and that's a euphemism to describe our relationship. Times were different, and even though I knew your father wasn't the love of my life, I chose to do what was expected of me. When you were born, he insisted very much that I stay at home; it was our first really serious argument..."

Leonor can't contain herself, "I understand, I understand that you're getting a divorce, but..."

"Your father grew distant, started drinking, having other women, and he didn't even make a secret of it. It may seem strange to you, but it was a relief... I channelled my energy into work, and then, a few years ago, I met someone... I won't describe her because that's not important now, but I want you to know that she's the best..."

"Her?" she asks under her breath.

Her gaze is perplexed, lost in the void. She stares at the window, frowns, and her lips are tight. For a moment, neither of us says anything, then her expression changes, her muscles relax, and her lips open in a welcoming smile. "It's good to know that you weren't alone! And to think that I was terrified to tell you, I should have talked to you before... if I had known."

I get up from the sofa and sit next to her. "Thank you!"

"Thank you for what?" she asks.

"For not judging me!" I say, stroking her hair. "But there's one more thing you need to know, something I would give anything not to have to tell you."

"You're making me nervous..." Her face tightens again.

I take a deep breath and muster the courage to begin, "I don't know how to tell you in a gentle way, but your father is aggressive towards me!"

"He's aggressive with everyone, he yells, orders, thinks he owns the world. He's the most arrogant person I know."

"I think you're not understanding. When I say he's aggressive, I'm not just talking about words..." Leonor opens her mouth as if to say something, but she doesn't utter a sound. She stays like that, mouth open, looking at me. "Your father is violent... especially when he drinks, and..." I can't finish.

"No! It can't be!" She remains motionless in the same position. I see a tear roll down her face, but she ignores it and keeps staring at me, lost. "He hits you?"

Finally, the question that demands the words I didn't want to say.

I hug her tightly, wipe her face with my hand, smile, and continue, "He doesn't deserve your tears. It's in the past!"

§§

"It was good that you told Leonor," Fili says, stopping his writing.

177

"Maybe. I would have preferred not to," I murmur.

Chapter 20

June 5th - In the Dark

Camila

"It's been so long since we've seen each other! You're thinner, Camila, are you okay?" Fili has finally returned from the psychiatry conference, it's the same every year in June.

"Maybe," I say distantly, my voice barely above a whisper as I struggle to find the words to express the turmoil inside me.

"Maybe not! You're definitely thinner, and it doesn't seem like it's just a pound or two. What's going on? You're not on a diet, are you? Vomiting?" His expression conveys his concern. He knows what happened.

"None of that. I have no appetite. I try to eat, but I'm not hungry. Every meal is an effort. I can't sleep either," I confess, my voice trembling slightly as I avoid his gaze.

"You'll have to explain to me what's going on," Fili says, prompting me to recount the last few weeks. I take a deep breath, steeling myself for the emotional journey ahead.

§§

I'm standing in line at the bar for lunch when I receive a call. The surrounding noise is deafening, and my brother speaks very quickly, tripping over his sentences.

"You're coming here? Really? When? Did something happen?" I ask my brother, surprised when I realize what he's telling me. "No, don't take it the wrong way, it's not that I don't want you to come. I really do, but I'm curious, why now? You haven't been here in years."

"You don't want me there, do you?" he asks, pretending to be offended, only to burst out laughing.

"Don't be silly... but you have to agree that it's unexpected, to say the least! Are you going to tell me why, or is it a secret?" I feel like there's something he hasn't told me yet, and my curiosity grows.

"Sis... you can't hide anything..." he teases.

"Come on, what's the news? Are you getting married?" I joke, trying to unblock the conversation.

"How do you know?"

There's a monumental silence. He doesn't say anything else, and I almost drop the tray of food I'm holding.

"I was joking... What do you mean? You're getting married?! Wait, let me put this stuff down on a table. I can't have this conversation like this, I need to sit down," the words come out of me in a jumble, but it doesn't matter, the correctness of my speech is the least of my concerns. "Okay, you can start explaining. You have a lot to say!" I exclaim. I see Esther in the distance, who has just entered and is waving in my direction. Not now, I think, as I return the gesture. I hope she doesn't come sit here.

"I met someone..." he begins, "He works here at Pediatrics. We started dating, one thing led to another, and we've been living together for a month. I didn't tell you before, so as not to give you false hope before I myself realized if it was really serious. He's amazing, he's an oncologist, gorgeous..."

"Well, your opinion on that doesn't count, I want a picture..." I interject to relieve the tension.

"Later, for now you'll have to take my word for it. Yesterday we had a party at our place, and at the end of the night, he proposed, with a ring and everything. The most cliché! What could I answer?!"

"Congratulations!" I shout as if I had finally understood the message. "But, you can't marry someone I don't know..."

"I agree, and that's why I convinced him to go there, what do you think?"

"When are you arriving?" I ask excitedly, seeing Esther approaching and standing with her tray in front of me, "Sit down, I'm talking to my brother," I tell her, making a hand gesture.

"What, are you talking to me?"

"No, sorry. It was a colleague who just arrived here. Go on, when are you coming?"

"We have to organize ourselves. It's not that simple. He's a widower and has a son..."

"What? A son? He has a son? You're going to marry him..."

"Are you okay? You're not making much sense," he replies with a laugh.

"Don't you think it's too much information in just one sentence?"

"We never needed to talk much to understand each other!"

"Right..." I'm unable to ask anything else.

"And you? How are you? Julia, Mateo?"

"Julia went to the cardiothoracic conference. Mateo is great... How old is...?"

"3 years old."

During the conversation, I even forgot to tell him about my mother's blackmail, but when he asks me about Julia, the subject comes back to haunt me.

"You won't believe what Mom did."

"Mom?" he asks, not hiding his admiration.

"Exactly! She went to the hospital to basically tell her that she could get her an extraordinary position in Boston if she left me. Julia didn't give in and put her in her place, you know the beast! But as if that wasn't enough, she came to me with the same conversation when Dad was still in the hospital. There's one thing that keeps hammering in my head, why? Why now?"

Distracted by the conversation, I almost forget that Esther is sitting across from me in complete silence. I shrug my shoulders, and she gives me a smile, continuing to eat.

"You don't know?" my brother asks, who surely has some information I'm not aware of.

"No, why? Should I know?"

"I think I know the reason. Favors are paid, and I think it's time for her to collect some. Don't forget that Mom was the brain behind several campaigns, she made people win elections. I wouldn't be surprised if this time she's running for party leadership herself. If that's the case, it's time to 'tidy up the house'..."

She hasn't changed in over thirty years, I think. We were the mascots at her parties, dressed the same with a smile plastered on our faces. Now, she needs a new family portrait and Julia can't be a part of it. If reality doesn't give her what she wants, then reality is changed!

When he finally hangs up, I focus my attention on Esther who has already finished her lunch, while mine remains almost untouched.

"Sorry, that was my brother," I say, feeling the need to justify myself.

"I understood."

"Is everything okay with you? I wasn't expecting to see you here."

"Actually, I came hoping to find you."

"What do you mean?"

--

No one is home. I have about two hours until Mateo arrives. I turn on the TV and the computer. I take the opportunity to check my email, nothing new. I open an article I'm writing and immerse myself in the text. A beep indicates the arrival of an email, diverting my attention.

> *Camila,*
>
> *After much thought about whether or not to write to you, I chose to do so, as you can see now.*
>
> *It's strange, even for me, who has experienced a little bit of everything, but what happened between us doesn't leave my mind. I know that anything I do from now on will only ruin that memory, and yet the urge to be able to talk to you prevailed over the most basic common sense.*
>
> *I have the advantage, I know who you are, and you know almost*

nothing about me. Still, I couldn't resist telling you that I can't stop
thinking about you.

A kiss (this time only in words), until one day,

A.

PS: I went for more tests and I'm waiting for results. Doctors...

I read the text again and get up from the chair. I walk around the room trying to make sense of what happened and what just happened. I sit back down and read the same words again. It has no name. It comes from a Gmail composed of apparently meaningless letters and numbers, at least to me. Who is this woman?

§§

Fili puts down the notebook and pen on the table. "Did you reply?"

"No. Actually, I tried. I wrote and deleted. I wrote again and deleted again. What am I going to say to a stranger? After that night she didn't show up on the morning train again. She doesn't want to meet me. Why?" I ask rhetorically, not expecting him to answer me.

"What do you want?"

"To know who she is!" I say immediately.

"Why don't you ask her?"

When I go out on the street I realize how hot it is. The air is stuffy and there is not even a breeze. I take a deep breath and think about Fili's last words, 'Why don't you ask her?'. Maybe out of fear, out of fear that it might break the spell.

Chapter 21

June 19th – Victims

Olivia

Fili is sitting across from me, legs crossed and glasses perched on his nose. Nothing new so far, but something is different. I don't know if it's me being impatient, but I feel like I need to tell him everything. "You know, Fili, Alexis has been tireless. I don't know if I'd be able to do this without her. She's the one who should be nicknamed the Iron Lady, not me," I confess, my voice trembling slightly as I try to convey the depth of my gratitude.

"Why? More problems with Javier?" he asks without smiling, his expression serious and attentive.

"I'll tell you the same thing I told Alexis," I begin, taking a deep breath to steady myself.

§§

Sitting in the chair on the other side of the desk, I look Alexis in the eye before dropping the bomb. "Javier left the house," I say, my voice barely above a whisper. "I came home and his things were simply not there. Not a message, a note, nothing. It's a perverse psychological game that he completely dominates. Our account is almost at zero, and there's nothing I can do. He even withdrew the money from my salary." Alexis looks at me and lets me speak while taking some notes. Sometimes I look at her and think she has a certain similarity to Fili's sessions.

"Listen, Olivia, he's smart and he's definitely being well-advised," she says, her voice calm and reassuring.

"To see how far things can go, yesterday, when I was leaving in the morning, the car wasn't where I had parked it the night before. I walked around looking for it, thinking I had gotten confused. The doorman was down here and came over to me, very nicely, asking if something was wrong. I explained that I couldn't find the car, I thought maybe it had been stolen... Do you know what he told me? That Javier had been there the night before, even talked to him about the weekend results, and told him he was going to take the car because it needed an urgent repair... Can you believe it?!" I exclaim, my voice rising with each word as the frustration and disbelief overwhelm me.

"And yet, your decision is the same?" she asks without looking at me, her voice neutral.

"I can't," I answer through clenched teeth, ashamed of myself. I feel like a coward, unable to stand up for myself, but the fear paralyzes me.

"Olivia, violence has to be reported. Silence is complacent, it's complicit. He's not going to stop. He thinks he can bend you," Alexis says firmly, rising from her seat and going to the window, looking out at the street for a moment. I watch her, feeling a sudden surge of admiration for her strength and resolve. I wish I could be more like her, more confident and assertive.

I remember the first time I told someone. Ursula called me in the morning while I was in a meeting, and I let the phone vibrate silently. On any other day, I would have asked to step out for a few minutes. We had only been together for a short time, and her calls made my heart race. But not that day. When the meeting ended, I felt guilty. I looked at the screen and had two messages saying she was waiting for me.

I didn't have the courage not to go. She opened the door, gave me a kiss on the lips, and asked bluntly, "What's going on? Are you okay?"

I didn't know how to respond. I couldn't say yes, but I didn't have the right words. Having no idea, she insisted, "What happened? Tell me, you know there's nothing you can't share with me."

And I did know! Unable to hold back the tears, I hid my face in my hands, trying to conceal what I was feeling. For long minutes, she said nothing. I sat on the bed and she, in silence, settled on the couch by the window and lit a cigarette. I knew she would wait as long as necessary.

I didn't know what to say. Without uttering a single word, I unbuttoned the shirt I was wearing and took it off.

"What is that?" she asked, visibly shaken. She dropped the cigarette, stood up, and stood still next to me, staring at my shoulder, saying nothing more.

"Sit here," I asked. She obeyed, never taking her eyes off the bruises that marked my arm, chest, and collarbone. "I have to tell you something I've never told anyone."

Without letting me continue, and with extreme care, as if I might fall apart, she leaned over and hugged me, in such an affectionate gesture that tears came to my eyes again.

"It happened again two days ago..."

"What do you mean, again?" she asked.

"It's a long and deeply sad story. Are you sure you want to hear it?"

"No! I'm sure I don't want to hear it, but I'm even more sure that I need to know." She ran her hand over my face, giving me the courage to continue.

"Javier has changed. He was always very ambitious, but he was an affectionate and kind man... With his career advancement, he gained more power and responsibility and started drinking more and more. Whisky became the cure for everything - for social events, for relaxing, for controlling stress, any excuse would do. He became aggressive and suspicious. The next day there was always an apology... a 'never again', and I... I kept believing."

I look back at Alexis, who remains standing. "I can't! I'm sorry if I disappoint you, but the truth is I can't!"

"No, I'm the one who should apologize. My role is not to force you to do what you don't want, quite the contrary."

"Javier took a lot from me. He destroyed my confidence, changed me as a person. I can't let him take anything else from me. If I report him, I'll be 'the victim', and I'll never be able to stop being one. Can you understand that?"

"Did you talk to Leonor?"

"I did," I say and take a deep breath. "There's something you don't know... only Ursula does."

"I'm not understanding, Olivia."

Sitting in the chair, I adjust my glasses on my nose and bite my lower lip until I feel pain. "Before I went to manage the oncology centre, I was an anaesthesiologist at San Joan. I liked being in the operating room. I was good at what I did. Until that day..."

"Go on... what happened?" Alexis looks me in the eyes and flashes a smile, trying to convey the confidence I need to continue.

"It was a simple surgery, a hernia. No one was available to administer anaesthesia in the general surgery room and I had nothing scheduled that afternoon. I ended up going. I didn't know the patient, but the colleague who handed over the case didn't give any special indications. No recommendations or warning signs, nothing. I trusted him. In the middle of the procedure, the patient started to decompensate." I stop, not knowing how to continue. "He went into cardiac arrest and no one could resuscitate him. He died on the table."

"What a terrible story. But it wasn't your fault."

"We were accused of negligence. The colleague who passed on the case to me denied ever talking to me about it." I get up from the chair and go to the window. I mechanically rub my hands together, trying to find the strength to say what needs to be said. "I told Javier. Instead of helping me, he convinced me that I would face a terrible process and that I would never be able to practice again. He proposed that I leave the hospital, and in exchange he would convince the administration not to sue me. He wanted me to accept the position as director of the oncology center, because he thought it could benefit him. I never knew exactly what happened, but the hospital reached an agreement with the family, they agreed to my departure, and they made everything disappear."

--

I don't know if it's just my impression, but Julia is different. She's distant, less attentive. In the last two weeks she has made and cancelled plans twice, each time with an implausible excuse.

I open the office door just as she's passing in the hallway.

"Still here?" I ask, looking at my watch.

"On call, again," she replies, coming over to me.

"Come in for a moment, I want to show you something," I say, pushing the door back to let her pass.

As soon as she enters, I close the door and kiss her. She reciprocates, but doesn't let the situation evolve. She takes a few steps back and starts talking about an unstable patient who may need surgery tonight.

"Do you want me to stay? I can help."

"No, it's not necessary. I'll see you tomorrow."

--

Already at home, after a shower and a change of clothes, I eat a slice of pizza in front of the TV and feel better. A movie I wanted to see is on. As always happens, fatigue wins out, and I fall into a deep sleep with the pizza box still on my lap. When I wake up it's two in the morning. I think about going to bed, but I anticipate insomnia. I go to the kitchen, drink some sparkling water and go back to the living room. I pick up the phone, which I left on the table when I came in, hoping to have a message from her. Nothing! I decide to go ahead: "How are you? Do you have a bed for me?" More than half an hour goes by with no response. On an impulse, I decide to go there and surprise her.

I enter the garage elevator and get off on the cardiothoracic floor. I walk down the dimly lit corridor and stop at the room door. I gently knock twice. I wait a moment, and when I raise my arm to knock again, the door opens.

"What are you doing here?" she asks in a harsh tone, not hiding her surprise.

"I thought you might want company to sleep..."

"The day didn't go well, and the night isn't going any better. I don't know if I'm in the mood for anything else."

I start to regret my decision. Unexpectedly, she pushes me against the wall, grabs my wrists with both hands, pressing her body against mine and, without allowing me to move, presses her mouth to mine, kissing me violently. I'm stunned and at the same time aroused. I can't move, but I try to follow her mouth seeking the taste of her lips. She kisses me and pulls away alternately, in a purely provocative movement. She pushes me away from the wall and makes me fall on the bed. "Turn over!" she orders.

I don't know what to do. Everything in this scene evokes the worst memories, yet at the same time I know it's her who's here, even though I can barely see her in this moment. Suddenly I feel a slap, the sound echoing in the silence of the room. Although not very hard, it's still a slap. "Didn't you hear me? Turn over!" Her voice sounds different. I don't know if she's serious or if it's part of the game.

"What did you come here looking for?"

"Slowly, Julia!..." I plead. She completely ignores my words as if she doesn't hear them at all. I force myself to react, but I can't. The image of Javier crosses my mind, his gentle smile and loving eyes haunting me. I know it will be impossible to feel anything. I swallow hard and fake, just wanting this to be over as quickly as possible.

She gets up, goes to the bathroom, and re-enters the room already fully dressed in a blue scrub suit. "I was called, sorry, I have to go," she says, her voice distant and cold. She places a kiss on my lips and leaves, leaving me alone with my thoughts and regrets.

The first thing that occurs to me is to lock the door again. What would happen if someone came in now? I shudder at the thought, pulling the sheets tightly around me as if they could shield me from the consequences of my actions.

I remember Ursula's words when she talked about Julia, 'she lives for the conquest.' I don't know how she knows, but that's of lesser importance now. If she's right, my story with Julia Garcia may be very close to the end.

--

"You know I don't like to gossip about other people's lives, you've never heard me talk about the office rumours, but this time..., this time I have to tell you..." Assunción says, her eyes wide with excitement as she leans in closer to me.

We're sitting together at one of the tables in the bar. I had a lunch date with Alexis, but she called me yesterday to say that she felt ill and wouldn't be working until the end of the week. I don't know what's going on, but she's already cancelled a meeting a few weeks ago for the same reason.

"What are you talking about?" I ask, not paying much attention as I savour a cheeseburger covered in melted cheese and a glass of Coca-Cola. I wanted a beer, but I decided it wasn't appropriate considering we're in the middle of a workday.

"About Julia!..." she says, stopping right after to drink almost half of her glass of water in one gulp. I shudder, but try not to show my interest. She has no idea what that name means to me.

"What about Julia? What did she do this time?" I ask, keeping a light tone.

"Last night, my husband arrived from a symposium sponsored by the pharmaceutical industry..., he was there for three days. You know...," she says with a proud air, "He was one of the invited speakers."

I'm not really understanding anything about the conversation. What does her husband have to do with Julia? Assunción knows how to make a conversation circular. I take a sip of Coca-Cola, pick up a French fry with my hand, and put it in my mouth, chewing slowly.

"He was telling me about it and I found it strange..., he can't keep secrets. But I have to tell you that this time, I wasn't expecting it, not even from Julia. On one of the days, there was a gala dinner and guess who he met? That's right, Julia! And why? Because she was none other than the companion of the company's president, a Swedish woman, a rising star. He says they were the centre of attention all night long. Anyway..., Julia at her best!" Assunción shrugs her shoulders, translating the inevitability of the situation into the gesture.

I feel my heart beating fast and a dizziness, I have the feeling that I'm going to throw up. I take deep breaths over and over again until I regain some control over my body. The news hits me like a ton of bricks, and I struggle to maintain my composure.

"You don't seem surprised...," are the first, and only, words I manage to utter, looking at Assunción, who is calmly eating her hamburger.

"And I'm not. I mean, it surprises me that she's with another woman in public dancing at a party. But I think not even Camila, if she knew, would be surprised. It's Julia! That's how she is, always has been, and always will be!"

§§

I tell Fili about my days, making reflections and omitting details. By the furrowing of his brows, I know he's uncomfortable, but he'll never say anything.

"You're right, you don't want to live life as a 'victim', but the most important thing is not to be one," he says, his voice gentle but firm.

Chapter 22

June 19th - Friendships and Loves

Camila

"Hello, how are you, Camila?" Fili greets me in a less lively tone than usual. Sometimes I wonder what his life is like when he's not sitting within these four walls. I've known him for so long, and in reality, I don't know anything about him. It's curious, considering he's one of the people who knows me best.

§§

"Your house is very nice," Esther says as she enters the living room, placing her bag on one of the chairs. Her ease contrasts with my nervousness. There was no way to refuse. We have to finish a presentation by tomorrow, and the worst part is that it was my fault we fell behind. Today, as I was leaving, Esther confronted me, and despite my arguments that I could finish alone, she decided it would be much better to do what's left together. I still tried to refuse, justifying that Julia is on duty and that I had to come to Mateo, but nothing dissuaded her; on the contrary, she insisted on coming with me.

"A tea? A coffee?"

"A beer, if you have one. After all, we're not going to operate on anyone, are we?" she says with irony.

"Of course," I say, returning a few minutes later with a glass. "I should be the one to finish, after all, I was the one who fell behind. I'm sure you have better things to do."

Mateo comes running in, darting out of the room as soon as he realizes someone has entered. "Mom?" he asks, still in the hallway.

"Don't run! It's Doctor Gonzalez, Mom's boss," I continue when he reaches us.

"Are you staying here? Are you having dinner with us?" he questions almost immediately. "I know who you are! I was at Grandma's house."

"No, Mateo, Doctor Gonzalez is not staying here, she just came to help Mom with some work," I say. "We're waiting for your friend's mother. Remember? You're going to sleep there tonight. Or do you not want to go anymore?" I ask, sketching a half-smile.

"Of course I'm going. The bag is ready." He states as if it were the inevitable, and disappears with the same speed with which he appeared.

"Shall we proceed? Where can I plug in the computer?" Esther asks questions but doesn't wait for an answer to settle in. At the same time, the phone rings and she answers immediately. "Yes, dear, no, I'm not at home, I came to finish a job." "I love you too. Of course I know you're coming this weekend, I'm waiting for you." She hangs up and almost immediately the phone rings again. This time she doesn't answer.

Before I can say anything, the sound of the doorbell is heard and Mateo reappears, this time with his bag on his back and his jacket on.

When I re-enter the room, Esther is already working. "Sorry, I couldn't help overhearing you just now, please don't stop doing what you were going to do because of me."

"Not at all. It was a friend, if she can't talk now, she'll talk tomorrow, nothing serious. It's essential to have our own spaces, don't you think?"

The question itself is nothing extraordinary, but it sounds somewhat inappropriate to me. "I don't know, maybe. But it can also make people drift apart. If everyone has their own world, then what's the purpose of being together?" The answer comes out without me being able to contain it. I think of Julia, and what she might be doing. Something happened at that congress. From then on, there are fewer nights she sleeps at home than those she spends at the hospital.

Time passes quickly and when I look at the clock it's already past ten.

"We're not going to be able to finish, are we?" I inquire almost rhetorically, looking up and facing her.

"Can I get another beer?" she asks, standing up. "No, don't get up, I'll go, it's in the fridge? I can find it."

It's impressive how she occupies the space, it seems like the house is hers, I muse.

"Of course we'll finish! We have until noon tomorrow," she says, handing me an already opened bottle.

"You found the fridge and the bottle opener. Full service, you're hired!" I joke.

"My computer battery won't last another half hour and I don't have a charger, besides we need to stop for dinner. I, at least, need to eat. How about we move to my house? Mateo is taken care of and Julia won't be back today, so I assume you're free, right?"

"To your house?"

"Yes. I promise I won't cook! We'll order something, and I'll open a great wine."

The apartment is beautiful and discreet. I can't help but notice the impressive amount of neurosurgery books neatly arranged on the bookshelf that covers the living room wall. When she goes to the kitchen, I approach the open desk. Scattered on the top, several articles and the hospital's surgical plan. I pick up the sheet, I'm scheduled to operate with her every day. On Wednesday, a highly complex surgery is scheduled. Why? Why does she insist on having me by her side in the operating room? Without giving me time for more thoughts, she re-enters the room with the udon boxes in hand. "Were you looking at next week's plan? We have an acoustic neuroma, we're going to try a microinvasive procedure, with a colleague from ENT. You're going to coordinate the technique."

"Please, Doctor Gonzalez..."

"Esther, here at home, my name is Esther."

"Right. Esther, I'm not prepared to take that on. What if I freeze up? You know it can happen again."

"And you know it doesn't happen to me when I'm by your side. How many surgeries have we done together? In how many did you feel unwell?"

It's true, after that initial episode, it never happened again. In fact, I've been feeling better and better.

My heart races as I confess my fears to her, the words tumbling out of my mouth before I can stop them. I've been trying so hard to prove myself, to show that I'm capable and competent, but the truth is that I'm terrified of failing again. The memory of my last surgery haunts me, the fear and panic that gripped me as I stood over the patient, scalpel in hand, unable to move or think or breathe.

Esther sets the food down on the coffee table and comes to stand in front of me, her eyes intense and searching as they bore into mine. "Camila, listen to me. You are one of the most talented surgeons I've ever worked with. You have a gift, a natural instinct that can't be taught. I know you're scared, and I understand why, but you can't let that fear control you. You have to trust yourself, trust your abilities, and know that I will be right there beside you, every step of the way."

Her words wash over me like a soothing balm, easing the knot of anxiety in my chest. I want to believe her, want to believe in myself, but it's not that easy. "I don't know if I can do it, Esther. I don't know if I'm strong enough."

"When we're together, there are always so many people, so much confusion. It's nice to be able to be here..." She interrupts her sentence halfway through and looks at me, continuing right after, "I've been thinking a lot about us," she says between two bites of food.

I don't like the direction this conversation is taking.

"I know you're in a relationship," I say, not daring to mention the phone call I just witnessed again, realizing how absurd my words sound.

"What's that supposed to mean?" she asks with a mischievous smile, placing her hand on my arm.

I take her hand and hold it between mine. "That you're with someone else, and I'm married..."

Without letting me finish, she gets up and hugs me. I feel the warmth of her breath on my neck. I don't know what to do; I should have anticipated this. "We work together. You're my boss, and I'm very grateful for what you've done for me..."

She presses her mouth against mine, preventing me from continuing. I slide my chair back and turn away. "I'm sorry, I can't."

When I'm about to argue, she puts her hand over my mouth, stands up, and cuts the moment short.

I look at her as she prepares two cups of coffee in the kitchen. She's an intense woman. I don't think I've ever seen her like this before.

Little by little, we become absorbed in analysing the images again and work in silence, if it weren't for the jazz playing in the background. It's two in the morning when I admit I'm exhausted. "I can't take it anymore. We'll have to stop. I'll finish it alone tomorrow."

She smiles and raises her head, closing the computer screen. "We'll do better. I have to go to the hospital tomorrow, and I'll finish it there. I know you're alone and you have Mateo... He's coming back tomorrow, right?"

"Yes, before lunch. But no way, I'll get up early and finish it..."

"I don't know what to do with you," she says, laughing. "And I don't know what I'd do without you," she adds as she stands up. She extends her hand to me and pulls me onto the couch. She holds my face with both hands and kisses me again. This time, a serene kiss, a simple touch of the lips.

"Esther, please. We can't do this. I'm married, and you're my boss. It's not right."

She looks at me, her eyes dark with desire, and for a moment I think she might argue. But then she sighs and nods her head, stepping back and running a hand through her hair.

As I step outside, I turn back to look at her, my voice soft and sincere. "Goodnight, Esther. And thank you, for everything. I value our friendship and our working relationship too much to risk it."

She nods, "Goodnight, Camila. I'll see you tomorrow."

--

Back home, I reflect on what happened. I fear that Esther will make my life difficult at the hospital, but I'll have to survive.

I can't sleep, despite the fatigue, my head is spinning. I grab my cell phone, maybe a game will help me relax. Distracted by a simple exercise, I let time pass. A signal of a new email arrival appears on the screen. At this hour, I think, it shouldn't be anything important. Despite that, I end up not resisting curiosity.

Camila,

I'm sorry to write to you again without you even having replied to me. I'm not even sure if this is your email. You know how it is, I searched the internet and this is what came up. Still, and because I have no alternative, I write to you again. I promise I won't show up unexpectedly at your hospital.

If you ever read these messages, you'll think I'm crazy, or just lonely. Maybe a little of both. I can't forget that night. It's true that there are things I don't remember very well. I passed out, didn't I?

When the lights came on, you fled. I don't know if you fled from me,

from yourself, or from the situation.

I would like to be with you again, but not in a morning encounter on

a crowded carriage. I want to be with you when you want to be with

me, even if it's simply through words written on a screen.

A kiss, until one day,

A.

It's three in the morning, who sends emails at this hour? She must be really crazy and lonely, I think, not avoiding a smile. I recall the kiss, the hug, and the cadence of her voice. Between fatigue and adrenaline, the desire to know more about her takes hold of me.

Reader of the Red Cover Book,

Not knowing your name, that's how I'll address you. Maybe one day

you can satisfy my curiosity and tell me what you were going to read

on the train on the many mornings we crossed paths.

You have the right email. Please, keep my hospital card to return it

to me when we meet.

Camila

Will she answer?

§§

Fili doesn't say anything. He takes some notes here and there but seems lost in reflections.

"Nothing can happen," I state with conviction, hoping to close the subject with that.

"It can't, why? You don't want to? She doesn't want to? Why 'can't it'?"

I have no answer. He's good at what he does, I think, smiling involuntarily.

Maggy McAndrew

Chapter 23

July 17th – Brussels

Olivia

Sitting in the waiting room, I take the opportunity to rest a bit. I'm actually glad Fili is running late. I close my eyes and recall the days in Brussels, but the thought doesn't last even a minute before being interrupted by his voice, "Hello Olivia, would you like to come in?"

I head to the office and sit in my usual spot.

§§

Finally in Brussels, after the invitation made so long ago, the day has finally arrived. Through the room window, all I can see is the completely gray sky and a drizzle that has been falling uninterruptedly since morning. That's how Brussels is. I convinced Ursula not to stay at the hotel in the center where she usually stays. We rented an apartment in Petit Sablon, facing a church with sublime architecture, so the view I have from the window at the foot of the bed is stunning, even on a day like today. Despite the rain, it's warm, and I put on jeans and a t-shirt to go down the stairs to the cafe. She left early for her endless work meetings. I take the opportunity to have a cappuccino with pancakes, sitting in one of the comfortable chairs covered with colourful cushions. The possibility of having time alone allows me to reflect on everything that is happening. I'm at a crossroads for which there is no way forward. I will necessarily have to change something and find a new balance. She arrives in the late afternoon, excited about the success of her meetings. "What did you do?" she asks, giving me a kiss on the lips. "Come, take a shower with me. Then we'll have dinner right here, in one of these restaurants on the square, they have a wonderful tartare, and you love it." She talks nonstop, not letting me answer, while undressing her suit and shirt. I look at her almost naked, I never get tired of admiring her.

I start undressing too, "I'll take a shower with you, but I can't guarantee we'll finish in time for dinner." She laughs and goes in, letting the water run over her head. We stay like this, embraced under the water, without saying anything, for a long time.

--

"So what did you do today? Did you think about me?" she jokes, rising slightly to kiss me.

At the table next to us, a couple chats animatedly, devouring a pot of mussels and completely ignoring us. Her small gestures never cease to amaze me. I can't remember the last time I was kissed in public. I look at the mirror on the wall in front of me and see a woman sitting at another table, watching us with a smile on her lips. I look away from the mirror and stare at Ursula, who is still waiting.

"I didn't do much, I woke up late, had a fantastic breakfast, read a lot, and thought...," I say, taking a sip of wine before continuing.

"Where are you? I'm still waiting to hear your thoughts..., or are they so improper that you can't tell me?"

"Maybe later, if you behave," I say with as much seriousness as possible, before bursting out laughing.

The arrival of two plates with steak tartare, covered with a very yellow egg yolk, which the waiter makes a point of mixing in front of us, makes me interrupt the answer.

I lean back and look at her. Ursula is a straightforward woman, sometimes so direct that she can be harsh. "I want to change jobs. I know you don't agree..., but I'm sick of it!" I sigh and put a potato in my mouth.

"You're wrong. I agree. You won't be able to take this strain for much longer. I didn't want you to leave, not like this. I wanted you to implement your plan and leave on your own terms, in your own timing... But, as I told you, I understand that you're fed up. More than fed up, exhausted." She looks me in the eye and continues, "Right now, the hospital is just a small part of the problems you have..., that we have, ahead of us, and maybe the easiest one to solve."

The change from "you" to "we" doesn't go unnoticed. I drop the cutlery and hold her hand, conveying the gratitude I feel. I don't know why, but I look at the mirror again. The woman from the reflected table has her gaze fixed on our hands.

"You're funny. You always think everything is very easy. Nothing seems easy for me to solve. Do you realize that I need a job, I need my salary more than ever."

"If that's your concern, you can forget about it right away..." In all situations, Ursula is lavish with mysteries and secrets, but today she wants to surpass herself... "There's going to be a party."

I furrow my brows, annoyed by the change of subject. Doesn't she realize how important this is? "Please, this is not the best time to talk about parties." She ignores me and continues her line of reasoning, "Several people who can help you will be there. I'm sure you'll like it. When your situation at the hospital started to get difficult, that is, as soon as you started...," she says, laughing, "I talked to a friend and I think there's an opportunity that might appeal to you."

"What are you talking about? What friend..., what opportunity?"

We are interrupted by the arrival of dessert, lemon sorbet covered with meringue. "Okay, if it's work, let's go to that party," I say smiling, wiping her mouth with a napkin.

Ursula touches my leg with her foot under the table and winks. "What did you think about the most?"

Her question brings a flush to my cheeks as I recall my earlier musings. Leaning in close, I whisper sultrily in her ear. "I was thinking about you, of course. About your lips on mine, your hands roaming my body..." I trail off, letting my meaning hang in the charged space between us.

Ursula's eyes darken with lust. "Is that so?" She traces a finger along my collarbone. "Perhaps you should show me exactly what you were imagining later." Her husky tone sends heat pooling low in my belly.

I capture her wandering hand and bring it to my lips, placing a sensual kiss on her palm. "Patience, love. I'm all yours."

She shivers at my promise as I release her hand. For now, I content myself with teasing caresses and innuendo-laden looks, thoroughly enjoying this seductive game.

--

To my amazement, Ursula brought formal wear and looks stunning in black pants and a mint green top with a slight shimmer. When I come out of the bathroom wondering what I could wear that would be appropriate for the occasion, I find a white box wrapped with a golden ribbon, resting on the bed. Inside, a dark blue velvet and silk dress that leaves one arm and shoulders exposed. Another surprise.

"Finally! Sit here!" Across the room, a young woman with very short, all-white hair waves at us. She speaks loudly and clearly dominates the environment. As we approach, she gets up, wraps Ursula in a hug, and gives her a kiss on the lips.

"Olivia, this is Sophia. Over there are Emma, Joana, and Catherine," she says, pointing to each one as she introduces them. "This is the famous Olivia!" I feel myself blush, surprised by the kiss. Sensing my discomfort, Ursula puts her arm over my shoulders, pulling me close. Her warmth soothes my nerves.

Everyone is drinking champagne, so I grab a glass too and take a few small sips, trying to hide my nervousness. Joana and Catherine are sitting very close together, one with her hand on the other's leg. Sophia looks at Ursula and bursts out laughing, "Don't make that face!"

"Sorry... I didn't know...," Ursula says.

"It had to happen...," Catherine kisses Joana, confirming in actions what they're talking about, "I've been chasing her for months, did everything possible, and she kept that idiosyncratic marriage."

"You left Sebastian?" Ursula asks, still trying to understand. I have no idea who they're talking about.

"I did. And you know what? I think he was relieved. We still work together, even better now," Joana smiles and pats Catherine's leg affectionately.

"They are administrators of one of the big pharmaceutical companies...," Ursula says, interrupting her sentence halfway. She looks at me, then at Joana, and smiles as if she had an important thought that she keeps to herself. Sophia changes sofas and sits next to me, "Olivia, Ursula talked to me about your situation at the hospital."

"I've already decided, and I'm really going to leave..."

"And do you know what you're going to do next?" she asks in a casual tone.

"I have no idea. I would like to practice again, to be in an operating room, but I also like the idea of being able to change something within the system, make it more humane, more personal." As I talk, I get excited, carried away by my own words, "Take the University Hospital, for example. I don't know if you know it, it's fantastic and yet it's completely hostage to the classic powers of the medical barons..." Beside me, Ursula lets out a laugh and looks at Sophia.

"She didn't tell you anything, did she?" Sophia asks with an enigmatic smile.

"You think?!" Ursula confirms, still laughing.

"What's going on?" I ask, confused by the smiles exchanged between them. No one says anything, which makes me nervous. Finally, it's Catherine who comes to my rescue, "They're messing with you. Sophia was appointed

president of the University Hospital. She takes office after the holidays."
They laugh out loud, and I can't hide my amazement.

"Sorry, I didn't know!" I say, embarrassed.

"Don't apologize," Sophia says, wiping away tears from laughing so hard.
"Besides, you're absolutely right. How about putting what you said into
practice and starting to change from within?"

"I don't understand?"

"It's an invitation, Doctor Olivia Lopez. Would you like to come work for
the University Hospital team?" she says in a solemn and formal tone, if not
for the smile on her lips.

"Are you serious? Are you kidding me?" I ask, looking first at Sophia and
then at Ursula.

"I think Sophia is waiting for an answer, and look, I know from experience
that she's not a woman known for her patience," Ursula looks at Sophia and
winks at her.

Without anything to make me hesitate, I accept the proposal without even
asking what I'm going to do. Hugs, applause, and toasts follow until
everyone calms down again. "Since we're talking about hospitals, Olivia,
what can you tell me about Julia Garcia?" Sophia asks, staring at me.

Tonight, I can't stop being surprised. What kind of question is that? "Well...
she's an exceptional surgeon! Sometimes she's a difficult person, and she's
not my biggest fan, but... what exactly do you want to know?" It suddenly
occurs to me that Ursula told me that Julia is part of the 'Sphere' group. If
that's the case, then Sophia must know her.

"I wanted your opinion. I've known Julia for many years...," she begins, only to be interrupted by Catherine.

"And well!" she says with irony.

With general laughter, Sophia continues, "You're making me embarrassed..."

"As if that were possible!" Joana replies immediately.

"Right, I know Julia, but that has nothing to do with her work." I notice Ursula looking at me out of the corner of her eye. She must be amused by all this!

"She's great at what she does. She's respected by everyone," I reaffirm.

"Even by you?" Sophia insists.

"Of course!" I exclaim without thinking.

The party goes on until dawn. I dance with Sophia and Catherine until Ursula finally challenges me to one last dance. As soon as she puts her arms around me, I realize that's not exactly all she wants. Her hands caress my dress, lingering at the small of my back. Her fingers follow the edges of the neckline, sliding softly along my bare arm until they intertwine with my hand in a gesture of complicity. She engulfs me in a lingering kiss, then presses her lips to my ear and murmurs provocative words, knowing perfectly well their effect.

"Not here," I answer softly, while pushing one of her hands away.

"Why? No one cares."

I start to realize it won't be easy to stop her. I feel my heart beating faster and my breathing accelerate. "I want you," I whisper in her ear, changing strategies.

"Can you be more specific?" she murmurs.

"Your mouth... where you know."

"Just the mouth?"

"Please..."

She plays along and raises the stakes, "And Julia?"

I shudder, "What about Julia?"

"You said she was extraordinary..."

§§

What happens in Brussels stays in Brussels. I look at Fili and describe what I can, omitting the details of the party. "You know, Fili, Ursula knows everyone. It's impressive. I ended up getting a new job."

"She's a good friend," he replies.

"Friend? Is that how you see her?" I ask, surprised.

"You tell me. What role does she play in your life?"

Without giving me time to answer, Fili ends the consultation, getting up and walking me to the door. Once outside, I pause to think about his question. What should I call Ursula - lover? Lover doesn't seem a strong enough word for what Ursula is to me.

Maggy McAndrew

Chapter 24

July 17th – Decisions

Camila

"I separated from Julia!" It's the first thing I say when I sit on the couch in front of Fili. "It took me a while, but I reached my limit..."

"What do you mean, you separated from Julia?" He is truly surprised. I think he's been waiting for this news for a long time, and yet, he didn't expect that one day I would show up with the fact already accomplished.

§§

Finally, the sound I've been waiting for so eagerly - the key turns in the lock. I hear the sound of her setting her things down on the entry table, and then her voice, "Camila?!"

"I'm here," I answer, waiting for her to reach me.

"Where's Mateo? Did something happen?" Looking at me and seeing the beer bottle in my hand, she goes to the kitchen and comes back with a beer for herself.

"He's fine, he's staying at Paloma's. We need to talk." As I speak, her phone

215

rings. She takes the device out of her pocket, looks at the screen, but doesn't make any move to answer.

"What do we need to talk about this time?" she asks sarcastically.

"I want to separate, Julia. I've already decided. I'm going to stay in an apartment hotel with Mateo, and then we'll see."

"You can't be serious!" she exclaims immediately, shouting. "What happened? Did someone tell you something?"

"Why? Is there something to tell?" My question is rhetorical, but that's not the reason for my decision. "No, no one told me anything. If your question has to do with the people you've been with, no one told me anything, but the messages on your phone are very explicit."

"Come on, Camila, it was one night, hundreds of miles from here. We had a few drinks, danced, and nothing else. She's a friend. You're the only person..." She approaches and presses her lips to mine, seeking a kiss. I reciprocate and let myself be kissed.

"We're not going to solve this with kisses, not this time," I say as I pull away, leaving my hand on her leg. "And you know why? Because this time, I'm not angry, I'm not jealous. I saw the messages, I saw the photos, and I felt nothing. Nothing, do you understand?" I look attentively into her green eyes, the eyes where I've lost myself so many times over the years.

She sits on my knees, grabs my hands with hers, and kisses me again, in an ancient dance, etched with memories. "I love you, and you know that!"

I pull away again, sliding to the side, letting her sit back on the couch. "I know you love me, but I also know that it's not enough. It took me a long time to understand. We have an obligation to fight to be happy... not just moderately happy, but as happy as one can be, and look at us, we're ambitious," I comment, forcing a smile. "I've come to the conclusion that we have to fight that battle each on our own."

When she intervenes, her tone is low and hoarse, unlike other conversations where she defended her arguments by shouting, "I don't want to lose you."

"You're not going to lose me. You need adventure, and I can't be that in your life, but I also can't be someone who has you in the interval between your conquests." I look at her. She's pale and biting her lower lip, a repeated gesture.

"I wanted to take you to bed..." Despite her words, she doesn't make any movement in my direction.

§§

"Congratulations, I know how difficult it must have been." Fili uncrosses his leg and crosses it in the opposite direction, a characteristic movement when he wants to relax. Right after that, he adjusts his glasses on his nose, using only his index finger.

"I don't know if congratulations is the right word," I say. "We ended up having dinner at home and continuing to talk. It took us deciding that there was no way to continue for us to be able to have a conversation. Life is curious!"

As I sit there, recounting the events of last night to Fili, a mix of emotions swirl within me. Part of me feels an immense sense of relief, like a weight has finally been lifted from my shoulders after carrying it for so long. I've known deep down for a while now that my relationship with Julia wasn't sustainable, that we wanted fundamentally different things. Another part of me aches with the pain of this loss. Julia has been such an integral part of my life for so many years. The thought of not having her there anymore, of truly letting go, is terrifying. Even now, I find myself questioning if I made the right choice.

§§

I arrive at Paloma's house just in time for dinner. It's a sublime late afternoon, and we sit on the balcony. It's the top floor of a seven-story building, with an unobstructed view of a garden that stretches out a short distance away.

"I have several things to tell you..." I take a deep breath before dropping the bombshell: "I separated from Julia."

Paloma leans forward in her chair, as if she hadn't heard correctly. "What?" she asks in disbelief.

"Exactly what you heard. I separated from Julia."

"But why? I mean, why now?"

"It could have been last week or next week, but it ended up being yesterday. I don't think there's any specific reason. It was just the right time."

"You deserve to be happy, and Julia... Julia doesn't live on the same wavelength as you." She interrupts and drinks the rest of the water from the glass she had placed on the floor. "Come on, let's go inside and get a glass of wine. I need something stronger than water." As we pass by, Mateo waves his hand and turns back to the TV, not before saying in his sweet voice, "Look, look, Paloma, see how many points I scored... I'm going to beat you!" She smiles and applauds.

We sit down again, this time with a glass of white wine.

"I still haven't been able to internalize it. Are you okay?"

"I feel relieved, free. But I miss Julia. I miss her even before I stop being with her." I take advantage of the moment of confessions and tell her what happened with Esther.

"She kissed you? I don't believe it!" she says with tears in her eyes.

"Great Camila! Dealing with Julia and Esther is not for everyone!" she says jokingly. "It's good, isn't it?" Without waiting for me to answer, she picks up the bottle and refills the glasses. "Mateo..." she calls out loudly so he can hear, "...do you want an ice cream?" Immediately, the sound of footsteps running on the wooden floor is heard. He enters the kitchen with the game controller in one hand and the other already outstretched.

Their relationship is fantastic, and that makes me happy. "What about you? Did you get any more massages?"

"I did."

"Really? You went back there?"

"Of course I did. But this time, when he entered the room, I got up and faced him. At first, he was startled. I don't know if it was because of the unexpected or if he thought I might be angry. I asked him to talk with me outside of there. We went out, and we ended up here at home. What can I say? He's great company. Too bad I lost my masseur!"

--

In the last few weeks, I've exchanged several emails with the Reader of the red-covered book. I think it could be the beginning of the most unlikely friendship. The fact that we've never spoken, that I don't know who she is, gives me a freedom I've never considered. After fainting twice, one of which was at work, she finally decided to take the situation seriously. Still, she's so afraid that I worry she hasn't done the necessary tests. I hope it's nothing serious.

Camila,

I'm on vacation in Rome. I think I never told you, but my parents were born in Italy, and I lived here for over ten years. It's strange to return. At the same time, it's funny to see how our memory holds onto what's truly important, without it ever being anything relevant in the grand scheme of things. Small details, a smell, a food, an image.

I remembered the first time I saw you on the train. You were wearing a blue coat, buttoned up to the top, and you were looking out the window without paying attention to who was getting on and off. At one point, you smiled. I don't know why. I noticed the dimples you make on your cheeks and the way your face lights up. I was captivated by that look. I had the feeling you noticed, and I pretended to focus on the book. Maybe one day, in person, I can tell you what I was reading.

See you soon,

A.

§§

"Could it be, Camila? Could it be the beginning of a friendship?" asks Fili, already at the doorway, as he says goodbye to me with a handshake.

His words keep hammering in my head long after I've left the office. What did he mean by that?

Maggy McAndrew

Chapter 25

August 21st – The Vacation

Olivia

"Fili, you look great! Your vacation must have been fantastic. You have a different glow about you." Time has given me the intimacy to speak to him like this. I often forget that this is a therapeutic relationship, and I feel like I'm talking to a lifelong friend.

"They were indeed invigorating..." is all he replies, immediately moving on to the counterattack, "And you?"

"Ursula rented a small house in the south of France, a paradisiacal place, a place made for us to forget about the world. We talked, we read, and... well, I don't need to explain..." I say, smiling.

§§

Finally on vacation. Although it's not as hot as during the day, you can't say it's cool. Ursula, in her immaculate white bikini that reveals the confidence she feels in her own body, dives in, reappearing on the other side of the pool. She shakes her head, shaking off the drops of water caught in her hair, and with four or five strokes, she reaches me. She rises out of the pool, splashing me all over, and gently kisses me on the lips. I slap her hand, laughing and pushing her to the side. "You don't waste any time, do you?"

"You've been in the sun for a long time. I was just trying to cool you down."

"And you think you can manage that?" We both laugh.

She lies down next to me and hands me a glass of juice that was on the table. I watch her as she drinks hers. After emptying half of it in one go, she puts the glass down again and, out of nowhere, asks me, "Have you heard from Julia?"

I'm caught off guard, as usual. Not only because I don't know how Julia is doing, but also because I don't expect this to be a topic of conversation. Better this way, it's none of my business.

"I have no idea," I reply, trying to better frame the context. It's the second time she's referred to her in a short period of time.

I recall our night in Brussels when, after the party.

We entered the room, and she asked me about Julia. "What do you want to know?" I asked. That night, I never ceased to be surprised by everything.

"I want to know what you were thinking when you said she was extraordinary... You're not the first person I've heard say that Julia Garcia is 'extraordinary'..."

"Have you never been curious to find out for yourself?" I inquired, treading all the risks.

Ursula didn't answer me. She took off her top and unzipped my dress.

"You're not wearing …!" she exclaimed in admiration when the dress slid down and fell to the floor.

"I had no choice. I didn't travel prepared." I stared into her eyes and recognized the sparkle in them.

As she kisses me eagerly, she puts her arms around my neck.

"Tell me about Julia..." she whispers in my ear.

My heart races again, a mixture of astonishment and desire. "Do you want to know if I let her?"

"Like this? Here?" she asks.

"Don't do that... I can't speak like this... Julia is used to being in control, but due to circumstances, in the few times we were together, she let herself go..." My words make her intensify her touch, the speed of her fingers increasing, realizing that this is not the time to be gentle. As far as I'm concerned, we're going to take this game to the ultimate consequences. "I felt her..."

Ursula stops. She knows how to provoke me and seems determined to test the limits. "Go on!"

"The great surgeon, so sensual, so vulnerable, surrendered to her own desire..." I sigh and recall the moment again. "I remember wanting it not to end." Although I try to continue, my voice grows weaker and weaker.

As if hearing my thoughts, Ursula holds me, leans in, and kisses me, again and again. With her mouth glued to my ear, she murmurs, "Liv..."

I feel my breath caught in my throat. She had never called me that before. These were Julia's words... How? There was no point in even trying to contain what was inevitable. I close my eyes and tilt my head back.

I return to the present, hearing her insist, "I want to understand better what's going on between you two." She lights a cigarette and continues, "Don't make that face. You know I like to know everything." She takes a deep drag, releasing a cloud of smoke. She brings her index finger to her mouth and places it between her lips in a provocative gesture. "But my question isn't as colourful as you're thinking. You can stop smiling..." she says sarcastically. "What do you think about Julia replacing you as the director of Central?"

"What?" I ask incredulously, sitting up in the chair.

"If you're going to University Hospital, someone has to replace you at Central, don't you think?!"

"Of course, but... what do you have to do with it? Julia, in management? Do you think she wants to stop operating?" I ask questions one after the other, not giving her time to answer. Continuing to talk is also a way of protecting myself from information I'm not sure I want to have.

"Are you done?! Do you want me to answer, or are these rhetorical questions?" She slowly smokes what's left of the cigarette, averting her gaze to the shimmering water in front of us. "I'll ask you again, what's going on between you two?" As she finishes the sentence, she stubs out the cigarette and kisses me.

I turn my face away. I stay still and silent. I don't know what she wants to hear, and even if I did, I don't know the answer to her question.

She doesn't let me pull away and, with tenderness, holds my chin. "I adore you in every possible way. We are us, and with her, it will always be something different," she states with unshakable conviction, kissing me again.

This time, I respond.

"I don't know how to answer you, or rather, there's absolutely nothing going on, and if you want to know, I don't think anything else is going to happen in the future. I haven't seen her in a long time. The last time we were together, I wanted to surprise her... It went terribly."

"Okay, then let me ask you the question another way. What would you like to happen?"

Here we go. Talking to Ursula requires the truth, no matter how difficult it may be.

"She has a magnetism, a seductive ability... I can't explain it... There's something different about her," I answer, for lack of a better explanation.

"You're not the only one saying that..." Ursula murmurs, almost imperceptibly.

"The contrast between the aggressive person she is at the hospital and the fragile, sweet Julia who surrenders in my arms... It leaves me captivated." I sigh. "But none of this is real! The reality is quite different... I was just another conquest, a trophy that means nothing, just one more on the shelf. That became very clear the last time we met." It's not easy to admit this out loud.

"I think you're wrong. I've told you, I've known Julia and her reputation for a very, very long time. I've heard many women describe their encounters and misencounters with Julia Garcia, and I'll tell you, there's one thing I've never heard before..." Ursula enjoys moments of suspense and takes an almost theatrical pause.

"What?" I ask anxiously.

"I've never heard anyone say that she surrenders!" She sighs and looks at me. "You should think about what that means."

The phrase keeps hammering in my head, "I've never heard anyone say that she surrenders." Trying to change the subject, I go back to the conversation. "What were you saying about the clinical management position? You didn't get to answer me."

"You asked so many questions and gave so many answers that I thought I didn't need to say anything else."

"Don't tease. Tell me what you were going to say..." I pout, pretending to be offended.

"The President of Central spoke to me... She's friends with Sophia. Knowing about your departure, she asked her what she thought of Julia for the position."

"And?"

"Sophia ended up suggesting that she talk to me, and she called me. I told her what I think, but I was supposed to get your opinion. If you tell me she doesn't have the profile, the matter ends here..."

I intervene, cutting off the sentence. "No, I didn't say that. In truth, I don't know Julia. We oscillated between screaming arguments and moans of pleasure, and we despised everything that could be in between."

"You two are extraordinary at that game. But, Olivia, don't forget, it's a dangerous game."

§§

"You know, Fili, that conversation with Ursula made me think about Julia in a different way."

228

"Are you in love?"

"It's a complicated word, but I wish I had met her under different circumstances. With all this, I forgot to tell you something important. The day after I returned to the hospital, Mateo, Julia's son, was admitted..."

As the words leave my mouth, I feel a sudden tightness in my chest. The memory of Mateo's arrival at the hospital, pale and fragile, his small body wracked with tremors, floods my mind. I remember the fear in Julia's eyes.

Maggy McAndrew

Chapter 26

August 21st – Point of No Return

Camila

When I enter the office, the first thing I notice is a new painting on the back wall, a black and white photograph of the horizon line on a beach, which given the lack of references, I can't locate. Was it Fili who took the photo? I know almost nothing about him, where he spends his holidays, with whom, nothing.

"How were your holidays?" he asks, sitting on the usual couch. He pushes his glasses back with his index finger, picks up his notebook, and crosses his leg. Immediately my eyes drift to his socks peeking out between his pants and sneakers, black socks dotted with tiny umbrellas of all colours. It's undoubtedly a good choice.

§§

Unable to go on vacation with Julia, I end up inviting Paloma to come with Mateo and me. The first week flies by. Paloma gets up at dawn to run and then dedicates herself to taking care of Mateo. They have breakfast, take long walks, play soccer, and build pools by the sea. For the first time since he was born, I have the privilege of lying on the sand without constantly having to lift my head.

Most days we have dinner at the hotel. After so much activity, he falls sound asleep before nine o'clock.

During the night, Mateo wakes up calling for me. When I get to the room, he's standing by the door and vomits before we can reach the bathroom. After calming him down, I put him in my bed, and he falls asleep. In the morning, he seems much better. He eats some cereal and lies down on the couch to watch cartoons.

"Do you think we should go back? Let's go to the hospital," Paloma says, looking at him as he falls asleep and snores lightly.

"Kids have these things, it's nothing. He'll vomit a few times and be fine." I've already called Julia, and she thinks so too. It's not worth interrupting our vacation. Speaking of Julia, did I tell you she told me she's already rented an apartment? She's moving in early October."

"Was she happy?"

"No! I mean, I think so, but she kept saying she wasn't. My life seems like a carousel, and Julia's is a roller coaster. I miss her," are my last words before I turn the conversation. "What about you?"

Mateo wakes up screaming, "Mom, Mom! It hurts a lot... here!" he says, pointing to his belly button, just before getting up and vomiting in a stream on the floor.

I run to him, "Calm down, Mateo! Calm down, you'll feel better soon," I say as I pick him up and take him to the bathroom.

Paloma stays in the living room and tries to clean up some of the liquid that has spread on the carpet, minimizing the damage. "Do you want me to go there? Do you need help?"

"Bring the thermometer, it's in the bag, in the side pocket."

He's pale and has deep dark circles under his eyes. He cries softly and clutches his stomach in pain. He has a fever of almost 39°C (102°F).

"We have to go to the hospital," it wouldn't even be necessary to say, as Paloma is already in the room packing the bags.

I call Julia and summarize what's happening, "It's appendicitis, isn't it? We should have gone right away."

"Calm down! You couldn't have known. He was just feeling unwell. Calm down. Come carefully, I'll wait for you here." During the nearly three-hour trip, Julia calls more than five times. On the last one, we're almost there.

"Camila, they called me to the OR. There's an emergency, I'll have to go. Everyone is notified that you're arriving. The paediatric surgery colleagues are waiting. Please, ask them to give me news as soon as they know something. You know I adore you both!" Poor Julia, I think. A victim of her own success.

One of the two surgeons who operated on Mateo appears at the door of the room. I jump out of the chair as if I had a spring. Although it's been just over two hours, it seems like an eternity to me. Paloma stayed here and remains seated by Mateo's bed, empty for now.

"It went well," he reassures me. "The surgery took longer than expected. The situation no longer involved just the appendix. Good thing you came. A few more hours and it could have been very serious. My colleague just went to the cardiothoracic OR, and Julia already knows everything went well."

I thank him, relieved. I wait until he leaves and face Paloma. "We should have come earlier!" I walk over to her and give her a hug. "Go rest, go home, I'll be fine. Julia should be arriving."

"Are you trying to get rid of me?" she asks, forcing a smile.

I shake my head, holding her tighter. "Never. I just don't want you to exhaust yourself. It's been a long day for all of us."

Paloma returns the embrace, her warmth enveloping me. "I'm not going anywhere, Camila."

In that very instant, the door bursts open and my mother, my father, and Julia, right behind them, barge into the room. The situation is utterly bizarre, all of us standing there looking at each other, not knowing what to say. Unsurprisingly, my mother is the first to react, and she does it in the worst possible way. She takes a few steps in my direction and screams, "How dare you not tell us that our grandson is in danger? I already know what happened. Mateo almost died because you decided to continue your vacation instead of bringing him to the hospital!"

"Don't talk like that! And don't talk about what you don't know!" Julia intervenes, her voice shaking with emotion.

"I don't need your advice, I'm talking to my daughter! You're never around, so if something happens, you're just as guilty as she is," my mother stretches an accusing finger, pointing first at me and then at Julia. Then she turns to Paloma, her eyes flashing with anger. "And you, who are you? What are you doing here?" The question is rude and directed straight at Paloma.

"Don't you dare talk to my friend like that," I say, my voice trembling with fury. "I won't allow it!"

"Friend, is that what we call it now? I thought it had another name! You were with your 'friend' at the hotel? And Julia, apparently, was working..."

Amidst the confusion, someone opens the door, enters, and closes it again. I recognize her, it's Olivia. She says a quick "good evening" and literally drags Julia by the sleeve of her coat to a corner. They talk for a few minutes, but from a distance, I can't understand what they're saying. Julia nods and then leaves without saying a word. I can't go after her and leave Paloma exposed to my mother's wrath, who continues screaming, seemingly unaffected by Olivia's entrance.

"If anything happens to my grandson..." The sentence is left unfinished. This is her modus operandi.

"Nothing will happen," Olivia states firmly, looking her in the eyes. "You probably don't remember me, I was in your husband's surgery..."

My mother doesn't let her finish. "I know exactly who you are..." Another suspended sentence. "The friend who called me didn't fail to mention that you were waiting for an anaesthesiologist to be available so you could enter the operating room... and look where we are now!"

So that's how she found out.

"They waited too long, first this one...", she says, pointing at me again, "...then you, who don't have proper teams..."

"I understand you're upset, but you can't be here screaming. Come, let's go to my office, it'll be more comfortable." Olivia demonstrates enormous composure amidst the tumult and maintains her poise.

"No way! I'm staying here, or better yet, I'm going upstairs to the recovery room." My mother doesn't lose her arrogance and continues in the same tone. In a flash, I lose my head and yell even louder than her, "Get out of this room immediately, both of you!" I point at both of them. "If you don't leave now, I swear I'll call security. I don't want to see you here or anywhere else ever again. Get out!"

My mother still tries to say something, but my father, who had remained silent the whole time, grabs her arm and delicately but firmly leads her into the hallway.

I'm very close to the edge, I held everything I could during the last few hours, but now... I let myself fall sitting on the bed and hide my face in the pillow where Mateo was lying. I want to cry, but I can't. I grab the pillow with exaggerated force and in a gesture of rage throw it against the wall. The pillow makes a dull noise and falls to the floor. Olivia, standing, leaning against the window, looks first at me and then at the white pillow lying on the linoleum. She goes there, picks it up and places it on the bed as if nothing had happened.

Moments later, Julia enters the room. Having no idea what just happened, she looks around, "Where are your parents?" she asks. She's pale, her face mirroring a concern that terrifies me.

"I sent them away," I declare. I'm not able to ask what's going on, because I'm sure something happened.

"Mateo is not well. He has a fever and low urine output. He was taken to the Pediatrics Intensive Care Unit." She sits on the edge of the bed and cries convulsively. It's a silent cry and, at the same time, a scream in its intensity. Olivia goes over to her and strokes her hair. I'm surprised by the gesture, but

I don't have the capacity to reflect on it. What did I do? What did I not see? My mother thinks it's my fault.

Paloma comes over to me with the water bottle from the table. "Drink! You're pale! You're shaking," she says, hugging me. "Listen, I was with you and I saw what happened, there was no way to know, it was very quick. It's not your fault at all. Please, Camila... I know you're listening and repeating your mother's words, but please stop! In a few days you'll be home and it will have been just a scare."

"I can't... I can't..."

"You can't what?" she asks me.

"I can't breathe..."

Olivia intervenes in her calm voice, putting her arm around my shoulders. "Of course you can. Keep the rhythm, breathe slowly, blow the air out through your mouth, you know how it is." In front of me she breathes at the same pace. Little by little I calm down and stop shaking. "Are you better? Let's go upstairs, I'll go inside and see how he is. Maybe at least one of you can stay with him."

We follow her down the hall and into the elevator to the seventh floor. When we reach the closed access door to the Intensive Care Unit, I feel my legs shaking again and it gets dark. Julia, by my side, anticipates and grabs me.

"You have to calm down. You couldn't have predicted this. Paloma is right, he's going to be okay," she says, already sitting next to me in the waiting room.

"What if something happens? What if there was contamination? He wasn't urinating, you said."

"There's no point in getting stuck in the 'what ifs', we have to believe that he's in the best possible hands and that he'll recover."

I raise my head and see Olivia walking towards us. "He has a fever, but he's already awake and seems much better. He called for you both. You can both go in, and then one of you can stay and spend the night with him. From what I understood, the appendix was in an unusual position. This masked the symptoms and made the approach difficult. The situation is under control. Mateo will make a full recovery."

§§

"Those were tough days!" exclaims Fili, interrupting my reflection.

"Very much so! Mateo stayed in the ICU for forty-eight hours, and now he's in his room, he should be discharged soon. Paloma is tireless, she's always there. Julia too, she seems exhausted."

"What about your parents?" he asks, knowing how sensitive the subject is.

"Remember when, a long time ago, we talked about how hard it is to break up?" I look at him, trying to figure out if he remembers this particular conversation.

"Of course I do," he replies immediately.

"This was my point of no return! It's over. The character I am, or rather the one I was when I was with them, died, killed by my mother's words and my father's silence."

Chapter 27

September 25th - Parallel Worlds

Olivia

"You know, Fili, when I passed through the large transparent glass entrance doors of the University Hospital, I was transported back to the day I entered Central Hospital. So much has happened since the beginning of the year," I say, closing my eyes for a moment, reminiscing on the tumultuous journey that has led me here.

"It's true, Olivia. These have been turbulent times, but not necessarily bad ones," Fili responds, pausing his writing to look at me with a reassuring smile.

§§

The atmosphere here is quite different from my previous hospital, I think to myself as I watch Sophia approaching with long strides. She comes to meet me in the atrium. Although we have spoken several times, I haven't seen her since Brussels. She opens a radiant smile and extends her arms, enveloping me in a hug. Despite being a more discreet and quicker gesture than others under different circumstances, it does not fail to be warm and welcoming.

"Welcome to the University Hospital, your new home! You don't know how much I enjoy having you here..." I don't hide my nervousness, and she perceives it on my face. "Don't be nervous. Come, let's go upstairs. I've gathered a small group of people in my office to introduce you. We know you're only taking over at the beginning of the year, but they're eager to meet you. Besides, we have a complicated issue, and I wanted your opinion."

"What happened? Is something wrong?" I ask, somewhat distressed, knowing that I cannot afford to fail in this approach.

Sophia leads me through the corridors and elevators in a labyrinthine route through the hospital's interior. "It has nothing to do with you, not directly. Two weeks ago, I presented the new plan for the hospital's organization. Although it was a general outline, it became clear that we're going to change our way of working. As always, there were voices that opposed it, among them, Professor Velasquez. I think you know her." Without ever stopping, although advancing at a slow pace, Sophia looks at me and asks, "Have you been talking to Julia?"

Again, the same question. "No, I haven't seen her since her son was operated on at the hospital."

"I heard she was going to accept a job offer in Boston..." The conversation doesn't continue because we enter the office. There are six or seven people seated at a meeting table. It couldn't be more different from my reception at Central, I think.

--

"Hey, how did you guess? I just said goodbye to Sophia and I'm leaving the

240

University Hospital. I think it went really well..." Ursula has a knack for guessing the right moments to call.

"Shall we have lunch?" she asks, seeming to ignore what I just said.

"Today? I won't be able to. I have so much to finish that I don't even intend to leave here."

"Cancel it. We really need to have lunch!"

Unable to argue, I end up agreeing.

I arrive at the restaurant, one of her favourites, just past one o'clock. The room only has six or seven tables, and they're all occupied. Ursula is already seated, but to my amazement, the table has three place settings.

"Are we waiting for someone else?" I ask, giving her a kiss.

Before she has time to answer, I hear a familiar voice: "Hello, sorry I'm late. How are you?" Alexis gives me two kisses and sits down, allowing me to recover from the surprise.

They immediately start talking, and I, without the courage to interrupt, contain my curiosity by sipping Chardonnay and eating toast with melted cheese. Under the table, Ursula plays footsie, taking off her shoe and running her foot up my leg, almost reaching my thigh.

"You didn't tell her anything, did you?" Alexis asks, finally perceiving my discomfort.

"No! You're the lawyer, you're in charge. I'm just..." Ursula doesn't finish the sentence. It's a shame; I'd like to know how she would have ended it.

"Listen, Olivia, I've been very worried about your divorce situation. Javier's lawyer has been relentless, not to mention inappropriate. I understand why they get along so well," Alexis comments, not failing to sketch a smile. "They allege a bunch of nonsense, but enough to call your rights to the assets into question. Javier even got hold of some documents about what happened at San Joan, and now he wants to use them as blackmail."

"That's not possible! This will never end! It wasn't my fault! I didn't know, and the colleague knows what he told me before the surgery."

"That's true, but your colleague is with Javier. For some reason, he gave him a written testimony where he tells the story in a very different way."

"Are you saying he has evidence to accuse me of negligence?"

"Maybe..." Alexis leaves the sentence unfinished and looks at Ursula, who remains silent and continues chewing calmly. "Come on, Ursula, stop making Olivia suffer. Spill it!" Alexis concludes with a smile.

She stops eating and runs her foot up my leg again. "I think I've found the solution to the 'Javier' issue," she says, keeping the suspense. "Do you know the story of Al Capone?"

"Ursula, I've known you for so long, but I had forgotten how Machiavellian you can be. Remind me never to be against you. But look at her... she's pale. Tell her at once before she has an attack," Alexis interrupts, unable to suppress a laugh.

"Okay, okay, I was just trying to add a little more excitement. Well, Olivia, I'm going to tell you a story. You know that Javier is preparing to go to Switzerland. He's already rented an apartment and even made a visit to the new office..."

"How do you know all that?" I interrupt, unable to contain myself.

"Contacts! Anyway, continuing,"She takes a sip from her glass and looks at me with the same mysterious gaze, "He thinks he has everything under control - a new job and many thousands of euros. The only detail he didn't count on is that before he assumes his new position, the company will do a brief investigation, ensuring there's nothing irregular that could bring them problems in the future..."

I intervene again, "Why? He's worked there for years. Why are they doing this now?"

"Because Ursula has friends in the right places," Alexis replies.

"Life has curious things. They won't be able to discover anything about the real Javier - a violent and malformed man - but they will find something much more frugal: fraud, financial fraud."

I'm stunned. "What?! Is that true?" I'm unable to continue eating, having lost my appetite.

"He deliberately evaded taxes all these years, on every bonus he received. We have proof of that," Alexis says, re-entering the conversation. "Ursula likes mystery movies, but I don't. Javier's company makes it easy for bonuses to go undeclared. Everyone knows that, and it's never discovered, or rather, almost never... It's best not to upset the company's administrators!" Alexis lets out a laugh that makes me smile. "Which brings me to the next answer to your questions. Why investigate Javier now? Because Joana and Sebastian are close friends with some of the board members of Javier's company... You remember Joana, right? Ursula told me you were with her in Brussels."

"Of course I remember..." I start to think that I should have accepted the invitations to the 'Sphere' parties much sooner.

"Joana is handling the case directly. She called me yesterday," Ursula interjects.

"I think the divorce will go better than we expected," Alexis concludes, raising her glass and waiting for us to do the same for a toast.

"Are you okay, Alexis?" Ursula asks, quickly getting up from her chair.

As white as a sheet, Alexis leans back in her chair and holds her head between her hands. "I'm fine, I'm fine. It was just a dizzy spell. It must have been the wine."

"Are you sure? Do you want to go to the hospital?" I ask, concerned.

"No, I'm fine."

--

I leave the restaurant feeling happy. I decide not to go to the hospital and, without a specific destination in mind, I end up coming to the seafront and choosing a terrace to have a coffee. Ursula had a meeting and went with Alexis. The weather is sunny, despite a late afternoon breeze. I feel my cell phone vibrate inside my bag. It must be Leonor. I haven't talked to her in a few days.

'I need your scent, your taste!' The message doesn't say anything else, nor would it be necessary... How many months have passed since the last one? I read and reread those words, feeling a wave of desire each time I let them echo in the back of my head. Her power is undeniable, far beyond anything I can explain.

I don't respond. I'm going to ignore it. Now that my life seems to be making some sense again, I'm not going to get involved in her web. At the same time, I remember Sophia's last words before we entered the office: 'I heard she was going to accept a job offer in Boston...' Could it be that she's leaving?

The prospect of her leaving the city, the country, generates a feeling of anguish in me, as if I were losing her even without having her.

Back in my new small apartment, I think about Ursula. After a bath and a salad, I sit on the bed watching the news. Before I even realize what they're talking about, the phone vibrates. 'I'm going to operate tonight.'

--

Life is made of coincidences, or so we call what we cannot explain. I have lunch at the bar every week with Assunción and I've never run into Julia, but today, of all days, we cross paths. She passes by us with her team. She looks me up and down, as if trying to assess if anything has changed. Assunción makes a head movement and also looks at me, leaving a clear feeling that she noticed something. The conversation is circumstantial and lasts only a few minutes.

"Did you know that Julia broke up?" Assunción asks almost casually when she walks away.

"What do you mean, broke up?" I ask, surprised.

"The other day I had lunch with her and she told me, without much detail, that she had broken up with Camila. She seemed at peace with the decision, but at the same time, I found her sad. I've worked with her for so many years and I don't remember seeing her like this. Her eyes were dull and her voice hoarser than usual. She didn't seem like the Julia Garcia we're used to seeing reign around here."

"Did she tell you anything else?" I ask, somewhat embarrassed.

"I think she's thinking about going abroad. She mentioned an invitation to Boston." Assunción sighs and looks at me, setting down the glass she's holding. "Look, Olivia, I'm going to speak frankly. Maybe I shouldn't interfere, but you're leaving the hospital, and I consider you a friend, so here it goes..."

I stop, surprised by the preamble. "I consider you a friend too..."

"If I hadn't known Julia for so long, I'd say she's in love."

"In love?" I almost shout the question. "With whom?"

"I don't know. I have my suspicions, but I don't know." She looks at me with her huge eyes. I can't decode if that look means anything else.

§§

"You know, Fili, I can't deny that every message affects me... but I didn't reply. I knew that if I wrote even a single message, it would all start again."

"And that's bad?"

"It's awful!" I state without thinking.

"Why? From everything you've told me, I wouldn't say that's the adjective that best sums up your story."

"That day at the hospital, the aggressiveness... the way she ignored everything I tried to say. I don't want another relationship..."

"I think you're comparing the incomparable." Fili changes position on the couch and uncrosses his leg, looking at me as he waits for an answer.

"And now?" Fili asks. "Knowing that she broke up changes anything?"

"I wouldn't want to tell you yes, but I can't say no," I reply.

"Don't you believe she could be in love?"

"That's not Julia Garcia's profile," I state emphatically.

Chapter 28

September 25th – Questions

Camila

"With so much happening, I haven't been here for over a month," I say, looking at Fili, who just nods, waiting for me to continue. "When we left the hospital, Mateo and I went home, and of course, Julia too. Her apartment will only be ready at the end of this month. It's strange, Fili, it seems like after we separated, many things improved..."

"Why do you think it's strange? It's common," he says without lifting his eyes from the notebook.

§§

Mateo fell asleep, but not before making me tell three stories. Julia stayed in the living room watching a movie, looking like she's going to stay up late, if not fall asleep on the couch. I tuck in the comforter, put one leg out, it's still hot, I reflect. I pick up my new book and turn the first pages.

"Camila, can we talk?" Julia asks, slightly opening the bedroom door. I look at her in her green striped pyjamas, shorts and t-shirt, there's no doubt she's an attractive woman, I can't help but think.

"Of course!" I reply, putting the book on the bedside table.

She sits on the bed, "I've been pondering everything that happened, everything your mother did to us."

"Don't waste time thinking about her. She's part of the past. The only thing I regret, and I apologize for, is not ending this a long time ago. Yesterday I talked to my brother, by the way, he sent you a kiss. He says he has fantastic news, but he can't reveal what it is yet, even with all my insistence, he didn't say anything." I stop, realizing that I still haven't let her say anything, and it was she who asked to talk.

"I had an idea, but I don't know if you'll like it..." she says, restarting the topic that brought her here. It's a dangerous start, but it makes me curious.

"Do you remember when your mother came to talk to me?"

"Of course. She's crazy!"

"Well, let's be crazier than her, and accept the offer! A place in Boston in exchange for letting you 'have a normal life'!" she exclaims with one of her laughs.

I can't grasp where she's going with this. "Are you kidding? We're already separated."

"It's true, we are. But she doesn't know! In fact, nobody knows. So, for all intents and purposes, we're together and, if we're together, we can accept the offer and separate. We can even put conditions."

"Are you serious?" I ask, incredulous. "And you? What do you gain from this? Is it just for the pleasure of making her look silly?"

Julia lets out another laugh, "It's not little. Think of Professor Amelia

Velasquez's face when she finds out she was fooled! Yes, because one day, she will find out!" Julia keeps laughing. She changes position and lies at the foot of the bed, her head resting on one hand. I straighten up to pay proper attention, and she continues, "I'll be honest, Camila. It's hard! I'm here laughing, but the truth is I don't have many reasons to laugh. I'm not well. Work helps, but the environment there is also terrible. I'm almost certain that Olivia won't be able to take it. There's more and more talk of her leaving and someone else coming. I haven't talked to her, in fact I hadn't seen her in a long time, when we met on the day Mateo had surgery..., she must have just arrived."

I remember our meeting that day. I was completely distraught, and there are many details I don't remember, but one I do remember is the fuss Olivia made over Julia's hair. She was loaded with something.

"I'm going to tell your mother that I'm leaving you in exchange for the place in Boston, it will do me good to get out of here for a while, don't you think?" she looks at me with her green eyes even greener with the glow of excitement.

"I think you're crazy!" I answer as I try to understand the consequences of what she just proposed. "But I won't deny that I love your craziness!" I don't want her to go, I reflect without saying anything.

Julia jumps out of bed and hugs me. Feeling her body glued to mine gives me a shiver that I haven't felt in a long, long time. She prolongs the hug, and when I think she's going to pull away, she makes an unexpected move and kisses me. First, a gentle kiss, a sweet kiss, a touch of lips. But immediately, both she and I feel the need for more. Without letting her turn away, I put my arms around her neck and pull her to me. The taste of this kiss is unmistakable. I had no idea how much I wanted her. Since we broke up I haven't been with anyone, and Julia, will always be, Julia!

"Are you sure?" she asks, her mouth close to my ear.

I have no choice. Desire is a thousand times stronger than all the reasons not to do it. "I am!"

§§

"It was a farewell, Fili. We both needed it, to know that even if we follow different paths, what we have together will not disappear. I woke up the next morning feeling lighter, freer..., do you know what I mean?" I look at him trying to gauge if he follows my words.

§§

"My mother called looking for me?" I ask surprised. "Why didn't she come here to talk to me?"

"I don't know. She says you don't answer the phone, and asked me to tell you that she operated on a patient this morning and the patient insists on talking to you, it seems she knows you." Esther relays the message somewhat irritated. The power of Professor Amelia Velasquez is indeed great, I think, to make Esther come looking for me to give me a message.

"Okay, I'll see what it's about, but only after I finish visiting the floor. Which room?"

"504."

As soon as she turns her back I continue my routine and go into the rooms of the patients who are in the ward one by one. All under control, I think, when I finish more than an hour later. I look at my watch, quarter to one. I'm going to have lunch before I see what my mother's patient wants, who could it be?

I find Vitoria in line at the cafeteria and tell her about my encounter with Esther. "Since that day at home, she barely speaks to me, but today she went to the trouble of coming to the ward just to give me a message from my mother."

"Who could it be? Aren't you curious?"

"Coming from my mother, not a bit. And you?"

"Me what?" she asks averting her gaze to take the soup and plate.

"You and Esther?"

"What do you want to know? Ask..."

"I don't believe it, you got back together with her!"

We resume the conversation already seated. "How can you? She treats you badly! And why didn't you tell me? When was it?"

"Camila! Stop! Stop asking questions!"

"I'm flabbergasted, I asked just to ask, I wasn't expecting you to have gone back."

"When I got back from vacation, she invited me to dinner. We had dinner and talked. From what I understood, she broke up with her partner for good. She apologized to me and told me she wanted to try, that this time it will be different..."

"And you believed her?" with the haste of the question I hit my elbow on the tray and spill half of the soup on myself, fortunately it's no longer hot. The coat is useless and the pants are also hit.

"Are you okay?"

"I am. Don't change the subject, did you believe her?" I insist, trying to salvage what remains of my lunch.

"I have no choice. I want to be with her. I have to try, even if it's for the last time. Don't blame me."

Her words sting, but I force myself to remain composed. "Never! When you need me, I'll be here."

I can't go see my mother's patient all covered in soup. I pass by the locker room in the hospital wing and put on one of the blue scrubs. Finally, I head for the elevator. 5th floor, general surgery ward.

"Lost?" asks one of the nurses, tapping me on the shoulder and letting out a laugh.

"You're here?" he asks, surprised. He used to be with us in neuro.

"Just this month, it's a swap. What are you looking for?"

"Room 505," I reply, glancing at the numbers on the wall.

"There isn't one... maybe it's 504, she was operated on by your mother. Alexis Conti."

"I don't know who that is."

"One of the best lawyers. She lived in Italy, but now it seems she lives here. Your mother must know her well."

I knock on the door. "Come in!" I hear.

I open the door. "No! It can't be..."

"Camila Rossi, pleasure to meet you, Alexis Conti," she says, flashing a smile and extending her hand to me.

I remain motionless, frozen halfway between the door and the bed. Shock courses through my veins at the sight of her.

Given my silence, she insists, "Please, come over here, I can't get up yet. Your mother did a good job, but still, I only got out a few hours ago."

I finally walk over to the side of the bed and give her a kiss on the cheek, ignoring her outstretched hand. "Why?"

"Why what?" she asks, furrowing her brow slightly. The expression makes me recall one of the first times I saw her on the train. I glance at the book resting on the bedside table - the same red leather cover.

"Why did you call me?" That's not at all what I want to say to her, but I can't seem to align the words. It's as if my head is blocked by the swirl of emotions.

"I'm sorry, I know I should have done things differently. Sit down, please. Are you going back to the ward?" she asks, interrupting what she was going to say and looking at my scrubs.

"No, I'm finished for today," I reply, not mentioning what happened with the soup. Relief mixes with lingering anxiety.

"Great. Then, if you're not in a hurry, I'd like to explain some things to you. Life plays tricks on us, there's no doubt about that."

I hear a soft knock on the door and then someone enters. "Alexis, how are you, did it go well? Sorry I didn't come earlier, but there was a board meeting at my hospital."

"Hi Olivia. It's good to see you here, and it's good that it's over..." She doesn't finish the sentence and says, "You know her, don't you?" pointing to me.

"We do. How are you Camila? I already know that Mateo is doing great."

I greet Olivia, as surprised as I'm still allowed to be, since the surprises keep coming one after another. Where do they know each other from? As if reading my mind, Olivia says, "Alexis is my lawyer. I'm in a complicated divorce, now it seems closer to the end." Turning back to Alexis, she continues, "How did it go? Do we know anything more?"

"Well, according to Amelia's words, really very well..." I can't help but notice that she calls my mother by her first name. I remember that outside, the nurse told me they know each other. I wonder from where.

"...I'll repeat to you what I heard, but promise you won't ask me any tough questions. 'It was small, in the head area of the pancreas, very superficial, she did a total excision,' that was more or less what I understood from everything Amelia said when she came here. They're going to analyze it, she thinks it's benign and that it's cured, but..." Once again, the sentence is left unfinished.

"Of course it's benign, don't think of any other possibility," Olivia concludes, patting her on the blanket.

For a long fifteen minutes, Olivia stays and chats with us. She tells us that it's now official she's leaving Central and has another project, although she can't talk about it yet. I think Alexis knows exactly what it's about, but they don't want to discuss it in front of me.

"Finally alone," Alexis jokes good-naturedly when Olivia leaves. "I'll explain before anyone else arrives," she says, still laughing. "I lived in Italy for many years, and that's where I met your mother. We became good friends, even long distance. I knew she had children, but seeing your name on the card you dropped, I never could have suspected you were one of them, at least not until yesterday. Amelia was here last night, we talked and she said your name, that was enough to make the connection. Incredible, isn't it?"

§§

"More than incredible, unbelievable," Fili concludes. Life is like that, that's why I never get tired of saying, there's no point in thinking we can control what's going to happen next.

This time I have the feeling I managed to surprise him, and that's not easy!

Maggy McAndrew

Chapter 29

October 16th - We Can't Save Everyone

Olivia

"'As much as I'd like to whisper other things in your ear... I need to talk to you about work.' The message arrived as I was leaving the hospital, it was already past eight o'clock at night. Coming from Julia, I never know what to expect or what to think. These last few days the messages have been piling up, and I keep wondering how long I can hold out."

"And how long are you going to hold out?" Today, Fili seems to be in a particularly good mood, there's something new that illuminates his eyes and his smile. He leans back on the sofa, he hasn't picked up the notebook or the pen yet, making me believe that we're simply having a friendly chat.

"I didn't hold out!..."

§§

I stare at the screen again and again. She wants to talk about work? We've never talked about work, except to fence with sterile and useless arguments..., and now, when we haven't spoken for months, she wants to talk to me about work?! She must know I'm leaving the hospital. Assunción spoke to me again this week, she's very worried about the possibility of someone from outside coming in and destroying everything we've done.

I feel like I've lived through this scene countless times. Sitting on the couch, with the TV on, not knowing what channel I'm watching, I slowly eat forkfuls of pre-prepared pasta that tastes like frozen tomato. It's been about an hour since the last message. I pick up the phone again and reread it for the twentieth time. I make excuses to myself, repeating that it's work, and type 'What professional matter?' I delete what I wrote... I don't want to make room for us to have a conversation by text. 'Can we talk about it tomorrow, at the hospital?'

My heart races as I hold the phone in my hand, waiting for a response that doesn't come. A few minutes later, I feel completely stupid... here I am looking at my phone, longing for a reply. I throw the device forcefully against the pillows and get up.

I put away the few things I dirtied in my improvised dinner and make some coffee. I can't let her, even without being present, have this hold over me. I go back to the living room and lie down to watch a soccer game, I don't even know which teams are on the field. For more than half an hour I think about everything and nothing, following the back and forth of players from one side to the other, as if it were a ballet without music. I'm interrupted by the vibration of my phone. Where is it? I remember that I threw it on the pillows, and it takes me a few seconds to locate it.

'I wanted to talk to you outside the hospital. Should we have coffee?'

Wow! What a sudden change of tone... was it really Julia who wrote this message? It doesn't seem like her. My desire is to write something provocative, and force her out of this candid tone that is definitely not hers. I restrain myself and choose not to respond, at least for now. I turn off the TV, take half a dozen steps to the bedroom, and get ready for bed. I stop in front of the bathroom mirror, put toothpaste on my brush, and brush my teeth with unnecessary vigour.

Already in bed, I look at the screen again. What are the possibilities? Schedule a coffee, force a meeting at the hospital? It should be an easy decision, but it's not.

I think about the conversation with Assunción. She said that Julia was in love, but she didn't say with whom. Was that why she broke up with Camila? She fell in love and it's not reciprocated? None of this matches the Julia I know.

I toss and turn in bed. Did she talk about us to Assunción? Many times, over these months, I had the feeling that Assunción knew more than she wanted to let on.

It's almost eleven o'clock, it's late to call... What will she think?

At eleven five I can't resist and I call. "Sorry. Good evening! Maybe you were already in bed?"

"No, not yet, did something happen?" Assunción is surprised, but also seems worried.

"No! Sorry to call so late, but I have to ask you a question and I couldn't wait until tomorrow."

"Of course, what's going on?"

I take a deep breath, and muster up courage. I know that after asking there will be no way to go back. "The other day... the other day, you told me that..." I'm not able to finish the sentence, but Assunción, with her characteristic insight, takes over the conversation. "You want to know about Julia, right?" A silence follows. Neither she nor I say anything for a moment.

Almost in a whisper, I end up responding, "Yes."

"You two need to talk! She's miserable, like I've never seen her before. She doesn't seem like the same person, she's thinner, she's lost the sparkle in her eyes, she's sad. Look, I've seen Julia charm a lot of people. I've seen many women cry over her, but I've never seen her like this." Assunción pauses, but it doesn't take long for her to continue. "And you don't seem to be doing very well either..."

"Are you saying she's in love with me?"

"What do you think, Olivia?! Seriously? Suddenly it seems like you've both gone soft in the head. Please, call her. You have to talk. I don't know what happened, but now you're going to leave the hospital, and she seems determined to go to Boston. Please, talk to her..."

"It's complicated."

"Of course it is. She's Julia, and she's in love."

"I can't understand how she works..."

"If she weren't the way she is, we wouldn't be in this situation. Part of her magnetism comes from that, from her aura of mystery, from her intelligence... she's a genius, but that comes at a price."

"I lived twenty-eight years with Javier."

"And you're getting divorced! You're the only person, perhaps along with Camila, who has conquered Julia's heart, touched her soul. If that's not being up to the challenge, I don't know what is. You are also an extraordinarily intelligent woman and you have a resilience that's hard to beat. Use it."

I hang up the phone, but I keep tossing and turning, unable to fall asleep. Calling Ursula is not an option. I return to the kitchen, but this time to get a glass of wine. I look at my phone again, and I'm faced with several new messages that I hadn't noticed. They must have arrived while I was talking to Assunción. The texts follow one after the other and are huge, taking up the entire screen, lines and lines:

'Olivia, it's time to call things by their names and assume our feelings...', 'I'm not the best person when it comes to emotions, but I owe you an apology, and a huge thank you, for the way you were there when Mateo had his surgery, even after everything...', 'The last time we were together I was indecent... and I know it.', 'There are no excuses that can erase what happened, but maybe one day you'll want and be able to talk to me.' , 'You were the strangest love story, the most complicated, and the simplest...', 'The matter I wanted to talk to you about is brief... I'm considering going to the United States, I had an offer, but I didn't want to accept it without talking to you first. We don't need to see each other, or have coffee, if you don't want to, but I couldn't help but tell you what I've had stuck in my throat for so long.', 'Liv... if you close your eyes...'

My heart beats wildly, my hands tremble, and I have to make an effort to keep breathing because the air doesn't seem to want to enter. I read the long text over and over again, with no idea what to do. I wish I had her here in my arms, to kiss her, and to assure her that everything will be alright. But that's not our story... Our story is made of misunderstandings, passion and anger, lies and betrayals. Is it possible to change a story halfway through?

'At Dune's tomorrow at ten?' My message is short and maybe even a little arrogant after everything she just wrote, but right now, I can't do any better. I feel completely overwhelmed. She's leaving?!

The answer is not long in coming, this time with only two words, 'I'll be there!'

§§

"A round of applause for Julia Garcia, it took courage to write that message. The more I listen to you, the more I'm convinced you're playing a dangerous game, but one thing is undeniable, you're elite players..." Fili utters these words in a serious tone. Unlike other moments, he doesn't try to lighten the speech with irony or smiles. He looks me in the eye and speaks very seriously.

§§

I wake up with the signs of someone who has slept no more than four hours. In the middle of the afternoon, Assunción comes to my office to see if everything is okay. In fact, what she wants to know is if there has been any progress. I don't comment on the messages and only tell her that we arranged to have dinner one of these days.

Interrupting the conversation, Julia herself bursts into the office.

"Olivia, please, come with me."

"What happened?" Assunción and I ask in unison.

"There are no anaesthesiologists. We have an infectious endocarditis. It hit the aortic valve. I know the patient. I operated on him a few months ago."

I literally run down the hall after her.

"I'm going to disinfect myself, I'll meet you on the other side," she says, trying to sketch a smile without success.

I rush into the room without having time to know almost anything about the patient.

"It's a good thing you came, Doctor Lopez. I was so distressed," says one of the interns who walks towards me.

"Calm down, tell me what you know."

"Not much... The man is 81 years old, he has already been operated on for this valve twice and now he has gone into failure. The valve is incompetent and the output is very low, the systolic function is terrible. I don't know how he is going to hold up."

"Do we have blood? Plasma expanders? Vasopressors?" The young woman answers yes to each of the questions.

I come outside to the disinfection area. Julia is pale and talking to two other surgeons who are also disinfecting themselves.

"Julia, did you consider ECMO?"

"He can't handle it. He won't resist. The only chance is to buy time and replace the valve. The agent has been identified and the antibiotic will take effect."

I go back in without knowing what the best plan is. This is not how I had thought I would end the day.

The music sounds in the room, and Julia coordinates the work of the team surrounding the patient. The vital signs are worrying, but stable. Little by little I am getting calmer. It seems to be going well, as much as possible.

They advance very slowly, mainly due to the adhesions from previous procedures and the need to avoid further blood loss.

A little more than three hours have passed since we started when one of the alarms goes off. The heart rate has risen, the urine output is practically nil.

"Julia, we have to speed up, he won't be able to resist much longer." I increase the level of medication and open the plasma expanders trying to increase the output.

"The old valve is falling apart in my hand, I have no cutting plane and even less tissue to suture." The voice, although subdued, does not fail to express the seriousness of the situation. "Aspiration! I can't see anything!" From one moment to the next, the surgical field is flooded with blood. All the alarms go off at the same time.

"It ruptured, Julia. You have a tear in the wall."

"I see it, I have my finger on the spot and I can cover it a bit, but I can't clamp, the tissue breaks as soon as I touch it!"

"Asystole!" I utter, knowing exactly what my words mean.

"Epinephrine. Manual massage." Julia literally has her hand around the heart and tries at all costs to recover some rhythm and maintain circulation. There is nothing more to do, but I can't be the one to say it.

"Come on, hurry up! Another ampoule!"

"Julia... Julia!"

"What is it?" she asks, shouting and looking at me.

"There is nothing more to do. Declare the death."

"No, I know him. I operated on him. It went well. He was fine."

"Julia, please."

"Time of death 22.04," declares Raul next to her, placing his hand on her arm and removing the instruments she continues to hold inside the patient's chest. "Julia, leave. We'll finish up."

My heart aches thinking about what Julia must be going through right now. I know all too well the weight of losing a patient, of feeling like their death is on your hands. And for her to have a personal connection to this patient, to have operated on him before and seen him doing well... I can't imagine.

Part of me wants to go find her, to hold her and tell her it will be okay. But the rational side of my brain knows that's not my place in this moment.

In the end, I decide to send her a simple text: "I'm so sorry about what happened. If you need anything, I'm here."

I stare at my phone, willing her to respond, to give me some sign that she's alright. But minutes pass with no reply. It's going to be a long night...

§§

"I stayed in the room a few more minutes after she left. I ended up going to the medical room. I was in there alone, I don't know for how long. I remembered another death, the accusations, the guilt. I don't know how one can deal with this. I didn't see Julia again..."

Fili, sitting in his usual position, took off his glasses, put down his pen and simply follows what I am saying, as if the subject was too serious to be simply jotted down in a notebook. "You did what you had to do and you were there. We can't save everyone." These few words are enough to make me breathe a little better.

Maggy McAndrew

Chapter 30

October 16th - What's Your Story?

Camila

"How are you, Camila? Did you find an answer to your questions?" Fili comes to get me from the waiting room and accompanies me to his office. He sits down on his couch and signals me with his hand to sit down as well, as if it were necessary!

"I don't know if I found answers, but I have many questions. I think, at least, I found the right questions."

"That's the best start. You'll never find the answer if you don't know what the real question is." He's leaning back on the couch and hasn't picked up his notebook or pen yet. Strangely, he hasn't even crossed his leg.

I change the subject, buying time. "Last week, Julia had dinner at my place. A glass of wine and a delicious tagliatelle."

§§

When Julia arrived for dinner, Mateo had already been asleep for almost an hour, but not before I had to promise that Julia would give him a kiss when she arrived. She moved to the new apartment three weeks ago, and it has been a period of adaptation for everyone.

"Sorry, I was delayed seeing a patient who was operated on this afternoon. She was alone, and I didn't have the heart to leave her. She told me things that made my heart feel tight... Her husband died last year, and she doesn't speak to her son. As a result, she had heart surgery and is alone in a hospital bed." Although the story is touching, what surprises me the most is the fact that she had been talking to a patient.

"Since when?"

"Since when what?"

"Since when do you sit next to a patient and talk? You don't seem like the Julia Garcia I know," I say, emphasizing the irony of the words.

"You're right. I haven't done this many times in the last many years. But today, I looked into those blue eyes the colour of the sea, all white hair, and she looked back at me, took my hand, and thanked me. I can't tell you why, but it moved me. I told you I lost a patient in the operating room... Anyway, I'm sorry. As usual, I'm late... It's the story of our lives!" She gives me a kiss on the cheek, smiles, and sits down at the kitchen table.

"Tagliatelle with shrimp. You'll have to wait because, as I've known you for too long to believe you'd arrive on time, I haven't put the pasta on to cook yet. Open a bottle of wine." I take the bottle of white wine I put in the fridge and hand it to her.

"A toast to your mother!" she says, letting out a loud laugh.

"Be careful. Don't wake Mateo up. By the way, go give him a kiss. I promised." Julia follows the order and gets up. When she leaves, I notice that she left her phone on the table. The device remains silent. Come to think of it, of all the times I've been with her, I've never heard the phone ring. There are more things that have changed about Julia...

"There, promise kept. He's sleeping so deeply that he didn't notice a thing."

Meanwhile, the pasta is ready, and I put a generous portion on the plates, which I cover with the shrimp curry sauce.

"Let me guess, you were with my mother?" I ask, tears coming to my eyes with the heat of the pasta I just put in my mouth.

"Bingo! That's right. I called her, told her I had a matter of interest to her, and we arranged to have lunch. As soon as we sat down, I informed her that I accepted the proposal, but with some conditions. You should have seen her face. I think she didn't understand if I was serious or joking."

"You said it just like that, directly?" I ask.

"Without beating around the bush or preambles. She was quiet for a moment but didn't show any weakness. 'Great, Julia. I always knew you were ambitious and wouldn't waste your career.' I took the opportunity to say what I had told you I was going to say. She responded by making remarks about Olivia's 'ruinous management'..."

"Speaking of which, I was with her," I interrupt.

"With whom?"

"With Olivia. Come on, finish. I'll tell you that story in a bit."

"Your mother talked and talked, and when she finished, she looked at me, waiting for the counterparts. I let her stay for a while without an answer, while we ate our salads, until I concluded the conversation: 'I'm going to separate from your daughter. Before I came to have this conversation with you, I talked to her...' If you had seen your mother's face, she even turned white... 'No, don't worry, I didn't say anything about your proposal.'" Julia laughs out loud. She laughs so hard that the sauce splatters, staining not only the tablecloth but also her white shirt.

"Stop laughing," I say, also laughing out loud. "The matter is serious. I don't know how you managed to keep a straight face!"

"A performance worthy of an Oscar! I told her that I had told you that I had come to the conclusion that I didn't make you happy and that we would be better off separated, so I could dedicate myself entirely to my career. I confess that part was really hard for me..." I try to intervene, but Julia doesn't allow it. "I know, I know, you're right. I understood your reasons, and everything I said to your mother is a lie, but I told her what she wanted to hear." Julia is silent for a moment and takes several sips of wine.

My heart aches seeing the pain etched on Julia's face. I reach out and take her hand in mine, giving it a reassuring squeeze. "You have to be able to fight your own battles, to conquer, and to win. I will always be here, and I adore you too." Julia bites her lower lip, a gesture she repeats whenever she gets anxious. "Come on, don't make that face. Who knows, maybe we'll be lovers from time to time," I say, making her smile. "Now tell me, how did the conversation end?"

"I told her I was moving out, that I was going to the United States, and we'd see. I had to make up a few lies about how you were devastated. She was thrilled. I told her she should never dare to interfere in anything that concerns Mateo again, and that you and I will be the administrators of the fund. If you had seen her face when I talked about the fund, I thought she was feeling unwell."

"And she?" I ask, still half-stunned by what Julia has just said.

"She agreed with every word."

"Are you going to Boston? Do you really want the job?" I finally gather the courage to ask what's been on my mind since the first time she shared her plan.

"I don't know... It's a good possibility. But I don't know if I can live away from Mateo... and from you..." She says the last words through gritted teeth, gets up, comes closer, and gives me a kiss on the lips. "What were you going to tell me a little while ago? You were with Olivia?" she asks, sitting back down.

"We met in the room of Alexis Conti, her lawyer, who was operated on for pancreatic cancer by my mother."

"The wife of the Italian deputy? Where do you know her from?"

"Who?" I ask, dazed.

§§

"Look, Fili, it was a complicated conversation. First, I was relieved that Julia wasn't sure she wanted to go to Boston. I don't want to think that she's going to live permanently in the United States..."

"Of course, it's important for Mateo that his mother is nearby..." he says with a laugh, not hiding his sarcasm.

I roll my eyes at his remark but continue. "Then there was the surprise when I realized that she knows Alexis. I changed the subject because I didn't know what to say, and with that, I also couldn't ask questions. But I ended up being with Alexis herself and was able to get some answers."

§§

I arrive fifteen minutes before the agreed time. She is already seated on the terrace by the beach where we arranged to meet.

"Are you okay? Recovered?" I ask, trying to hide my nervousness.

"More or less. I have some pain but nothing special. Apparently, I'm cured. Thank you!"

"Why are you thanking me? I didn't do anything."

"You said I was letting myself be carried away by fear. You didn't know me at all, and you couldn't have been more right."

I drink a beer, and she has a tonic water. We chat as if we've known each other, until a silence settles that's hard to break. Alexis looks me directly in the eyes and puts her hand over mine. Not only do I not withdraw it, but I place my other hand on top of hers. "Camila..." "Alexis," we both speak at the same time, bursting into laughter.

"You first," I say.

"When I woke up from the surgery, I knew I had to see you. I had to tell you what I'm feeling, even if it doesn't make any sense, even if you say I'm crazy and run away from me, which, by the way, wouldn't be the first time."

I smile, remembering the stormy night, but I don't interrupt her.

"When you ran out, I tried to go after you, but I felt so dizzy that I couldn't. I sat back down and saw your card on the floor. When I got home, I searched and found your email. It was difficult; there's not much about you online."

"I'm sorry for the way I left, but I got scared. I am married. Or rather, I was married. Nothing like this had ever happened to me before. I panicked. The kiss plus the thunderstorm was too much for me. I thought about you many times. I had been observing you on the train for months."

"The Reader of the Red Cover Cook!"

"Exactly. I invented a life for you. I thought you could be a surgeon, maybe a pianist." I look at her fingers, now intertwined with mine.

"And it turns out I'm just a lawyer, what a disappointment!" she says ironically.

"I think you already know everything about me. I'm the middle daughter of Professor Amelia Velasquez, a neurosurgeon, now divorced, mother of a 4-year-old boy. And that's it, there's not much more to tell!"

"What a capacity for synthesis," she says with a laugh.

"And you, what's your story?"

"A little more complicated than yours. Right now, I'm Olivia's lawyer, and I'm totally committed to that. Olivia and Julia..." Alexis interrupts what she was going to say and looks at her watch. "I have to go. Let's arrange another day, and I'll tell you my story, what do you think? It's always a pretext to see you again."

My heart flutters at her words. "You don't need pretexts. I want to be with you again. Shall we have dinner over the weekend? Mateo is staying at Julia's."

§§

"And now? I was happy that we arranged to have dinner, but I'm afraid," I say through clenched teeth, raising my head to face Fili.

"Afraid of what, Camila?" he says, closing his notebook and taking off his glasses, showing that our time is up.

"Of what might happen."

"What do you want to happen?"

Fili wouldn't be Fili if he didn't answer my questions with more questions. I leave the office knowing there's no point in insisting. He's not going to make my life easier.

But as I step out into the bright sunlight, a sense of excitement mingles with the fear twisting in my gut. Deep down, I know exactly what I want to happen with Alexis. I'm just not sure I'm brave enough to admit it to myself yet.

Chapter 31

November 6th - It Doesn't Get Better with Time

Olivia

"Hello Olivia, good afternoon. How are you? How were these past few days?" Fili sits down and turns on the light of his small lamp. I like these days when the office is illuminated by this yellowish light, which gives the whole environment a more intimate, cosier atmosphere. Not that it's necessary; he's always warm, but I've gotten used to associating this luminosity with a feeling of inner peace. The first time I sought out Fili, it was winter, the days were short, and most of our sessions took place in this same setting, with the window blinds closed and the small lamp lit.

"Hectic, but good..." My response is laconic. I know that Fili's question is just a welcoming greeting and that he will try to make me talk.

"What have you been up to? Or should I ask what has Julia been up to?" Fili sketches a smile and picks up his notebook.

§§

In front of the bathroom mirror, with wet hair and water droplets dripping, I let myself get lost in thought, towel in hand. I have to hurry if I don't want to arrive wrecked. In fact, I want to get there before her and watch her enter. Without further hesitation, I finish drying my hair with the towel and put on a little gel, giving it a tousled look. No makeup, just a little perfume, I choose black pants and a colourful, casual shirt, a short cotton jacket, and that's it. I feel the adrenaline rushing and my legs shaking. I call an Uber and give the address of Dune's.

It's 9:50 when I look at my watch. After the surgery, Julia insisted again that we meet, and we ended up scheduling for today at the same time. Standing in the middle of the street, before pushing the door open, I raise my head, fill my chest with air, and enter with determination. I look around for an empty table when I see that Julia is already sitting in one of the corners of the room. She seems distracted and doesn't see me enter.

"You arrived early..." I say, coming up behind her and startling her.

"Oh, sorry, I was distracted. How are you?" she says in her low, husky tone. I sit down, signal to the young man who is on duty again, and order a whiskey. "Well..., but you know that since we were together at the hospital..." I hold my breath and stop talking. Are we really going to do this? Small talk?! "And you?" I take off my glasses, place them on the table, and rub my eyes. Without giving her time to answer, I continue, "It was tough losing that patient. I imagine it was even harder for you, since you knew him."

"We never get used to it. I think it's worse; it gets harder every time. Each time, I question what I could have done better. What could have been different?"

I feel a tear run down and hurry to wipe it with my hand. I pick up the glass and take a sip, hoping she hasn't noticed.

Of course, it didn't escape her. "Have you lost someone? I mean, of course, you must have lost many patients over time, but someone special?"

She can't imagine the size of the wound she's poking at.

"Tell me. When we let our ghosts out, they become less frightening. Tell me!"

A tear runs down my cheek that I no longer try to hide. "So many years later, I still think it could have been different. I went into the operating room because there was no one else. I quickly heard the story and read the little that was written in the file. I didn't think much. It was a simple procedure, a hernia. It should have taken less than an hour; we went in and out. Minutes after being anesthetized, the respiratory rate increased, the jaw began to stiffen, but I didn't notice right away. The heart rate changed. I remember the sound of the monitors. The other day, in the room, I had exactly the same feeling. It seems that nothing we do will change the course of a story that is already written." The tears are now flowing without being able to contain them. At the same time, I feel an enormous relief in sharing this story so many years later. "In no time, the patient had a temperature of 104°F, 105°F, 106°F. The two surgeons had little experience and panicked. Malignant hyperthermia. I couldn't do anything."

Julia remains silent with her eyes fixed on mine and the glass in her hand. "You couldn't have known. It wasn't your fault."

"I did; the truth is, I did. Later, when reading the entire file, I saw that there was an indication that a brother had complications with anaesthesia, and he himself, in a previous intervention, had already had an episode that was never fully understood. If only I had talked to him... if I had read the history as I should have, and not just the words of a colleague saying 'there's nothing unusual.'"

"And then?"

"The hospital opened an investigation. Javier, my husband, was friends with one of the administrators and managed to convince him to close the case. For him, it was perfect. He had wanted me out of the operating room for a long time. I was a wreck. I accepted it."

"Just like that, without fighting, without responding?"

"I tried. They were all against me. I was the most obvious scapegoat. It exonerated the surgeons and let all the blame fall on me. They said they had informed me, that I had access to all the information. I was alone."

"I don't understand... You like what you do in the operating room. And you're good at what you do. If you tell anyone I said this, I'll deny it, but you're one of the best I've ever worked with," she says with a smile, squeezing my arm with her hand.

"I heard you separated."

"Camila came to the conclusion that we couldn't continue. She's much more self-aware than I am; it must be from all the hours spent with Fili," she says with a somewhat forced laugh. "It was terribly hard to hear everything she said to me, especially because she's absolutely right. She knows me well, so well that she's able to expose my soul and confront me with my conscience. She says I live to conquer..." Julia pauses for a moment, finishing her drink. She signals to the waiter and orders another one.

Curious, I think, it's exactly the same thing that Ursula said; they seem to agree on the subject... "And is it true? During these months when we didn't talk, I thought exactly the same... I felt like a trophy..."

She interrupts me in an affirmative tone, "Don't say that..., no! You weren't a conquest."

"Of course I was, Julia, think about it... You did everything, and I have no doubt that, at that time, you would have done the impossible to have me, and when you got me..., what happened? You lost interest. I became just another one who crossed your life, your bed."

I wanted to stay quiet and listen; after all, it was she who asked for this meeting.

"You weren't just another one in my bed; you weren't just another conquest..." Julia looks at me in such a way that I feel myself tremble inside. "If I remember correctly, it was you who seduced me!"

I let out a laugh, letting the atmosphere become lighter. Meanwhile, she spins the ice cubes around in her glass. "You said you wanted to talk about work..."

"It's true, I wanted your opinion. I had a proposal to go to Boston. It's an almost irresistible invitation, a very long story that involves Camila's mother..."

I interrupt her again, "After what I saw at the hospital, I thought you and Amelia Velasquez didn't exactly get along."

"She's an exceptional surgeon and an execrable person, but this time she was tricked at her own game. She offered to help me get this position in Boston if I broke up with Camila..."

I can't believe what I'm hearing; despite everything I know about her, I never imagined she could stoop so low. "I don't understand..."

"I decided to tell her that I accepted the offer..., she hasn't found out yet that when she made her 'deal,' we were already separated." Julia lets out a laugh, and we both laugh for a moment.

I stop laughing and look at her, "Are you really going to Boston?"

"I don't know..., I was hoping you could help me. A few weeks ago, I was surprised by an invitation to lunch..." She falls silent and waits for me to say something.

"Should I know who invited you to lunch?" I ask Julia, my curiosity piqued.

"Well..." Julia pauses, a mischievous glint in her eye. "I had lunch at Fred's with our President, Sophia, and Ursula. From how much they talked about you, I assume you know them. I don't dare ask how well you know them though..." She laughs, her green eyes sparkling with the same intensity as when I first saw them.

"Quite the interesting group! Was it a party?" I joke.

"Not exactly, they called it a working lunch. I assume you know what the conversation was about. The mystery of where Doctor Olivia Lopez is going has been solved. But it didn't stop there - 'if Olivia leaves, someone has to replace her'. Our President was absolutely convinced that person should be me. I can't even imagine how many conversations Ursula and Sophia must have had with her about it."

"And you? What did you say?" I prompt, eager to hear more.

"Nothing, I was stunned. Ursula explicitly stated that you had been one of the voices in my favor, and suggested I talk to you before accepting. In that moment, it dawned on me... I knew that night couldn't have been your first time with a woman..."

I feel myself blush. "I think you could be a great clinical director..." I can't tell her that I don't want her to go to Boston.

"I don't want to leave the operating room." Julia raises her arm to signal for another drink. I pull her arm back down and gesture to the waiter to cancel the order.

"That's enough... I want to hear the story to the end and for that I need you to stay sober," I say firmly but gently.

§§

Even though I stopped Julia from continuing to drink, she was already quite tipsy. After listening to her insist she can't accept the position, that she has to keep operating, after swallowing the likelihood that she really is going to Boston, I managed to convince her to go home, but not before promising we would have dinner together soon.

Which reminds me - I have a question for you. When Julia spoke of her separation, she mentioned Camila was "very self-aware", alluding to "hours spent with Fili". That's not just a coincidence, is it? I ask rhetorically with a knowing smile.

Maggy McAndrew

Chapter 32

November 6th – Invitations

Camila

"So Camila, any news? New dinners?" Fili is sitting on his couch, illuminated by the yellow light from the lamp.

I set my bag down and take a seat as well. "Sorry I'm late... you can't imagine how bad the traffic was," I say, taking a deep breath before continuing. He stands up, goes to his desk, and returns with a new notebook in hand. He sits back down and I find myself wondering how long it will take for him to cross his legs. He turns, grabs a pen, writes something down, maybe the date, and there it is! He crosses his leg. Immediately, my gaze fixates on his socks. Champagne flutes, dozens of little flutes toasting in pairs on a black background.

"How have these past weeks been?" he asks, lifting his eyes from the notebook.

"Unusual!" I reply, before going on.

§§

"Really? And here I thought I had news for you. You kissed her without knowing who she was?" Julia is seated across from me. Over the past few weeks, she hasn't ceased to surprise me. Two days ago, she called and invited me out for a drink after dinner. It's an unusual invitation, to say the least.

"Stop it. Yes, it's true... but then my Mom operated on her, and you know the rest," I say with a laugh, seeing Julia's astonished expression. "Actually, you know more than I do. The other day when I mentioned her name after the surgery, you said she was the wife of an Italian congressman. How do you know her?"

"It's a very long story. Maybe one day she'll tell you herself."

"I won't insist, but what about you? What's with this invitation?"

"I have something to tell you, but we're waiting for more people."

"Who?"

"Calm down, you'll see. But first, there's something else I need to tell you."

"You're making me nervous with all this mystery," I say, taking a sip of my Irish Coffee.

"I've been seeing Olivia." She says the words like a declaration, offering nothing more. She runs a hand through her hair and sighs.

"Olivia? The same Olivia from the hospital?"

"She's going to be leaving the hospital."

"Yes, I know. That's not what I meant. Are you talking about the same person you hated until yesterday? The one who was homophobic?"

"Maybe I made some hasty judgments. Yes, Olivia!"

I recall the day Mateo had his surgery, and the fuss Olivia made over Julia's hair. It makes sense now.

"Well... congratulations! You seem happy." I'm not exactly sure what to say. But it's true, Julia seems more at peace, more content.

"I had to tell you, especially since she's going to be here in fifteen minutes. Her and Sophia."

"Sophia? The new administrator at my hospital?" I ask, not understanding anything about this conversation.

"You're starting to sound like Mateo. I don't think even he asks questions this quickly. But yes, that's the one. They want to talk to you."

"To me?" I finish off the rest of my drink and signal to the red-headed young man to bring me another.

"Take it easy. It's a serious conversation."

"Can you just tell me what's going on and stop messing with me?" I say, knowing full well she won't tell me a thing.

Minutes later, Olivia, Sophia, and... Alexis walk in. As she passes by, Olivia waves to the young waiter, showing she's a regular, and heads toward us. Julia stands up, gives her a kiss on the lips, murmuring "Camila already knows," as if the comment was necessary. Olivia smiles and greets me. If she's nervous, she doesn't show it. For her part, Sophia jokes around with Julia, making insinuations that go over my head but make Julia blush.

Alexis still hasn't sat down. She stands there, waiting for the others to get settled, before circling the table to give me a kiss on the cheek. Next to my ear, she whispers, "It's good to see you." I'm happy to see her too, but I can't figure out what she's doing here.

"Ladies, let's get to the point. We came here to work, after all," Sophia says, bringing her champagne flute to her lips.

"To work?" I ask, not understanding.

"You really didn't tell her anything, did you? You're terrible!" she says, making a face at Julia. They laugh out loud, leaving me more and more perplexed.

"Sorry Camila, Julia was supposed to give the introduction, but you know how she is! The thing is, as you already know, I recently took the reins at our hospital, and there are changes that need to be made, people that need to leave and others that need to come in."

For a moment I get worried. She's not going to fire me, is she? I look around and realize that can't be the context. I take a deep breath, have a sip too, and wait for whatever is coming.

"Come on, Sophia, don't be like that," says Olivia, who had been quiet up until now.

"You're being indecent!" says Alexis in a commanding voice. "Enough joking around. Listen, Camila, I'm the attorney for the University Hospital. Sophia hired my firm when she took over."

"Okay, Alexis, I'll say it..." Sophia jumps in, not letting her finish.

"Olivia is going to stay on as clinical director and I'd like you to be the director of neurosurgery. What do you think?" Sophia looks me in the eye with a penetrating gaze. She has big, sweet, provocative eyes.

I refocus on her words. "Wow!" escapes me before I can contain my enthusiasm. "I can't accept," I say, biting my lip.

Alexis rejoints the conversation, "I don't know if this helps, but there may be some things you should know before answering. When I lived in Italy, I got to know your mother and Esther well. I know how brilliant they are at what they do, but I also know the other side. It doesn't matter. What I want to tell you is that both of them are leaving the hospital at the end of this year."

"My mother and Esther? What happened? Esther just got here."

"Nothing, they have other challenges and it's time."

"It's good to see you in action, Alexis! And it's good to see you haven't changed!" says Sophia, not adding anything further.

The information is so abundant and unexpected that I remain silent. Julia places her hand on my knee and gives it an affectionate pat.

"I'll make the offer again. Will you accept being our new director of neurosurgery?" Sophia reiterates.

"Of course! Of course I accept, I don't even know what to say."

We leave close to two in the morning. We spent hours talking. Sophia has endless stories and an ability to joke about everything, including herself, that brought us to tears of laughter.

--

I can't sleep. It was too much information for one night.

'Are you awake?' 'Feel like chatting?' I send the message before giving myself time to think better of it.

More than ten minutes pass with no response. Of course, what was I expecting? She's probably sleeping or worse, not interested. I get up knowing I'll be unable to fall asleep. I open the freezer, take out a pint of vanilla ice cream, and eat directly from the container with a soup spoon. I return to bed feeling more comforted. Nothing like a hefty dose of sugar. I pick up the phone I left on the sheet and see that two messages have arrived.

'Can't sleep?' 'Did you doze off...'

Damn! Why didn't I take my phone with me? I take a deep breath. 'Sorry, I went to the kitchen to eat.'

'What?'

'Vanilla ice cream.' Right after, I send another message. 'What are you doing?'

The response arrives immediately. 'What are you wearing?' I feel a shiver and reread the message. 'Pyjamas, a white shirt with blue stripes and blue pants.'

'Take it off!'

Despite my astonishment, I find myself doing exactly as she asks. 'Now I'm cold,' I tease, playing along.

'No. Not if you imagine my hands,' 'Feel my fingers. Gaining courage to move higher...' I never would have imagined Alexis having a conversation like this.

'If you were here, I could give you courage to continue.'

For a few minutes, I don't receive any response.

Then a message comes through: 'It's almost three in the morning, I need to sleep or I won't be able to work tomorrow.'

'Of course! Talk another time?' I reply, lacking any arguments to keep the conversation going.

§§

"Did you set up a date?" Fili asks, not looking at me.

I move one of the pillows and cross my leg before answering, "No. But I'm going to call her to set one up. I want to be with her."

288

Chapter 33

November 20th - 'Fairy Godmother'

Olivia

"Hi Olivia, good afternoon. How are you?" Fili looks at me, waiting for a response.

"Fine," I say, unable to continue.

"How monosyllabic..." He crosses his leg and takes off his glasses, cleaning them with the edge of the sweater he's wearing. "May I ask what happened?"

"You can always ask anything..."

"That sounds like someone who doesn't want to answer everything..."

§§

"Olivia, I need to tell you something," Alexis's voice is grave. She called me early in the morning and asked me to come over to her place, without saying anything about the subject.

Seated on one of the couches in the living room, I distractedly touch the fringe of one of the pillows with my fingertips, and look at Alexis, seated in front of me. "What did he do this time?" I ask, staring at her.

"He had an accident, last night."

"An accident? Is he okay?" I ask, standing up.

"He was arrested!"

"Arrested?" I repeat, unable to follow the conversation.

"Last night, in the early hours of the morning, Javier hit a person with his car and fled. He was caught shortly after and it was confirmed he was over the legal alcohol limit. He was arrested. I didn't have a chance to tell you, but the divorce decision is being announced today. He must have found out yesterday."

"And the person he hit?" I ask cautiously.

"They're in the hospital, but out of danger. He has no way to escape this. He's facing multiple charges, on top of the complaint filed by his own company last week for tax evasion." I'm left speechless. Maybe I should feel relief, but all I feel is pity.

"Olivia, from here on out, you have to let it go. It's no longer about you. You're officially divorced and you have to move on with your life."

--

I take off the shirt and leave it haphazardly on the bed. It's the third one I've tried on, and nothing seems suitable. I look in the mirror, then at the wardrobe, still as undecided as when I got out of the shower. I glance at the black dress I wore months ago and smile. I opt for gray pants and a black shirt. I even grab a scarf but give up on it. Finally ready to leave, not a moment too soon as I'm running late. I turn back to put on perfume, take one last look in the mirror, and grab my phone.

I enter the restaurant and she's already seated at the table. It's becoming a habit, her arriving before me. Maybe it means something has really changed. There's a bottle of water on the table, and she's drinking slowly, playing with the glass in her hand. She looks younger, wearing tight jeans and a light blue shirt with the sleeves rolled up to the elbows. A brown leather jacket hangs on the back of her chair. I slow my pace to admire her for a few moments.

She looks at me and waves as I approach. I greet her with two kisses on the cheek and sit beside her. I've never been to this restaurant before.

Before we even have a chance to start talking, a waitress comes over to ask what we're having. I choose a pad thai and she orders a green curry. "You're drinking water? Do you want to choose a wine?"

"No, I don't think so... At our last meeting, you said you had things to tell me, but only if I was sober. I took your comment very seriously and decided not to drink alcohol today." She turns her head towards me and smiles.

I end up ordering water too. I'll have to find the courage for this conversation without a glass of wine. When we're alone, I feel her eyes roaming over every part of my body. "I'm going to accept Professor Thompson's offer," she says, making my blood run cold. "After our dinner the other day with Camila and Sophia, Ursula called me..."

"Ursula?" I ask, uneasy. I don't feel at all comfortable with this closeness between them.

"Yes... we've known each other for a long time. It's not that strange for her to call me." The answer seems harmless, but it's far from it. I don't know exactly what Julia knows, but I'm sure she knows more than she's letting on.

"And, if I may ask, what did she want?"

"To convince me not to go to Boston..."

"Seems she didn't succeed," I state ironically.

"Maybe..."

"With 'maybe,' you just said you were going to accept." To hell with Julia's mysteries, Ursula's riddles, I'm getting fed up, I think, without saying anything.

"I don't know the details, but Ursula knew about Professor Thompson's new lab and the invitation for me to go there... Don't make that face. I gave up trying to figure out who knows who and where they get their information long ago. You should do the same. Be content to know the outcome."

"But then? What does she have to do with it?" I ask impatiently.

"You know she works for a financial consulting firm. That company is one of the project's funders, and so by some magic, they proposed that the lab operate split in two - one part in Boston and the other here."

"Are you serious?"

"I am. In fact, I already accepted Professor Thompson's offer. Of course, I'll be based here, still able to operate, and go there when necessary."

"Ursula..." I shake my head, unable to finish.

"It wasn't exactly her plan. She wanted me to take your place as clinical director at Central, but that's impossible."

"Congratulations! Seriously, congratulations!" I lean over in my chair and give her a hug. Wasting no time, she turns her face and presses her lips to mine.

The arrival of our dishes interrupts the conversation. The aroma of the curry invades the space, an intense and provocative scent, a bit like Julia herself. When we resume, she changes the subject and asks, "You were saying you came by Uber. The other day you didn't have your car either. Did something happen?"

She's undeniably a keen observer, or perhaps more accurately, has a mind adept at steering the conversation where she wants it to go. I take the cue, breathe deeply, and reply, "No, I don't have a car now..."

"Don't tell me you've converted to bicycles?" she interjects smiling, her fork suspended in mid-air between the plate and her mouth.

"Not exactly. It's a bit more complicated."

"I can handle it. I like complicated things!"

In my head, images flash by. I don't know where to begin. I need her to know this side of me... Ultimately, it's also part of who I am. Lost in my silence, I don't see her movement and I'm startled when her hand rests on mine. I let go of my fork and allow our fingers to touch in a gesture of affection.

"You never asked anything about my life, so I assumed you knew everything you wanted to know. You met the deepest part of me, without having the slightest notion of what was on the surface... It was only when we stopped seeing each other that I realized."

"I missed you," she cuts off my speech because she senses the tension in every word. It's a characteristic move.

"You accused me of being homophobic, without having the slightest idea who I was. We started a relationship at the end, missing the chance to enjoy the journey, the joy of arrival. Maybe this is the moment to start at the beginning..."

"I never apologized, but you can be sure I deeply regretted everything I said. I was gripped by fear. Fear turned to anger and anger turned to aggression.

A disproportionate force against someone who, as you say, I didn't even know..." Julia purposely leaves the sentence unfinished and looks at me, without removing her hand from mine. The green of her eyes is so intense that I have difficulty holding her gaze. I gently withdraw my hand and pick up my utensils again.

"It hurt terribly, but it passed. That night I got out of bed and lay down next to you, knowing exactly what I wanted, and the risk I was taking... What if you didn't want it? What if, the next day, you reported me?"

She doesn't eat, and remains almost motionless. For the first time since we met, I feel she's listening to me.

"You asked what happened to my car. Well, the truth is Javier stole it."

"You didn't file a complaint?" Her expression fluctuates between astonishment and indignation. If only she knew everything I still have to tell her.

"No! Alexis handled the divorce. It's in the past. I don't want to hear about Javier ever again." I pause for a moment. I need to drink water and think about how I'm going to start what I really have to tell her. Unlike usual, Julia doesn't say a word.

"Do you remember the night you took me to the hospital room?"

"Of course!" she says impulsively, having no idea where I'm going with this.

"That night you grabbed my arm, and without meaning to, I screamed. You asked me what was going on and I gave you a vague excuse about having hit it somewhere. You didn't ask any more questions, and I was grateful I didn't have to give more explanations..."

She looks at me again with that fixed stare of someone trying in vain to anticipate what follows.

"A few days before, I had a huge argument with Javier. He found out our daughter is living with a woman and lost his head. When I got home I heard him yelling at her on the phone and I went back out, hoping he would calm down or leave. I returned two hours later and found him sitting in the living room waiting for me with a bottle of whiskey beside him. I'll spare you the details of what followed... But that day I decided it was the last time he would lay a hand on me." As hard as I try, I can't hold back a tear. I didn't want her to see me cry, but when you get right down to it, that's also part of who I am.

Raising my head, I wipe my face and face her. She remains silent, her eyes brimming with tears, biting her lower lip so hard it turns pale.

"Why didn't you tell me?" are the only words she utters.

"Out of shame... out of guilt."

The food has grown cold on our plates. Around us, the hustle and bustle is great. The restaurant has filled up and the conversations mix with the music, giving the room a touch of humanity that I find somewhat comforting.

"You're not going to eat?" If I ate little, Julia seems to have taken no more than one or two bites of the curry.

"I can't," she smiles and signals to the waitress, asking for another water.

"You never told me how you know Ursula. I have to say I was surprised... I didn't imagine..."

"Didn't imagine what? That I knew Ursula?"

"Let's just say, from what I heard, from her herself, it's a little more than that."

"Ursula was the most important person in my life in recent years... I met her at a fundraising party, we ran into each other smoking on the balcony, and by the end of the night I was a different woman."

"Ursula is always Ursula!"

"What do you mean by that? The first time I spoke to her about you, she said she knew you."

"I joined '*Sphere*' many years ago, through Francesca, I don't know if you know her... I was at a conference in Italy, and I fell madly in love with her, an Italian much older than me, a Diva. Ursula was always an unconsummated flirtation, a promise of maybe someday. Now I'm convinced that day will never come..."

Julia looks at me and lets out a laugh, the first one worthy of the name since we sat down. I have a lump in my throat and a question that has to be asked. I take a deep breath, as if I needed an extra dose of oxygen for what I'm about to say, "What about us?"

Julia lowers her head and looks at the table, "You were the person I gave myself to!"

The waitress interrupts the conversation at the worst moment. Now that she's gone, so has the intensity of the moment.

§§

"You know, Fili, I didn't want that night to end. I knew her more in those hours than in all these months."

"And nothing else happened? The dinner ended like that?" Fili smiles, as if he's visualizing other possibilities for our night in his mind.

"Nothing like what you're imagining... no."

Chapter 34

November 20th - Courage

Camila

"You're being mysterious, Camila. What is it?"

"You're right Fili. I spent much of my life trying to control everything, afraid of what might happen, afraid of my mother, of Julia, of difficult surgeries, and in the end, in the end we're never prepared for what comes next," I say with a smile.

§§

"You promised that if you were with me you'd give me the courage to go on, remember?" Alexis says, recalling the messages exchanged a few days ago. I place my hand on hers, press a little with my fingers and slowly pull it up. I feel my breathing quicken, this time it's not anxiety. I lean towards her, bringing my face close to hers, until we're only inches apart. We let the position hold, and she's the first to break the distance between her mouth and my lips. First with hesitation, then she kiss me with such gentleness it feels like something might melt. One first kiss leads to another, and another, only

297

interrupted by the urgency to breathe.

"No, don't do that..."

I'm surprised, and look at her for an explanation.

"I have a rule of never going to bed with anyone on a first date," she states with a forced smile.

Alexis agreed to come over to my place after dinner. Mateo is at Julia's house, actually I was hoping this could happen.

"You're scaring me," I don't know if it's her tone, or her look, but I feel like she has something to say, like someone keeping a secret that could jeopardize what follows.

"I lived in Italy for over ten years. I was married..."

Suddenly I remember that Julia referred to her as "the Italian congressman's wife".

"...I was married for almost twenty years. We met in Paris, lived there, then in London, until we settled in Rome. He's a lawyer and made a political career, until he was elected congressman. A good person, a good friend."

Alexis stops and looks at me. I don't know what to say, I drink some wine and hold her hand.

She shrugs, shakes her head and gets up going over to the window. I follow the movement, remaining seated. Right after, I get up and go after her.

"What's going on?"

"It's not worth it. I can't do it. I can't! I better go."

"You're kidding?" I say surprised.

Alexis turns to me, she's livid, with tears in her eyes. "I can't!"

Taken by an assurance I don't usually have, I decide the story isn't going to end like this. I need to know what's going on, and I have a feeling she needs to tell it too. I go back to the couch and sit down, drinking what's left in the glass. "All right. I'll stay here. Don't go away, stay here, keep me company." I take my cell phone out of my pocket and put on some soft music, avoiding the silence settling in.

"I loved him, married him in love, and we lived well. He's fantastic, a man like few others. We had been living in Italy for a few years when I met a woman. She was also a lawyer and also connected to politics. We got closer, got to know each other. She introduced me to Esther and Ursula, they were friends. Later, she introduced me to your mother. They all knew each other. She was married and had two children. Nothing was strong enough to stop it and we ended up getting involved. I had never been with a woman. She seemed to know what she wanted and how she wanted it. It lasted two years and three months. One day a journalist photographed us. And suddenly it was on the internet, it was in the newspaper. Not that the press made a big fuss, but it was enough. I got divorced and ended up leaving Italy, without arguments, without fights, a separation as friendly as our relationship had always been. He continued his career, apparently without much damage, on the contrary, it even brought him closer to a certain electorate."

"And her?" I can't resist asking.

"She went through a contentious divorce process, lost custody of her children and, a year later..." Alexis has tears rolling down her face, but she contains her emotion and continues, "...a year later she killed herself."

"How long ago was that?" I ask, running my hand over her face.

"Almost five years ago."

"You haven't been with anyone since?"

"No! Do you understand now? I can't! I can't do it!"

--

Vitoria invited me over for dinner. From her tone, I knew I couldn't refuse. It didn't even take five minutes for her to start pouring her heart out.

"I just don't understand. Things seemed to be getting better, I told you. She came after me. She swore she had ended everything, and now..."

She goes on about Esther while I stay quiet. I'm not sure if I should tell her what I know.

"Listen, I can't keep this from you. We're friends and I owe you honesty."

"What are you talking about? Did you see her?"

"Esther? No! Esther stopped talking to me the day I turned down her advances. I told you, lately she's barely said a word to me, only what's strictly necessary."

"So?"

"Alexis, a friend of mine. The other day we went out and ended up talking at her place until the early morning. We talked about everything and nothing. I told her about Mateo and Julia. I complained about my mother, although cautiously because I still haven't figured out how they know each other. And out of the blue, she brought up Esther. She knew we worked together in the OR, and she's known Esther for years, since she lived in Italy. From what I gathered, Esther never officially came out, but she's been living with someone for over twenty years, her partner in Madrid. Alexis knows them both and said theirs is a lifelong relationship. Based on that and other conversations at the hospital, it seems Esther requested a transfer and is moving to Bilbao, maybe because her partner was invited for an artistic residency there."

"She left? Without saying goodbye?" she says, not sounding as surprised as the situation would warrant.

"I don't know. I only know she officially leaves the hospital at the end of the year."

"I wasn't asking. Now that you're telling me all this, I realize last week at her place was a goodbye."

--

Alexis calls me just as I'm getting home. It's past eleven.

"Did you finish what you had to do?" she asks when I pick up.

"It never ends... They're people, and problems. This job never ends. Did you finish what you needed to turn in today?"

"I did. Did you have dinner with your friend?"

Our nightly phone calls have become a routine. Between Mateo and work, we haven't had many chances to see each other since the day she was here at my place.

"I did. She's not doing well."

"What were you doing?" I ask, changing the subject.

"I was flirting with someone I met on an app... when I remembered I had plans with you..."

I can't believe what I'm hearing.

"Speechless? That's good... I was joking! Of course I wasn't talking to anyone, I was waiting for your call. I'd give anything to see your face right now!" Alexis's laughter rings through the phone.

"Idiot!" I smile to myself, sitting on the couch. "Are you in bed?"

"Yes."

"Naked?" I ask, knowing I'm pushing it.

"No! Of course not!" she replies, clearly shocked.

"Take your clothes off!"

"What?"

"You heard me." From her quickening breath, I'm starting to think this game might work after all, since she started it the other day.

"Done."

"Are you sure? All of it?"

"Do you have a camera?!" she responds, making me believe it's true.

"Do you feel it? I know you do. Show me the way..." She doesn't say anything, but I can hear her breathing heavily. "Slide it up... Feel the warmth." As I speak, I can't stop thinking about what she might be doing herself.

It's past midnight when we decide to end the call, but not before making plans for dinner at her place on Saturday.

--

When she opens the door, I stand frozen outside. I'm completely drenched - coat, shoes, everything. In the distance, the muffled rumble of thunder can be heard.

I've never been here before. Alexis's apartment is in an old building, an attic with no elevator. Definitely a good workout, I think as I climb the wooden stairs. The living room is warm and cosy. At one end, the sloped ceiling has a skylight revealing the sky.

"Getting to your place requires being in shape!" I say as I finally step inside, leaving a trail of drips behind me.

"We need to talk..." Through the glass, a flash of lightning splits the dark night, followed by a loud clap of thunder. Alexis nervously grabs the edge of her coat. I move closer and hug her. She's stiff and doesn't move at first. Then she wraps her arms around me and lets herself be held. When we pull apart, we're both wet from my drenched hair.

"Before anything else, you need to dry off. Take a shower, I'll lend you some clothes. Yours are soaked." I look down and see she's right.

I feel much better, and warmer, stepping out of the shower. I wrap myself in the towel she left on the sink and glance in the mirror.

"Alexis! Alexis, can you come here please?" I call out loudly to be heard.

I hear footsteps, then her voice outside the closed bathroom door, "Yes, do you need something?"

"Come in, please..." I say as if I really need help.

When she opens the door, I pull her to me, letting the towel drop. I kiss her without allowing for second thoughts and step by step, I push her until she falls back onto her own bed.

"You're right, we have unfinished business," I murmur softly in her ear.

"I want you so badly," she whispers.

"That's all I need to know right now."

Alexis has definitely left her doubts behind and doesn't take pity on my words.

She pulls the sheet up to cover us both, a gesture filled with affection and intimacy.

"No, Camila!"

"Yes!" I say rhetorically, and it's all it takes.

§§

"You know, Fili, that day I realized I would be able to move on without Julia," I conclude, leaving out much of what actually happened. Fili sets down his notebook, looks at me, and smiles without saying a word.

Chapter 35

December 4th – The Rules of the Game

Olivia

"You know, Fili, I have a feeling that with everything I've told you about Julia, you already know her."

"Maybe you're right, Olivia. Sometimes I feel the same way." Fili looks at me, smiles, and shakes his head.

"This time it was different..."

§§

Julia's apartment isn't very big, but it has extraordinarily good taste, combining modern features with classic objects in a mix of styles that is totally her. I arrive at the appointed time, bringing a bottle of wine. After much hesitation, I couldn't resist and ended up wearing the same black dress I had on when we met months ago. She looks at me and gives a smile that shows she noticed. She doesn't comment and kisses me on the cheek while taking the bottle to the kitchen.

The table is set with a grey linen tablecloth, matching napkins, white plates, red placemats, and champagne flutes, showing the importance given to the occasion. A beeping sound in the kitchen signals that something is ready. Minutes later, Julia crosses the room with a tray of baked fish. The aroma is delicious, and so is the appearance.

"Today we have to eat," she says, referring to our last dinner.

"You may want that, but I didn't know you had these skills..."

"There are many skills of mine you don't know about," she replies, reminding me of who I'm talking to. A master of rhetoric, she uses irony wisely, turning it into a mirror of her intelligence. At this moment, I remember Fili's words: "It's a dangerous game..."

To the sound of Kissin's piano, we chat about the hospital.

"The administration has already chosen the person to replace you as director," she says, showing she knows something I don't.

"Really? Do you know who it is?"

"Actually, I do... If Sophia doesn't play around at work, Alexis plays even less!"

"I'm not following you," I reply, completely lost.

"Alexis's ex-husband has a lot of influence, even here, and he supported Amelia Velasquez's candidacy for national party leadership in the next elections." Julia shows a huge smile and the tone of someone who has won a battle. "But it doesn't end there. Professor Velasquez wins in politics but has to swallow a bitter pill at the hospital. Do you know who's going to replace you as director? Camila's brother. He's coming from the United States with his husband and son and will be the new clinical director at Central."

I'm happy with the news, and I don't even dare ask how many strings were pulled to make this double move happen.

We're already drinking coffee when she starts a very different topic out of nowhere. "After everything you've told me, I've been trying to understand some things. We never talked about the night you came to me at the hospital..."

I cover her mouth with my hand: "No, we're not going to talk about that day... It's over."

She affectionately removes my hand and continues, "We have to talk. I want to explain, and I want to understand. That night, everything that could go wrong did. I operated on a patient, a routine procedure, and for no apparent reason the situation got complicated and the patient had to go to the ICU. He was okay. But it's always the same feeling, the feeling that something escaped me, that I should have been more attentive... That night it was a 25-year-old young man. I went personally to talk to his parents, and I couldn't hold back the tears when I saw the despair on their faces." She pauses, taking the opportunity to finish her coffee, which must be ice cold by now. "A few days before, Camila's mother had come to me with that amazing proposal, and I couldn't stop thinking about it. At the same time, you..."

"I what?" I ask, surprised by the twist.

"You had told me you were going to get divorced. I felt like I was in an impossible position..." Julia's speech is choppy, as if she's weighing every word she utters.

"Why? I never asked you for anything."

"It's true, but when you told me that, I wanted more. It was a dead end. I decided to do what I do best, throw myself headfirst into another conquest."

"Did it work?" I ask without looking away.

"No! That night you showed up, I was in a bad place, I knew I hadn't answered your messages, I thought I would never be able to give you what you wanted. Every time we were together, I surrendered in your arms, I had never done that with anyone. Your attitude on our first night set the pace, you earned the right to have me completely, and I gave in. Sometimes I felt like you weren't giving yourself over, it was as if there was a barrier you didn't dare cross. That night..., that night I wasn't thinking about you..."

Her gaze reveals what she's feeling, it's hard to hold back the urge to hug her, but I contain myself. "That night I felt terrible, suddenly I was with you and at the same time I wasn't, all the ghosts, all the fears took over me... I remember you held me tight, and at that moment I froze, I was no longer there."

"I had no idea..."

"I know..."

Julia gets up and goes to the kitchen, leaving me alone in the living room. I notice she's turned up the volume on the music, I close my eyes and let myself be carried away by the sound of the piano. I feel her hands on my shoulders, but I don't open my eyes, I know what's coming next. I kiss that finger again and the others, one by one, not letting go of her hand. Finally, I open my eyes and face the immensity of her gaze, losing myself in the magic of that green.

She stands up, reaches out her hand to me, picks up the unfinished bottle of champagne still on the table, and leads us to the bedroom.

She stares at me, waiting for a gesture, an indication. I stay for a moment, then lie down on the bed, showing that I'm willing to change the rules of our game.

"You're going to have it all, but not yet..., not until you can't take it anymore.", "Stay still!", she murmurs each word next to my ear, pausing now and then to kiss me.

She seems to be in no hurry, but I'm starting to feel like I need more..., I want everything she has to give me. She purposely stays dressed, leaving no doubt about who's in control. She picks up a silk ribbon I hadn't seen before and runs it over my body. The soft contact of the silk gives me goosebumps. I need more. She pretends to ignore it and continues with her plan.

"I need you, I want more..."

"What do you want? Say it!"

I feel inhibited, struggling to speak, but gradually I gain confidence.

She drops the ribbon, sliding it one last time. She stops and waits for further instructions.

"Lower..."

She advances at a deliciously slow pace. I find it difficult to control my movements.

"Open your eyes."

As soon as I do, I feel her, knowing exactly where and how to touch.

"Like this..., I can't..." The words come out in sobs. I can no longer keep my eyes open and I close them, and I let myself get lost.

"I love you Liv!" I hear her murmur through clenched teeth.

I wake up startled, not knowing exactly where I am. I open my eyes slowly, blinking until I get used to the sunlight streaming through the window. Images and sounds from last night flash through my mind... I smile and look to the side, but the bed is empty. I get up, find her shirt thrown over a chair and put it on.

I walk out of the bedroom and head to the kitchen. Julia is sitting at the small white table, holding a coffee mug in her hands. On the counter are two orange juices, a bowl of strawberries and a plate of scrambled eggs.

"Good morning... today you're more like Sleeping Beauty..." she says laughing, a laugh that lights up her face, as if mobilizing all her muscles for that smile. "I'm hungry," she states, turning on the toaster, where I deduce she has already put the bread.

"I can see that! You prepared a feast! You're going to spoil me..." I immediately regret using that expression. It may seem like I'm assuming this will be repeated.

Julia gets up, puts down the mug, goes around the table, and kisses me. "I love that shirt... I love your smell..." she says, making me blush as I remember last night. "What is it? Are you surprised that I know how to make eggs, or that I'm hungry?"

"Neither one nor the other, I just didn't want you to think that I believe this can become a routine, that's not what I meant. Don't be scared, I'm not going to start having Sunday breakfast in your kitchen," I say ironically.

She doesn't follow the joke, on the contrary, she forces a pause in the conversation, butters the toast and puts everything she prepared on the table, starting to chew the bread.

"Liv, we have to talk seriously. Let's not make the same mistake twice." I can't help but notice that she called me Liv. "Is it too cliché if I tell you that last night was one of the best of my life? So, I have no choice but to play this game..."

"It's not a game! What do you want me to answer without sounding, as you say... cliché?"

She stops chewing, takes another sip of juice, and smiles, "It would be very childish of me to tell you that I love you above all else, and that we're going to be happy no matter what, but you made me see life through another prism, details that I had never noticed, and a few things about myself. Camila is right when she says that I will always need to conquer, it can be work, it can be someone, if I deny that, I stop being myself, and I will be lying to both of us, condemning this relationship from the start..."

"I respect that!"

"What do you mean by that?" she asks, holding a strawberry in her hand, which she doesn't put in her mouth.

"I love you too, Julia Garcia. I know who you are, and it was you, the way you are, that I fell in love with. I don't want a relationship of lies and betrayal, but I want to try a relationship with you. I respect your battles, your conquests, and you respect that Ursula is part of my life." It's my turn to let a silence settle. I take some strawberries and eat them one by one, while taking a sip of the coffee with milk that she prepared for me.

"It's always a game, and you just defined the rules of this one!" she declares, giving me a kiss.

§§

"I spent the rest of Sunday at her apartment. It seemed like we had been living like this for years. We watched a movie and made a thousand plans for the hospitals. Julia managed to convince me to present a joint proposal to both Administrations, ambition is something she will never lack." I look at Fili, who is still taking notes in his notebook.

"Olivia, when I once told you that you were both players of excellence, I never imagined that you would be able to take the game this far, let alone that you would be able to get Julia Garcia to play by your rules."

Epilogue

It Was Inevitable

Camila

I'm waiting in the room, Fili is running late from his previous appointment. It's very rare for this to happen. The office door is closed, I can hear voices, I realize one is Fili's and the other is a woman's, but I can't make out what they're saying. I often wonder what the other people who sit on that couch are like. Alone and with nothing to do, I look out the window and let myself get lost in memories of the last few days, a wistful smile playing on my lips as I recall the moments of joy and connection.

Tired of sitting, I go to the bathroom at the end of the hallway. When I return, the office door is already open and Fili signals for me to enter. I missed the opportunity to see who was in there. My curiosity piques, but I push it aside, focusing instead on the session ahead.

"How are you Camila? Sorry to have kept you waiting, the previous consultation took longer than expected..." Fili says apologetically as I step into his office.

We haven't even sat down yet when the door opens again. "Sorry, Fili, I forgot my phone..." a familiar voice rings out.

"Olivia?!" I utter in astonishment, looking at her as she freezes when she sees me. My eyes widen in shock, trying to process the unexpected encounter.

"Camila?!" Olivia exclaims, equally surprised.

Fili smiles and shakes his head, "It was inevitable, it was going to happen one day!" He seems amused by the coincidence, a knowing twinkle in his eye.

I look at him as he sits in his usual place, adjusts his glasses with his right index finger, and crosses his leg. His pants rise slightly, revealing his socks, as always. Today they are black, sprinkled with movie clapperboards with small letters saying 'The End'.

[The End]

Table of Contents

About the author

Maggy McAndrew is a physician, mother of five, and a passionate writer based in Lisbon. With a diverse portfolio that includes scientific publications and captivating works of fiction, Maggy's true love lies in creating heart-breaking lesbian romance novels. Drawing from her extensive experience in the medical field and academic settings, she expertly weaves together "slices of daily life" with the intricacies of hospital and university dynamics.

Maggy's unique perspective and keen understanding of human relationships allow her to create authentic and emotionally resonant stories that showcase the joys, challenges, and triumphs of women loving women. Her novels offer a powerful and unapologetic representation of lesbian love in all its forms.

To stay connected with Maggy and receive exclusive offers, complimentary excerpts from her upcoming works, and the latest news about her writing journey, please reach out to her at maggy.mcandrew@gmail.com. She cherishes the opportunity to engage with her readers and appreciates any feedback, comments, or questions you may have.

Printed in Great Britain
by Amazon